FAMOUS SUICIDES OF THE JAPANESE EMPIRE

Famous Suicides of the Japanese Empire

A NOVEL

DAVID MURA

COFFEE HOUSE PRESS
Minneapolis

2008

COPYRIGHT © 2008 by David Mura
COVER AND BOOK DESIGN by Coffee House Press
COVER ART *Night Watch #3*, © Roger Shimomura
AUTHOR PHOTOGRAPH © John Noltner

COFFEE HOUSE PRESS books are available to the trade through our primary distributor, Consortium Book Sales & Distribution, www.cbsd.com or (800) 283-3572. For personal orders, catalogs, or other information, write to: info@coffeehousepress.org.

Coffee House Press is a nonprofit literary publishing house. Support from private foundations, corporate giving programs, government programs, and generous individuals helps make the publication of our books possible. We gratefully acknowledge their support in detail in the back of this book.

To you and our many readers around the world, we send our thanks for your continuing support.

LIBRARY OF CONGRESS CIP INFORMATION
Mura, David.
Famous suicides of the Japanese empire / by David Mura.
p. cm.
ISBN 978-1-56689-215-5 (alk. paper)
1. Japanese American families—Fiction. I. Title.
PS3563.U68F36 2008
813'.54—DC22
2008012526

PRINTED IN CANADA
1 3 5 7 9 8 6 4 2
FIRST EDITION | FIRST PRINTING

For my *nisei* parents, uncles, and aunts
For my *sansei* sisters, brother, and cousins
For my *yonsei* children, Samantha, Nikko, and Tomo
For the No-No Boys, for the *nisei* veterans
For the legacy we all share

"History is the tale of the victors."
—WALTER BENJAMIN

POSTCARD FROM ANOTHER DIMENSION

When Tommy and I were boys, we loved watching our father shave. We sat on the toilet seat as he lathered up, his face flushed with white foam. Thick spires of hair sprouted on his chest from beneath his sleeveless T-shirt. When we picnicked at Montrose Beach with relatives, I often noticed how my father seemed more darkly bearded than the other *nisei* men. To me, this made him more manly, more of a tough guy.

I always asked my dad if I could shave too. So did Tommy. One day he said that *I* could but that Tommy would have to wait. My dad was old school about these things. I was the oldest son. That meant something. Tommy got furious at his dismissal. He started whining and almost crying, and this simply proved my father's point. Tommy wasn't ready.

Like any older brother, I didn't protest my brother's secondary status. With Tommy banished, I felt I'd magically left the world of boyhood and little brothers behind. As the hot water streamed from the tap, my father lathered me, then lifted me up so I could see myself in the mirror. He swiped away the steamy film. We both laughed at our twin white beards, both grown into Santa Claus in an instant. Then he plopped me down and shaved himself first, long strokes for the cheek, short for above his lip.

"Damn," he said. He'd cut himself. "You didn't hear that." And then, "I don't want you to use that word."

He toweled himself off, then dabbed a toilet paper patch on the cut.

"Too many things on my mind, Ben. Too many things on my mind. You've got to pay attention when you shave."

Now it was my turn. He slipped the blade from the razor. I had wanted to use the blade, just like him. He told me it was too dangerous, I was just a boy. "A little shaver," he dubbed me and smiled. The blood had already reddened the toilet paper on his cheek.

He held up my mother's small hand mirror. I liked seeing my face all lathered and how the razor scraped away the foam. I used the razor just like him, long strokes for my cheeks, short ones above my lips. "Don't cut yourself, Ben," he said, and for a second I believed the razor still held a blade. "Just pray you don't get a beard like mine," he added, as he toweled me off. "You'll have to do this twice a day." He rinsed off the towel, then placed it under the water, wrung it again and splayed the hot cloth on his face. He glanced at me.

"Don't you ever ever use this razor when I'm not around, you hear? And don't even think about taking out the blade and using it. You understand?"

I nodded.

"You hear me?" he repeated, as he picked up the razor again. He flipped open the housing and pinched up the blade between his fingertips.

"See how sharp this is?"

With that he made a quick abrupt motion, almost as if he were swinging the razor at me. He flicked it across his left pointer finger, slicing open a thin red line.

For a moment we both stared at his finger. Blood pooled about the wound and trickled down his finger. I kept thinking it must hurt, but his face didn't register a pitch of pain. He seemed lost somewhere inside himself.

"Damn," he muttered. He yanked another few pieces of toilet paper from the roll, dabbing the wound, absorbed now in dressing the cut.

"Go on now," he barked, without looking at me. "Go play with your brother."

Back in our room, I told Tommy about Dad swearing.

"Oooh. That's bad."

"You're such a baby. Dad can say anything he wants. He's a grown man."

"Not if Mommy hears him."

"What do you know? I bet you don't even know what that means." Not that I knew exactly either.

"I do too."

"O.K., squirt, what does it mean?"

His face scrunched. "It means you're going to H-E-double hockey sticks."

I suspected he was right. But how in the H-E-double hockey sticks did he know?

Back then I'd already started to notice something different about Tommy. He wasn't yet in first grade, and he could already read as well as I could. He always seemed to know odd things, things you wouldn't think a five-year-old would know, like who Nikita Khrushchev was or that the Earth was the third planet from the sun or that monarchs came all the way from a valley in Mexico. (I thought he was making the last one up. Only years later did I find out he was right.)

"What else happened?"

"I got to shave. Only without the blade."

"You already told me that. Tell me everything."

"There's nothing more to tell." I looked out the window. "We need to get to the Empty. The gang's waiting."

I started down the hall of our apartment toward the back door. "He cut himself, didn't he?"

I looked at him. How did he know that?

Tommy stood there, as if still waiting for something more. I just turned and walked away, knowing he'd follow. He was my little brother. That's what little brothers did.

I'm an itinerant historian (i.e., no PhD, still untenured), and there's this book I've been working on for years, in a dozen notebooks and in the back files of my computer. In some ways it's not quite a real scholarly work, but it could help me jump several academic rungs if I did manage to finish it. I sometimes excuse my delay by saying only a trip to Japan will finally allow me to complete it. After all, the book is entitled *Famous Suicides of the Japanese Empire*.

My title and subject betray my lifelong fascination with the origins of my family's grief and madness. Under Western eyes, grief and madness are popularly associated with the Japanese— samurai *seppuku*, kamikaze pilots, the author Yukio Mishima, even *Madama Butterfly*. As for my tribe of Japanese Americans, well, compared to the *honto no nihonjin*, we're rather obscure creatures. So obscure even some of our own can't quite admit we exist.

Were she alive, my mother would still be torn about this project. She'd always envisioned a bright academic future for me, worthy of a Japanese American eldest son. But she let me know, at times subtly, at times not so subtly, that she thought my book a more than dubious idea. She sensed what I was up to. Oh Ben, why look back? Why drag the past around after you?

But I'm a history teacher, Ma. That's what I do.

Like a diligent scholar, I've done my reading, ranging both West and East. In Dante's *Inferno* there's a special ring in hell for suicides. Sentenced to the seventh circle they're transmo-grified into bleeding trees. Harpies gnaw ravenously on their damned and restless souls.

In some cultures they buried the corpses of suicides at night at crossroads. The traffic pounded the corpses down; the inter-section confused their sense of direction, made it more difficult for them to navigate their way home to haunt the living. In the days of Salem's colonials, they tossed cartloads of stones on these crossroads, to keep them burdened in the earth.

In other cultures they pounded a stake through the heart of the deceased, like a vampire. It was thought that the corpse of a suicide was unusually heavy, their coffins so ponderous that even horses could not pull them.

Of course I supposedly come from a culture where suicide is honored. *Harakiri. Seppuku.* A glorious samurai death. Full of honor and courage, a warrior's glory. Perhaps if my father had been a samurai that might have made a difference.

But he wasn't. He was American, as American as they come.

Only back in the day, the government didn't quite see it like that. To them, he looked just like the enemy. A case, one might put it, of mistaken identity.

But perhaps all that had nothing to do with his demise. Who's to say? Still, the old customs and cultures got it right. To the living there's something unfinished and unnerving about such deeds.

I know, I know. At my age, a handful past forty, even dealing with such special circumstances, I should be shriven of my dead. But they won't let me alone. They belong to me in ways I still haven't fathomed. They crowd in from all sides, the way the underworld spirits crowed and clawed at Ulysses and the blood he sacrificed to get the hell-bound Tiresias to rise from the dead.

But perhaps, of all my ghosts, even more than my father or mother, my brother Tommy remains the most unsettled. Tommy, who vanished ten years ago in the desert somewhere between L.A. and Vegas, whom I still picture wandering there with his restless soul. Who, just before his disappearance, had traveled to Japan and penned me letters about Kabuki-cho, the famed red-light district. Who seemed, for a brief span, to have found a place where he could escape the complications of our mutual past and our nearly invisible notch in our own country—"you really should come here, Bro, it's like some mysterious other dimension where everyone looks like me, a Bizarro world where I'm no longer bizarre."

At the time I told myself Japan for Tommy was just another one of his side trips, another zigzag away from anything substantial and responsible, from making something of himself and his genius. He and I had argued before he left for Japan. About his drug use, his gambling, women. Our places in the family, our place in America. Any number of things. When he came back, we still kept our distance from each other, wary, mutually suspicious and accusing. I suppose that's why, when he dematerialized out in the Mojave, part of me accepted it as inevitable, following a line of descent first established way back in our childhoods. He had drifted too far away for me to look into his absences.

And then, one day last winter, a decade too late, I received a postcard with a Japanese stamp. When I saw the handwriting, I freaked. A hundred zillion emotions pulsed through me; I thought for an instant that my brother had played a trick on us all, had vanished to the hinterlands like Huck—or in this case to the ancient homeland to make a new Nipponese start. The card didn't say anything spectacular, just, "Greetings from Kobe. It's nice to be here in this quiet coastal city, away from all the madness of Tokyo (though of course I still miss Kabuki-cho) . . ."

I recalled that my mother's family was from Kobe—maybe that's why he'd gone there.

But then I saw the date on the postmark. 1989. Ten years ago. How in the hell did it get here so late? Where had it been? Perhaps it had been lost in the American postal service (or the Japanese, though that was less likely; they're too efficient for such a mistake). Maybe the *kanji* on the front of the card threw it off course, languishing for years in some dead-letter bin until someone took the time to peruse it again and notice the address was, after all, in plain old American English.

Or maybe, as I hear my brother laughing in my inner ear, it spent a short while in the Twilight Zone.

About *Famous Suicides.* Often, as I've puzzled over all my research and notes, there seems too many deaths to cover. As any freshman comp instructor might advise, I should narrow my topic. Soldiers like General Maresuki Nogi or Shinji Takeyama and the young lieutenants of the February rebellion. Rebels like Sugako Kanno. Authors like Ryunosuke Akutagawa or Yasunari Kawabata. Parent-child suicides—*okako shinju*—like Fumiko Kimura. Troubled youths like Misao Fujimura. All those samurai and kamikaze, their death poems and letters to their disciples and loved ones. Add to these the odd and even fictional *seppuku* that crop up in my notes. Toshio Fujimoto, Dr. Serizawa. The forty-seven *ronin* and *Chushingura*, from the first Japanese samurai film I ever saw, back in college when Grace and I first started dating.

But perhaps that too is part of the problem. The origins for this book took place many years past, too long ago. Way back in linear time, as Tommy the astrophysicist would put it.

Blessed and cursed with a brilliant and lunatic mind, Tommy used to speculate endlessly about time and the existence of dimensions other than ours. He viewed these dimensions as alternative versions of our own, ever unfolding universes, each moving toward different conclusions, different fates. Perhaps, he said, *God* was just one name for the perception of other dimensions. God as the chess master, the überprogrammer. God conducting the grandest of all experiments through these multiple dimensions, seeking the best of all possible worlds.

But unlike Tommy, I'm stuck in this world, in this dimension, in a temporal universe. Past, present, future. So I go back to go forward. That's as complicated as I can get. I'm not my brother, I'm not a genius.

So from time to time, uneasily, reluctantly, I feel myself called back to confront my unfinished book.

Like last year when Venus and Mars came perilously close together in our far northern skies. On that occasion I took my two sons to a park near our house. We climbed the hill at the park's center, where others had gathered. We took a telescope we'd just bought for my youngest, who, like my younger brother, possessed a keen interest in astronomy. We set up our telescope and took turns peering at those bright vivid dots on the horizon. Brighter than any stars, the planets of love and war, woman and man, which never quite meet or see eye to eye. And as I watched my boys argue about the position of various stars and constellations, I wished Tommy could be with us.

Tommy would have had so much more than me to say to my boys, Takeshi and Kengo, about the bright blazing behemoths that appear to us as tiny pinpricks of light. He even, for a brief time, worked at the famous Palomar Observatory; it was part of his postdoctoral fellowship after his studies at Berkeley.

When we were younger, he'd astonish adults with half-hour lectures on the planets and constellations. He so loved not just the stars and planets, I think, but the empty spaces between them, cold and lifeless and pure. Their purity comforted him, that and the possibilities of life elsewhere—that in some other cluster of stars or galaxy, someone or some thing was looking down on us with pitiless curiosity, the way we on Earth inspect insects crawling in the dirt. Those moments he spent gazing through the telescope at the observatory provided a sense of peace and purpose he could find nowhere else in his life.

Most likely he was gazing at the heavens that night, in his early thirties, shortly after he returned abruptly from Japan, he walked out into the desert. And never came back. He'd been living in L.A., but from the cache of unpaid bills he left, it was clear he'd given himself one last bender in Vegas, then headed back toward Gardena. He never made it, his rented car abandoned deep in the Mojave. His body was never found. Nor a note.

So that is what he left. Nothing.

But absence never troubled Tommy in the way it did me. That's why the infinite blank spaces and their cosmological theories comforted him. "The universe is far more empty than full," he used to say, "unimaginably so. Nothingness—that's the essence of our universe. And yet within that nothingness? There are dimensions of possibilities, Ben, dazzling theologies."

In the end though, those theories and theologies could not save him. Nor could I, his dimmer older brother.

TRACKING THE PLANETS

For several weeks I tried not to think much about Tommy's postcard from Japan. Like my book, it seemed something best left in a drawer, covered by papers of more pressing importance. Then came a chilly evening in March, the wind whipping off Lake Michigan, the frozen heart of our continent. I could say it was simply the weather. Indeed, I'd been telling myself that for weeks, the brutal Chicago winter holding on with a ferocity that belied any possible spring. Snow lingering and getting blacker with the bituminous exhaust; the fetid smells when the temperature rose above freezing, only to plunge back toward zero, as if playing a cruel joke. I couldn't see taking several more weeks of this. But it had been more than a few weeks or a few months; the paralyzing fear, the lethargy, a too-familiar sense it wasn't going to get better, only worse.

And so, as we drove to a talent show at my kids' school, I brooded. On my unresolved past, our unaccounted history, on my unfinished book, my blocked career. Brooded silently, hoping no one would notice. But then Takeshi and Kengo—aged ten and eight, a two-year spread just like that between Tommy and me—started squabbling.

Grace scolded them. I could feel her waiting for me to bark at them too, especially when they started up again. I knew I should have. After all, it's a basic premise for Grace and me: Stick together. Be on the same page, otherwise the inmates overrun the asylum. The boys got louder and louder; Kengo started slapping Takeshi's arm. I could hear Grace snap something and then address me, this time directly, telling me to throw my two cents in, to bring in my roaring deep-bassed dad voice like a bullhorn, putting down the incipient chaos.

But even though I was aware that both she and the boys were tugging at me in their own ways, I couldn't respond. I felt enshrouded by a bubble, through which I could barely see them. I couldn't tell whether the bubble was enclosing me or them, but I knew that membrane, invisible, palpable, and surreal, now seemed to me impenetrable. It was as if they, my boys and Grace and everyone else, existed in another world, light years away and beyond me.

All I could think of was how I did not want to go to the boys' school on this cold dark night. I didn't want to talk to the other parents and pretend I was one of them, one of their tribe. I could not do simple polite chitchat about our kids' performances and how the Bulls were faltering again and the constant bad weather. It was all babble to me, a world I wasn't a party to. I should have just let Grace take the boys and stayed home, slogged my way instead through Masao Miyoshi or Jameson. Zoned out on *Law & Order* or ESPN. Taken off on a run, pumped my free weights in the basement.

And yet I knew I had to go. We had to go to their damned school or it would be even worse. But I couldn't bring myself to yell at the boys to stop their yammering and bickering. I couldn't say a thing. I kept waiting for Grace to say something. Perhaps I wanted her to yell at me, to ask me what in the hell was wrong with me. But instead, all she said was, "You know, Ben, you don't have to go if you don't want."

"Who said anything about not going?" I snapped. "Did I say anything about that? You think you're the only parent here?"

I looked at her, annoyed. Just once, I thought, I'd like for you to lose it, for you to need to get a grip on yourself. Who are you to be the one who always has it together, who's always so sympathetic, so long-suffering and saint-like? Why don't you for once, goddamnit, tell me how you really feel instead of this insipid, insufferable mask of superiority and fake compassion? When what you really mean is, "My god, you can't even do this simple normal everyday event for the sake of your children? What gives you the right to act like this?"

And then it hit me: that was what my mother, in her own way, was always saying to my father. Pull it together, Tak. Stop feeling sorry for yourself. Get up and do something. Start acting like a man.

My father, my mother. What a tough act to follow. Even for someone like Grace.

I still feel a bit guilty about not telling Grace about the postcard. But I knew how'd she'd react, and I didn't want to alarm her. Not that she wouldn't be justified in her suspicions. She would say that I was treating her as an outsider, going all tribal on her again.

Somewhere back in her past, growing up Irish Catholic in a Baptist Pensacola suburb, Grace stepped from insider to outsider, from the pure white descendant of old Eire, to something more wayward and off-kilter. Of course, it was the late sixties— all over America white kids were drifting darker for a while. But she was from a family of Northerners in the South—which is a hell of a lot different from being a McMullen in Boston. Good liberals that they were, her parents marched when the fights for desegregation bubbled over into the school system, and the first blacks appeared at her junior high like unannounced travelers from another galaxy.

So perhaps it wasn't too surprising that she made a more unconventional choice along racial love lines. After all, her first crush was the star of the football team, a black boy bused in from across town. She never followed up on it; that was too taboo. But though she didn't quite know it back then, she'd gotten that crossover jones in her bloodstream. Eventually she realized she didn't want to be with some middle-of-the-road white guy; she didn't want to order from off the usual corporate All-American, All-Caucasian menu.

Of course she didn't realize I'd come with my own peculiar baggage. After all, what could she have known about Japanese Americans?

The college I teach at is located in a remote new suburb, just recently erased cornfields. It's a ways off from the ivy-coated walls of Northwestern or the University of Chicago, the sorts of institutions my mother once pictured me teaching at. I only teach one or two history courses a semester; the rest composition. I'm a good teacher, but the students there aren't attending for higher academic purposes; it's just a stepping stone to a slighter better job or a four-year institution. Neither they nor I take it too seriously.

So, the day after the event at my kids' school, I cancelled my classes. I just couldn't get myself up to face my students' bored, mechanical responses to my questions, or lecture mostly to myself. I needed some respite, to get away. But rather than trekking out to the hinterlands, I headed to the city.

A twelve-minute drive and I passed Northwestern, then swept down Sheridan, taking that curve around the old cemetery, the one at which we used to sing, "the worms crawl in, the worms crawl out," as we passed on school field trips. I was in the city now, edging past Devon, past Loyola. Then onto the Drive, past Foster Beach, where we used to swim when Montrose Beach got really crowded. The lake to my left spilled its aquamarine sheen, a huge hunk of turquoise beneath the early March sun. I knew the old neighborhood was a dozen blocks inland. I could have taken the next exit, headed right and I'd have been there, the three-story walk-ups I hadn't seen for years and never want to see again. Instead, I moved farther down the Drive, to another old haunting place. The grand Museum Campus on the lake, just off Grant Park. But I wasn't interested in all the museums there, just one.

I hadn't been there for years. It looked pretty much the same. Back then I don't think they had those photos of Stonehenge. Who knew those megalithic slabs of stone actually constituted a Bronze-age supercomputer to view the stars? And there certainly wasn't Alan Shepard's space suit from the Freedom 7 Mercury Capsule. Shepard wasn't history; he was a brand-spanking-new breakthrough in human exploration. Though two years younger, Tommy took more notice of him than I did, projecting outward from this first little puddle-jump off our globe and envisioning future light years of space exploration, stretching his imagination outward, past the Milk Way into the whirling galaxies beyond.

As I passed beneath the display planets hanging overhead, I thought of Tommy's lectures that he'd give when company came over. How my mother always seemed a bit embarrassed by her son's precociousness. He used to beg her to take him here, to the planetarium, almost as much as I begged my dad to take me to Wrigley Field. But Wrigley Field was close enough that I could just hop the El and go there myself. The Adler Planetarium was too far away.

Once, tired of pleading with my mom, Tommy got into a hell of a lot of trouble by taking off there by himself. He sat for hours beneath the artificial dome of stars, looking up at that light show of the heavens, before he finally made it back home, taking the El. He arrived at our apartment to find my parents, a few neighbors, and the police, all thinking he'd been squired away by some predatory prince of darkness, when all the while he'd been seduced by the stars. A false alarm.

My mother always said that Tommy came from some other family. And as I looked at the planetarium's panels on the history of astronomy, I could believe that. Perhaps, in another incarnation, he'd been some Polynesian ancestor who steered by the stars. Or some adviser to the Pharaoh, predicting eclipses and guiding the planting of crops. Or one of those Druid engineers who spent their nights on their backs, memorizing the courses of celestial bodies.

After wandering through the halls, I came to a new exhibit—the timeline of astral theories, from the myths of the constellations to the first glimmerings of scientific observations and the advances in our tools of vision. Then the theories of Einstein and Hawking. The ascent into more abstract realms, the ones my brother dwelt in, the big bang and alternative dimensions and strings of energy, phenomena no human eye will ever see and few human minds can wrap themselves around.

Why go off on some wild goose chase? I thought. Perhaps this is as good a place as any to look for my lost brother.

And then I was in the auditorium, leaning back with the rowdy schoolkids, just like I had years ago. They gradually hushed, their rambunctious energy magically slowed by the dimming into darkness and first pinpricks of light overhead. In an instant I flashed back over the years. Suddenly I am eight and my brother six. We are sitting here with our dad, who still possesses the energy and verve to tell us to shush and to let us know that if we got out of line he'd haul us out of there and give us what we had coming to us. Tommy's nudging me, and I know I shouldn't butt him back, but I do, and my father takes my arm and squeezes it. I can barely make out Tommy's smirking mug, and I hate him for luring me into his trap again.

Then, a couple rows before me, a teacher came barreling down the aisle, grabbed a kid, and hauled him up and pulled him out of the auditorium. He was probably one of those like me, a classroom troublemaker who could never keep his mouth shut.

Seconds later the narrator's voice started up, calm with wonder and a hushed urgency. The Pleiades. Orion the Hunter. The North Star. I could feel this urge to fall asleep, a warmth settling in my body, a long downy coat of fatigue wrapping me in a cocoon. Yes, why not sleep.

I woke to the face of a young black usher, shaking me gently.

"Sir, sir. The planetarium's closing now."

His face looked vaguely familiar. Where had I had seen him before? My leg was asleep, and I had to shake the burning numbness away. I got up gently, and the usher asked if I was all right.

"Yes, thank you. I guess I was more tired than I thought."

"I'm sorry, sir. I hate to rush you, but the doors are already closed."

Great. I could have ended up spending the night here. Just what Tommy would have wanted back when we were kids. When was the last time I took Takeshi and Kengo here? I thought. I should really bring them back.

Suddenly I had a moment of panic. Then I remembered that it was Grace's turn to pick them up. Of course I wouldn't tell Grace about my little sojourn to the past. I knew how she'd take my canceling my classes. It would only confirm her fears that I was starting to stray off into my own inner dark.

On the steps outside the skyline of downtown was lit up before me. There were only a few people milling about, among them a young Asian kid, maybe Southeast Asian, maybe Filipino, probably eight or nine. He didn't look lost, but there was no one else with him. I thought about going up to say something to him, but then I wondered if that would scare him. After all, I know something about scary, strange grown-up men. But because of that, I thought I should say something to him, make sure he could get home safely.

"Excuse me, son. Are you O.K.?"

He looked at me like he didn't understand what I was saying. I wondered if he spoke English. He shook his head and turned away. I wasn't quite sure of what he meant by this so I persisted.

"Is anyone coming to get you?"

He looked back at me and said nothing.

"I said, 'Is anyone coming to get you?'"

He glanced to the side as if help might be coming.

"Yeah," he finally said.

"Who?"

"My older brother. He should be here already."

I could tell that I was making him nervous. "Are you sure he's coming?"

He wiped his nose. "I'm not supposed to talk to strangers."

"Yes, of course. You shouldn't. I don't want to scare you." Now why did I say that? That's exactly the wrong thing to say. "I just want to make sure you're O.K."

I had this urge to tell him that there was a reason I was worried for him. That I knew what dangers were out there. That I knew what it's like to think the world is safe and always will be, when exactly the opposite is the case. I wanted to tell him that he could trust me. I had two boys of my own. It was just natural that I would look out for other boys. But of course I knew that would only sound creepier.

The boy just stood there, saying nothing. I glanced around. I noticed that there was this guy in a parka who seemed to be lurking at the other end of the horseshoe. I decided to stick around.

A few seconds later the boy turned to me.

"It's o.k. My brother's picking me up."

I looked at him and saw a hint of fear in his eyes, though he was trying to hide it. He saw I was going to speak again and he beat me to it. "I'm going back inside," he said, nodding toward the planetarium doors. "To call my brother." I knew the doors were already locked, only I didn't want to point that out to him.

It was his words that threw me. They somehow reminded me of my brother, though I couldn't remember how or when Tommy might have said something like that. And then it began to flow up inside me. I knew I should stop it, knew it would only scare the boy more. I wanted to say something, something casual, like, sure, I'll just hang around till he comes. But I knew how that would sound, and that only brought the surge farther up my throat, and I felt suddenly cold, very very cold, the wind slicing in off the lake, and the two of us standing there in the dark, and that guy over there in the shadows, and it was not going to help things one bit, but I couldn't stop it. When the first sob started, I managed to stop, but another rose up in its place, and I couldn't shove it back; all I could do was try to keep any vocalization from erupting, and my chest, my throat, broke into silent seizures, the tears starting to slip out, and I hoped to god that the kid thought it was just the cold shivering my body and the wind searing the wetness from my eyes.

He looked up then. His face was no longer scared, just concerned, worried for me when I should have been worried for him.

"Are you all right, mister?"

I didn't say a thing, I couldn't. I just stood there, frozen, unable to move. I stood there, shaking, and I prayed for the boy's brother to come get him. Soon.

The next day I told Grace that I was starting in again on my long-abandoned tome on suicides. At first, she was skeptical. Part of her was not too keen about my book project; she knew its troubled origins. And given my family's history, she's understandably wary of any impulse on my part to wander off.

"Do you really need to go? Can't you do your research at Northwestern or the u of c?"

"They don't have the collections like the ones out in L.A."

I said I needed to get a new perspective on my subject; being away from familiar surroundings ought to help. I really should be taking a trip to Japan, but the West Coast would have to do for now (we couldn't afford such a trip and my traveling across the Pacific would have set off too many alarms for Grace). And as she well knew, I only had a few years of academic viability left; I needed to complete *Famous Suicides* soon or it wouldn't make any difference.

In the end, she didn't fight it. Maybe she wanted to take it as a good sign that I seemed interested in my career again. I'd left so many tasks unfinished.

So I made plans to go out to the West Coast when the semester ended. I'd do some research at the libraries there, their stacks on Asia and Asian Americana. And if, while I was out there, I might make a few belated inquiries about my brother's disappearance, well, there was no reason to trouble Grace about that.

That was several weeks ago. Now, here I am driving from L.A. to Vegas, just like Tommy, thinking about how I didn't know back then where my research would lead me. Didn't know I would be contemplating, like my brother, my own run to the middle of nowhere. Didn't know I'd risk getting myself hopelessly lost, or that I'd envision doing my own vanishing, going way off the grid, playing with the odds out here, as so many do.

But perhaps it's only off the grid that I could possibly see how much I've never understood about my past, our past, the currents deep beneath the surface of our years together, hidden riptides pulling us further and further apart, dividing us more than we realized or, certainly, wanted. All the questions I've never ventured to voice, not just about Tommy, but about my father and mother. Or the hard many-angled answers I'm just starting to engage—debts, obligations. Crimes. Prisoners. Punishments.

I've got hundreds of miles to go, and the next mountain range looms ahead. I push my rented Taurus a bit faster, knowing I have to drive all night and perhaps the next. As the Nevada desert barrels behind me, I tell myself I'm just a *ronin*, one of those masterless samurai, in the old black-and-white Toho films. A solitary warrior, fighting for himself, for honor's sake.

No, that's hardly what's going on. I'm just a kid here, whistling in the dark. Making my way back home, step by step.

2

BOYHOOD BATTLES

From notebook No. 7, *Famous Suicides of the Japanese Empire*:

What to do with this treacly letter from the kamikaze pilot Lieutenant Sanehisa Uemura to his child ("When you grow up and want to meet me . . . if you pray deeply, surely your father's face will show itself within your heart . . . Even though something happens to me, you must certainly not think of yourself as a child without a father . . . ")? Of course one can admire the lieutenant's courage, but the problem lies both in sentimentalizing and in Orientalizing such gestures. The man is a common soldier, not a philosopher or a psychologist, much less a writer. And soldiers of all countries, not just the Japanese, go off to battle, sometimes without any hope of surviving, giving up their lives to destroy the enemy or save their fellow soldiers. It's just too easy to view these acts strictly through bushido and the way of the warrior—as opposed to taking into account the military's propaganda machine or the dictates of a desperate imperialist-driven government . . .

Beyond all that, what to make of the differences between the father and the mother suicide? Take the case of Kimura Fumiko, the Japanese housewife who tried to drown herself and her children last year in the waves off of Santa Monica. All three were dragged ashore by some college students passing by, but only the mother survived. She was charged with murder, ensuing some debate about cultural norms. But I think too much can be made there of Japanese cultural views on parent-child suicide, oyako shinju. *As if the Japanese don't view such acts as criminal—which they do. Or even that they regard the mother's view of the children as an extension of herself as a definitive mitigating factor in sentencing; when sentences in such cases are more lenient, it tends to be more from the parent repenting and recognizing their crime than from the avowal of a certain cultural or psychological disposition. Of course there was that petition signed by both Japanese and Japanese Americans in southern California in support of Kimura, stating that "the mother's intent is to save the child from a life of suffering without her." (Perhaps this is a side issue, but I can't help but wonder which portion of those 20,000 signatures were honto no nihonjin and which Japanese American? And of those J.A., what generation were they?—the newspaper accounts don't say, once again blending all these divisions; why bother? A Jap is a Jap, anywhere you find them, as that old redneck Senator Tom Stewart put it, once upon a time.)*

Reading this over, it's not clear to me what the real subject of these notes is. Too many elements bleeding into each other, including my own unscholarly personal concerns. I need to be more organized, rigorous, and objective. I can't keep wandering off into a past that has nothing to do with my original thesis . . .

We lived in Uptown, a couple blocks from the El. It wasn't quite what you'd call a ghetto but—to use my father's expletive—damn close. Crumbling three-story walk-ups, yards with bare dirt and cinders. Cracked walks and trash-littered streets. The rickety wooden steps at the backs of buildings with their lines of laundry. Fences with huge gouges or bent over with no hope of repair. Alleys of broken glass and rancid odors. All surfaces dark and grimy, as if motor oil or some foul industrial soot had silted down upon everything. It certainly wasn't like the neighborhoods up near Lake Shore Drive.

I didn't think of us as poor. My mom would always proclaim that next year we were going to move out to the suburbs. That was where my Uncle Hank and Auntie Yo lived with my cousins Brian and Mark. She usually said this right after something went wrong with the apartment, like when the toilet clogged or the radiators leaked. She'd tell my father he ought to go up and yell at the landlord, Mr. Johnson. My father would say that it wasn't Mr. Johnson's fault—that it was an old building.

"It's his building," my mom proclaimed. "He ought to keep it up."

"O.K., O.K."

"Well, are you going to go tell him?"

"I said O.K."

"Are you going to yell at him?"

"I'll tell him."

She glared at him. "The trouble with you," she said, "the trouble with you is that you're afraid of *hakujin*."

When I think back, it seems strange that I didn't quite know what the word *hakujin*—white people—meant, though I sensed it referred to outsiders, people not like us. I didn't think much in those days about what *we* were. The other kids in the neighborhood were mostly what we called hillbillies. Poor whites from Tennessee or Kentucky or West Virginia. They were tough kids who slicked up in jean jackets and shoes with cleats and spoke from the sides of their mouths. They flashed greased pompadours and slipped combs from their back pockets, slid them back through their hair all the way to their ducktails as if prepping armored helmets for their battles with the world.

Here and there were a couple of Puerto Rican kids, but we never hung out with them. Sometimes we got in fights with them. They were even tougher than the hillbillies. One Puerto Rican kid next door would watch us all the time from his upstairs window.

He must have been only five or six, but he told us once that he had a switchblade. We didn't know whether to believe him or not.

But when Bobby Jo Watkins told us his older brother Jackie had a zip gun, we believed it. Jackie sported long sideburns and he'd sometimes flick open his switchblade to pique us if we were over at their house and he was in a good mood. Jackie was real tough, even tougher than the Puerto Ricans.

I wasn't very tough. A lot of the kids thought I knew judo like Michael Nagata. I used to tell everyone I had a brown belt. But I had to do this when Michael wasn't there. One time he heard me telling Jimmy Pearson about judo class and he punched me in the arm. Not real hard but hard enough so that I wanted to cry but didn't. Michael said that I was a sissy, I didn't know judo, I didn't go to class with him at the Buddhist temple, so stop bragging.

After Nagata left, I told Jimmy Pearson I wanted to fight Nagata, but my *sensei* said that a good warrior never triggers a fight and always tries to walk away from one. That's what my dad's *sensei* had told him back in L.A.

I didn't really like Michael Nagata. He was the only other Japanese American in the neighborhood, and he always seemed bent on putting me down. But I could never challenge him. He was older and bigger and had been taking judo classes since he was seven and had already chalked up a brown belt.

For years I kept begging my father to let me take judo classes. Sometimes when I did this, he'd talk about the judo classes he used to take in L.A. He'd go on about all the matches he'd won and how he'd earned his black belt by beating his *sensei*. His *sensei*, he said, was a real character. When the *sensei's* blond girlfriend showed up, he would always arrange a match between him and my dad's friend Tao, the biggest guy in the class. And then the *sensei* would beat the crap out of poor Tao. "Tao used to say he hated it when that *hakujin* gal showed up."

But no matter how much I begged, my father never took me to judo classes at the Buddhist temple. "Later, *boichan*. Later."

Now of course I know why he put me off. Why he didn't like us having too much to do with other *nihonjin*. And I have my doubts that he ever was a black belt or that he even took judo classes back in L.A.

That fall, when I was eight, Tommy and I would return home from school and find our father sitting—or more often lying—on the living room couch, watching TV. The Cubs game or an afternoon movie.

I still wasn't used to his presence at this time of day. I wanted to watch cartoons. The host was this pretty *hakujin* girl named Susan. She sported a flouncy polka-dot dress and her blond hair was wavy and cut with bangs. Her companion was a talking table who flew through the air like a magic carpet. A rather crusty sort, he jabbered about traveling somewhere else, like England, where tables were respected. Or Persia, where he could live with other flying pieces of furniture.

The year before, I'd watched the show every day after school. My mother often had a glass of milk and a plate of Salerno butter cookies waiting for me. I dipped the cookies in the milk and savored their beveled edges bite by bite. In her checkered apron, my mother stood at the stove or the sink, asking me a question or two about my day. Then I'd be off to the living room to watch TV.

But that fall my father was the one home in the afternoon, and my mother was working. My father's old job was at the Chicago Transit Authority. Now my mother worked there.

It was strange, this switch. But neither of my parents talked about it. It was as if over the summer between my third and fourth grades they'd exchanged places. My father, though, did not greet me with a glass of milk and Salerno butter cookies.

When I looked in from the kitchen, the living room would be dark, all the shades drawn. The only light the gray glow of the TV. If he sensed me peeking in, he'd make a vague wave of his hand. He wouldn't actually turn and look at me, his gaze constantly directed toward the screen.

Tommy would complain to me that he wished Mommy was here.

"You're such a baby," I told him. "Just eat your cookies, kindergarten baby." We were sitting at the kitchen table. I was the one who got the milk and cookies now for both of us.

"I'm not in kindergarten. I'm in first grade."

"Well, kindergarteners cry for their mommies." I told him that when I first went to kindergarten, I told mom she could leave a block before we got to school. When I got to the class, all these kids were clutching their mommies, some bawling like babies.

"I bet you cried for Mommy just like that. Just like you're doing now."

Tommy got the message. He just sat there, sullenly dipping his butter cookies in his glass as if he were fishing for something that wasn't there.

One afternoon I found my father taking in a war movie on TV. A squad of American G.I.s were trapped in a Buddhist temple. A huge brass Buddha towered over them. The soldiers arrayed themselves about the statue or, if they were wounded, rested at his feet. When the enemy soldiers rushed the temple, the noise was terrifying, not just rifle and machine guns but airplanes diving overhead. How could the G.I.s withstand such an onslaught, what with the planes and the enemy storming up the hill in wave after wave? But time and again the Americans just mowed their enemies down.

I slipped in and stood next to the sofa and watched awhile. I squeezed down near my father's feet. He didn't move to make room but he didn't shoo me away as he sometimes did. As always, he wore a T-shirt and faded khakis. Brown slippers. A five o'clock shadow grizzled his face; his hairline was already starting to recede. He swept his jet-black hair straight back off his forehead. He had a one-inch scar that seemed to dangle from his lip and always made me think he looked like a tough guy or a gangster. But in truth he never seemed that tough. He always seemed tired, tired and far away.

On the screen the radio operator kept rasping for reinforcements.

"They're not going to get out," said my father. "Poor bastards."

I asked him if this was the war Uncle Elbert fought in. He turned and shot me a stern look as if he were about to get angry. But then he simply said, "No, this is the Korean War. Those aren't Japanese attacking them, *boichan*. They're Koreans."

To this day I can't remember ever seeing what the enemy in that movie looked like. All I recall are the American soldiers, firing away and killing dozens, hundreds of their unseen enemy, all the while knowing that they were never going to make it, never going home. How I admired those soldiers and wanted to be like them, brave and fierce and true. They had names like Jones and Kowalski and O'Hara. I thought that was odd since our name was Ohara, though the O'Hara in the movie looked nothing like anyone in my family.

A short while after my father and I watched this movie, he went away. I'd come home and there'd be no one there and I could watch whatever I wanted. Then he returned for a while. Then he went away again. This happened off and on for the next few years.

And then he never came back. Just like those soldiers in the temple.

LIAR, LIAR, PANTS ON FIRE

At night before bed, my father would tell us stories.

Momotaro, the Peach boy who fought the *oni*—ogres—who raided his village. Issunboshi, the one-inch warrior who dueled with a needle and protected a princess many times his size against the *oni*, piercing their tongues, sticking his needle in their eyes. I loved these two guys. Like most boys, I wanted to wield a sword and to stick it to the bad guys; I wanted to be a hero. So of course I hated the story of Urashima Taro, who fell in love with a mermaid and lived with her under the sea while time slipped away and everyone he knew died. When he finally returned to his village, no one knew him. He hadn't aged. But two hundred years had passed. The story seemed pointless to me. Who cared about mermaids anyway?

But it wasn't all Japanese tales from my dad. He mixed in American ones too. Paul Bunyan and Babe the Blue Ox, Pecos Bill, and Davy Crockett at the Alamo, another great warrior. A few were silly little things he'd make up, like a tale of Popeye and the three monkeys who pelted him with coconuts. He'd also recite odd things, like the Gettysburg Address or the opening of *A Tale of Two Cities* or the ghost speech from *Hamlet*. (He once said he would have liked to have been an actor.)

Tommy and I didn't understand these recitals—well, at least I didn't—though my dad sometimes made me try to repeat them, telling us we should learn them by heart. But all I remember now is a few lines, such as old Hamlet's ghost going, "List oh list . . . what a falling off was there." Tommy somehow memorized most of them. He would recite them after Dad left, annoying me to no end. I felt he was showing off. But he also liked these speeches, even more than the stories my father recounted. He said he was going to grow up to be president or an actor. I told him he'd have to choose (of course this was before any of us knew what would happen to the actor who hosted *Death Valley Days*).

If he was in one of his brighter moods, my father would sing to us, songs from Glenn Miller or Tommy Dorsey or Cole Porter. "Long Ago and Far Away." "Begin the Beguine." He had a good voice, baritone, richer and more manly than you'd think, given his slight stature, like some barrel-chested Italian had been hidden inside him, some Pavarotti or Caruso. He'd talk about how they were playing "Don't Sit Under the Apple Tree" on a record player at the *nisei* dance when he met my mother. "I took one look at her and said to my buddy Tosh, 'Tosh, that's the girl I'm going to marry.'" My father laughed. "Tosh said I was too ugly for such a pretty girl, but I proved him wrong, didn't I *boichan?*" And then he launched into "Don't Sit Under the Apple Tree," his eyes gleaming as if he were again seeing my mother for the first time.

After a while, though, Tommy and I didn't quite enjoy this singing so much since we'd learned that such bursts of ebullience would sometimes lead to more morose moods. And those darker moods often preceded his periodic disappearances. In his melancholic moods, he'd move from swing tunes to Japanese ballads, songs his father had sung while playing the *biwa*, a Japanese stringed instrument. The songs were fluted with a mournful quality and quavering half-tones, almost bluesy in character. (I could imagine how our grandfather must have sounded, out in the country, like some Mississippi Delta singer, soulfully bringing back the great battles of the Heike and the Genji in syllables of that foreign tongue.)

Neither Tommy nor I spoke any Japanese. But Tommy was young enough that he seemed to respond to the songs more deeply than I. He'd sing along with our father, mouthing the syllables, though not understanding their meaning. In another way, perhaps he did understand their meaning, absorbing the ballads in ways I could not.

My father sometimes explained to both of us the outlines of the epic tales. How the Heike were finally defeated in a great naval battle. How the young Prince Atsumori was beheaded by Kumagai, who did not want to kill a boy of only fourteen. But Kumagai knew other warriors from his side, hungry for glory, would not spare the boy. And so, almost weeping, Kumagai took on the deed. Afterwards, hauling up Atsumori's body, he lighted upon a flute, proof of the boy's delicate nature, further cause to rue the cruelties of war.

For some reason my father liked to dwell on the defeated Heike, not simply their dead, like Atsumori, but those who survived, like the Empress. She felt so ashamed not only to have tumbled from such former glory—even her house physically collapsed in an earthquake—but for surviving when others had fallen in battle or committed *seppuku*. She shaved her hair and became a nun and moved north to the mountains of Ohara. "That's where our people came from," my father said (though my mother later said that this was all nonsense). "She thought it would be good to live in a place remote from the troubles of the world. So the wives of Nobutaka and Takafusa—far lower in rank than she—sent a palanquin to fetch her."

"What's a palanquin?" Tommy asked. I couldn't have cared less; I wanted to hear more about the battles.

"A palanquin is like a miniature stage coach, only it's not pulled by horses, it's carried by servants."

So she still had servants. I couldn't figure out why she was so sad then.

"They took her to this ancient temple, surrounded by mossy rocks and a garden of reeds. It was winter, and everything was covered in hoarfrost, and the whiteness seemed to the Empress a premonition of death."

I worried Tommy was going to ask what a premonition was. I didn't know but didn't care. Actually, he probably knew what it meant; he always had a much bigger vocabulary than I did.

"And so there she lived the rest of her days, in a ten-foot square cell."

"Was she happy?" Tommy asked.

"Happiness wasn't a question. She'd lost everything. She was there to renounce the world."

"So why didn't she just kill herself?" Tommy chirped.

My father looked at Tommy, then looked away. Why would Tommy ask such a stupid question? I thought.

"I don't know, Son," my father said. "Maybe because she was a woman."

I don't remember exactly when I discovered that telling a few lies made the world an easier place to live in.

For years I thought that I learned my ways of twisting the truth from my mother (I couldn't see then that my father had his own share of lies). After all, she had told both Tommy and me to lie to get us into school a year early. "This is just our secret," she told us. "No one else has to know. Just say you're five. And if they ask what year you were born in?"

"1954?"

"No, 1953, Ben. 1953. That would make you five."

She did the same drill with Tommy, only he got it much quicker than I did.

I recall my mother once talking to Auntie Satsu on the phone. Satsu was married to my uncle Elbert. My mom was telling her she would like to come over and visit on Saturday, but with her new job, she had to work even on Saturday. It was the post office, she said, the job she took after the one with the CTA. Rain or shine the mail has to go through.

But when Saturday came around, my mom didn't wake up early to go to work. When I asked her about this, she said it wasn't her turn to work that Saturday. Then why had she told Auntie Satsu that we couldn't go over to her house because she had to work on Saturday? She gave an exasperated sigh. She said that sometimes we have to tell little lies not to hurt other people's feelings. They were called white lies. She added that only grown-ups could do this, not kids.

Whatever my mother thought, I liked going over to Auntie Satsu and Uncle Elbert's house. I didn't understand why we gradually stopped going there. But even before we stopped, I noticed my father never went with us.

My uncle Elbert had been a soldier in World War II. He'd fought in the famed 442nd, the division of Japanese Americans, the most decorated unit in Europe. He himself had won a Purple Heart. Every time we visited, I asked him to show it to me.

Sometimes I'd even ask to see the scar on his belly, where he'd been wounded. My mom always told him not to do this, so did Auntie Satsu. But I'd persist in pestering him, and so would Tommy. Uncle Elbert would tell us we'd seen it before, we didn't need to see it again.

But Tommy figured out a way to get to him.

"I bet you don't even have a wound," he said.

"Tommy, don't say that," I whispered. I was afraid he was going to make Uncle Elbert mad.

"Maybe you never even fought in the war. Maybe you're making it all up."

Uncle Elbert looked at Tommy. For a second I thought that he was really angry, maybe even going to hit him. "You little whippersnapper."

"Tommy, Mom and Auntie Satsu said not to bother him," I said, trying to disarm the situation.

A slight smile slipped across Uncle Elbert's face. "That's O.K., Ben. This is men's business." And he winked at me.

When our uncle pulled up his shirt, I could see the rolls of fat. He would get even larger as the years went on. The scar was starting to inch its way into the folds. It was purple and splotched and looked like a repulsive pink worm.

"See. That's where the Gerries got me."

My uncle's scar made me feel a bit queasy but also thrilled me. To think that his skin had been pierced by Nazi shrapnel. My mind flashed to TV war shows like *Combat* and *The Lieutenant*. I pictured Uncle Elbert huddled in the foxhole with Sergeant Saunders, both breathing heavily after scurrying across a field. Faces sweating, beards unshaven, grimy and black. They'd glance at each other and nod and leap out over the top, screaming and shooting and gunning right at the Gerries, who didn't stand a chance.

Both Tommy and I tried to get Uncle Elbert to talk about the war. He always said that there was nothing much to talk about. He'd been wounded, he'd gotten a Purple Heart, but a lot of his buddies had gotten Purple Hearts. It was nothing special. In fact, he was one of the lucky ones.

I read his talk as the usual grown-up attempt to slough off a kid. Now I see that there was more to it, something that happened when Tommy and I really pestered him and made him tell us about his experiences as a soldier. Usually Uncle Elbert seemed nothing like my dad; Elbert was louder, lighter, more jovial. But when he talked about the war, even a little, he reminded me of Dad, though they weren't even related. Maybe it was the look that came over his face when he talked about the 442nd and his time in Europe. Something grainy and somber in his voice.

With Uncle Elbert's gentle demurral, I thought we were finished for the afternoon. After all, Tommy couldn't accuse our uncle again of not having been in the war. We'd already seen his scar. But Tommy was one step ahead of me.

"Jackie Watkins said there weren't any Japs on our side," Tommy blurted out. "They all fought for the enemy."

"Who's Jackie Watkins?" my uncle asked.

"One of the gang," I said.

"Well, tell him he doesn't know what he's talking about."

"Yeah," I chimed in. "The 442nd was the best in all Europe."

"I don't know about that, Ben. It's hard to compare such things." He paused. "There were a lot of good soldiers on our side; that's why we won. You can't just single out any one unit. A lot of good men died in those places, Anzio, Bruyeres, the Vosges. One thing though about us Buddhaheads you could be sure of. When you moved, the other Buddhaheads moved with you. You could rely on them. The first day going across the field back in Bruyeres I sensed that."

"But why were they like that?"

"Why? Well, we were Japanese, Ben. *Giri* and *gambare*. Obligation, hard work. You get this sort of thing in elite corps. The Marines had it. I don't think most of the ordinary *hakujin* soldiers had it. It gives you a sense of confidence. Maybe even a feeling of immortality, that you're not going to get hurt. And yet all the time you're still afraid. God only knows why you continue. It's not the notion of pride. Duty, yeah. You're a soldier, you keep the line moving. If you didn't, you couldn't face the other soldiers afterwards. And it wasn't like they were *hakujin*, strangers. We were all *nihonjin*. It was more like family."

He looked at me. I liked that. I thought he was doing this because I was the oldest. He was talking to me.

"You're young, Ben, I know how boys think about all this. Like in the movies, like John Wayne. But no soldier goes up there to sacrifice themselves. That's crazy. Oh, there were a few guys, they'd walk around as if nothing was going to happen to them. Like in the Iliad, like Achilles. A war lover. In some ways I admired these men. But they made me uncomfortable too. Their way of fighting, that was something you didn't do if you wanted to survive. And there were some battles, like in the Vosges, mortar fire coming in all night . . ."

My uncle got this look, like he was thinking about something. Tommy asked him about being wounded. But my uncle didn't seem to hear him. He was talking to himself.

"In the morning, after all the shelling, you became a soldier again. The light changed, and it was like waking up from a dream. If you hadn't slept, if you couldn't sleep, it wasn't a problem. You had other things to do."

He sat there for a second, looking nowhere in particular. Then he told us to scat to the kitchen to get him some *mochi*. "I can smell the *shoyu*," he said.

When we came back, he'd turned the Cubs game on, and we knew all talk of the war was over. My uncle had been a semi-pro in baseball after the war. He could talk a good game. He knew his stuff.

Later I told my dad all about what Uncle Elbert had told us. He didn't seem that interested though. I figured he had heard it all before.

We called the lot out back the Empty. The Empty was just that, dirt and cinders and broken glass, dandelions and ragweed. We played baseball and football and dodgeball there. Or we'd go out with Hellman's Mayonnaise jars to catch monarchs and viceroys and cabbage whites and the occasional tiger swallowtail. We'd creep up to the weed where the butterfly had landed and snap the top over the bottle. We snatched grasshoppers the same way. After we trapped them, we'd slip a grass stalk in the jar and the grasshopper would perch there and spit out its brown saliva. *Tobacco juice,* we called it. Occasionally we hunted dragonflies. They darted so quickly that we went after them with cardboard boxes hocked from the back of the IGA.

Jimmy Pearson was my best friend. Besides Tommy, who didn't really count, Jimmy and I were the two youngest of the gang. Jimmy wasn't tough like Bobby Jo Watkins, whose older brother Jackie was always beating the crap out of him. Jimmy had blond hair and a cowlick just like Dennis the Menace. A lot skinnier than me. Michael Nagata called us Laurel and Hardy. I was Hardy, the fat one. Or as Michael Nagata dubbed me, the Crisco Kid—fat in the can.

"You know what the Japs did at Pearl Harbor?" Michael Nagata asked me one day.

I shook my head.

Suddenly he goosed me. "Sneak attack." He howled with laughter when I shrieked. He called me a little girl.

He did this over and over, long after I knew what was coming. At ten, he was two years older than me, and that meant a lot in those days.

Nagata liked making up nicknames for other kids. Sometimes they were nasty, sometimes they were just his way of giving his stamp on things. One day the gang was sitting on the back steps of our building, and I was scrambling down to join them. "Hey here comes Harry Karry," Nagata shouted. I felt uneasy, like I should walk back up the stairs, but I knew I couldn't do that.

"You know what that means?" he asked.

I shook my head.

"It's when Japs kill themselves," piped Bobby Jo. "Like Jap warriors. Or Jap soldiers after the war."

"They kill themselves?" Jimmy Pearson asked.

Michael Nagata said it had to do with honor. I didn't understand what that meant. He said they *had* to kill themselves. It was their duty.

Then, to set the other guys straight, he proclaimed, "We're Americans. We don't do things like that." Part of me was taken aback. It was one of the few times Michael Nagata ever acknowledged that he and I had anything in common. *Harakiri?* That was a Jap thing. We were American. It had nothing to do with us.

Later Nagata left to go to his judo class, and Jimmy, Bobby Jo, and I played war in the Empty, crouching behind some bushes, firing at the Gerries. We argued over who would be Sergeant Saunders, and Bobby Jo cried out, "first dibs," and so got be the hero of *Combat*. I said that I was Sergeant Rock from DC Comics, and Jimmy said that he was John Wayne in *The Sands of Iwo Jima*. Bobby Jo said we were fighting Gerries not Japs, but Jimmy said Bobby Jo got to pick Sergeant Saunders first so he could pick whomever he wanted.

After a while we charged from the bushes, and each of us fell, dying glorious deaths, shivering like worms on the ground and giving out our last groans. Then we rose up and charged once more, overrunning the enemy in their foxholes, stabbing them with our bayonets.

As we walked back home after our battles, I told them all about the Purple Heart that my father had won in the war and the story of how the 442nd had saved the Lost Battalion of Texans. I explained the way the *nisei* soldiers held their line, and how my dad said that it all had to do with their being Japanese Americans, and how it wasn't that they weren't afraid but they couldn't let each other down.

I didn't know why Michael Nagata always had it in for me. That was just the way things were. Some kids got picked on, some kids did the picking.

The worst time was probably when we'd been over at Bobby Jo Watkins's, and his older brother Jackie was there. Jackie was showing us his magnifying glass. He told us he could make things burn with it. We went outside to the see how it worked. He put a piece of newspaper on the sidewalk. We held our breath as Jackie concentrated the rays of the sun on the headlines of another Cubs loss. "The Cubs ain't no good," Jackie joked. "Let 'em burn." Gradually the headlines started to smoke and blacken. Finally a tiny flame caught and swept across the scrap of paper.

Someone found a green, fuzzy caterpillar and placed it on the walk. Jackie shot the rays into it as it tried to crawl away. Dozens of tiny legs scurried and flailed in the air. It tucked and twisted to right itself. Then it began to smoke and blacken and it gradually twisted slower and slower, smoking but never bursting into flames. Somehow this made me queasy. I think that I said something about not doing this. Maybe that's what started it.

Anyway, the next thing I knew Michael Nagata said that they ought to try it on my head. I immediately stood up from the burnt caterpillar.

Michael Nagata shouted again, "Let's burn up Harry's hair." I began to back away.

"Look how scared he is, what a scaredy-cat," said Michael, pointing at me.

I stared at him, frozen, terrified. My legs suddenly felt heavy, ponderous, as if they weren't a part of me. A burning sensation crawled up my arms and my scalp began to itch and I felt the sun beating down hotter and hotter.

I turned and ran. I knew it was useless—Michael was faster than me, and he was going to catch me and burn through my skull. I didn't look back, just kept running. Where should I go? If only I could reach the door to our apartment building I might be safe.

I heard Michael Nagata yell, "Grab him, grab Harry." I kept running. "Get him!" I stumbled and fell. My knee and palm scraped the sidewalk, something ripped in my pants. Pain shot up from both places, and I tried to get up. But it was too late. I put my hands over my head and curled into a ball on the sidewalk, the way the caterpillar had twisted in on itself and its fate.

Balled up with eyes closed, I heard Jackie Watkins tell Nagata to let me go. I forced myself up and started running again, pumping for all I was worth.

I made it to our apartment and locked the door. From the couch my dad looked up. He asked me why I was locking the door.

"Just because," I said.

I hurried off to my bedroom, before he asked anything else.

One day Jimmy Pearson, Bobby Jo Watkins, this new kid Billy Blevins, and I went over to Michael Nagata's apartment.

I'd never have done that alone, but since the gang had decided to call on him, I would go along. We spent the afternoon playing football in the narrow hallway. We really didn't have much room to maneuver there, so we simply tried to bowl each other over.

I was big for my age. Well, actually, Michael Nagata was right. I was fat. My mother had to buy husky corduroy pants from Sears and then, to make them fit, cut them a few inches shorter. But in the hallway football game, my bulk made up for my lack of speed. I could pull guys from the other side along the corridor. Michael even had a hard time bringing me down. I scored four touchdowns. Every time Michael Nagata called me a scab, meaning I'd scored because I was lucky, not good. Once he called me a big fat ape, and I would have burst into tears if we'd been alone and if Billy hadn't said to him, "Come on, Nagata, cut it out."

"Big fat ape," Nagata said again, but Billy said nothing back. Jimmy said that *Combat* was coming on, so the rest of them ambled down the hall into the living room.

"You gonna cry, baby?" asked Michael Nagata, glaring at me.

"No," I mumbled. I tried to make my way around him without touching him.

"Harry's so fat he can't even fit through the door."

I just hurried on, trying to catch up with the rest of the gang. I knew what could happen when Michael Nagata got going; I'd borne the brunt of his bullying too many times before. I didn't want something like the magnifying glass chase again. Now, here in his own house, I'd scored four touchdowns and beaten him in football. I could sense that he was still angry when he went to the bathroom and came back and barked, "Move over, Harry," so he could sit on the couch where I was sitting. I scooted down to the floor next to Jimmy Pearson.

In that episode of *Combat*, they were trying to take this hill, only a machine gun kept laying down fire, pinning them to their position. They couldn't even get close enough to toss a grenade.

"They ought to bring up them mortars," Billy said. "That'll fix 'em."

But the squad had used up all its mortar shells, so they squatted in their foxholes, trying to figure out what to do.

"Your dad would know what to do, wouldn't he, Harry?" said Jimmy.

Sometimes Jimmy would call me Harry too. Only it never sounded like it did from Michael Nagata.

"What would he know?" scoffed Nagata.

"Oh yeah," said Jimmy. "Harry's dad was in the war. He was a real hero. He even got a Purple Heart."

"Yeah, sure," said Nagata. "Liar, liar, pants on fire."

"He was. Tell him, Harry. Wasn't your dad in the war?"

Michael snorted. "Sure. Old scaredy-pants has got a real live hero for a dad."

I knew I shouldn't say anything. Maybe I thought my four touchdowns meant something. Maybe it had given me a swelled head and bloated my brains.

"I'll show you his medal if you don't believe me."

Michael Nagata looked at me. An odd look, as if he couldn't believe I was saying this.

"Come on over to my house. I dare you."

"Your old man doesn't have any medals."

"I double dare you."

"You spazz. You're lying. I know you're lying."

"Yeah, I triple dare you."

Michael Nagata started laughing. I didn't know what to make of this. Why had I said that? But I couldn't back down now.

"I'm not going over to your house," said Michael. "No way."

"'Cause you know he's right," said Jimmy. "It's in his dad's drawer."

I thought Michael Nagata would back off now that I had the upper hand. Some part of me knew that it was insane to think this. There was no Purple Heart in my dad's drawer. But ever since I told Jimmy Pearson and he'd believed it, I'd started to believe it too.

"You jackass," said Nagata. "You don't know what you're talking about." I couldn't tell if he was talking to Jimmy or me. "You know what his dad is? You know what his dad is?"

We all sat there waiting for him to answer his own question. I had no idea what he was going to say.

"His old man's a No-No Boy."

What the hell was that? I felt like laughing almost. He was trying to insult my father, but his insult sounded stupid.

"You spazzes. You don't know what a No-No Boy is?"

Jimmy shook his head.

"His dad's a deserter. He was never in the army. He was too scared to fight. He wasn't in the army in World War II—he was in jail."

"You're lying," I yelled. "You're lying."

And then I didn't care if he was two years older, I didn't care if he was a brown belt in judo, I didn't care if he'd threatened to burn a hole in my skull with a magnifying glass—I jumped on top of him, right there on the couch.

I think I surprised him, because I managed to get him in a headlock. I squeezed him as hard as I could. I felt his fists punching me on my back and on my side, and he managed to hit me real hard in the head. I burst into tears and loosened my grip, and he jerked out from under me and got me in a headlock. I couldn't breathe.

That was when Michael Nagata's dad came into the room.

I don't exactly remember what happened next. I know he yanked us apart and slapped Michael, and then he slapped me and I started crying even more. When I stopped crying, he tried to sort out what had happened. He asked Jimmy, Bobby Jo, and Billy, and then he asked Michael.

But when he asked me to tell him what happened I said something that made him angry. He told me I'd get in trouble if I said that again. But I didn't care—he wasn't my father. So I said it again, and the next thing I knew he had yanked me over his knee and wailed on my butt. I started crying again.

Finally he stopped spanking me. I rolled off him and stood back up. I knew he expected me to take back what I said or apologize, but I didn't. I just stood there blubbering and wiping my nose.

"I'm going home," I said.

Then I was out their back door onto their porch landing. It had grown dark, the air autumnal and cold, and it had started to rain. I wondered if Mr. Nagata was going to tell my parents about what had happened. How could he have done that? I wasn't his son, what right did he have to spank me? I knew I'd done something wrong but already I'd forgotten what I'd said to him. But he was wrong, he was so wrong.

In this way I almost completely forgot what Michael Nagata had said.*

---

* Years after Michael Nagata barked out that mysterious slur, I read about them—the No-No Boys. I was a history major, after all. But that hardly sufficed. Indeed the deeper you dig into history, the more skeptical you become about the whole enterprise. Maybe that's why I never did get my PhD, why I never became the scholar my mother and I envisioned.

Spies and double agents—that's what they thought we were. Enemy aliens, traitorous Japs. Scapegoats for fear mongers. Wartime hysteria. Hearst headlines branding us a "fifth-column force." Editorials and senators telling

America, "A Jap is a Jap no matter where you find him; you can't trust any of them; the racial strains remain, undiluted, the pure Nipponese line . . ."

So what were the Japanese Americans to do when Executive Order 9066 swept them up and jailed them behind barbed wire and under armed guards in rifle towers? Go along with the government? Show their patriotism and loyalty by not resisting? Or protest and proclaim they were being imprisoned illegally, against the laws of the nation and the Constitution?

One day, after they'd interned all the Japanese Americans on the West Coast, prompted in part some say by the JACL (the Japanese American Citizens League), the government came up with this loyalty oath. A little Kafkaesque afterthought. They administered it to all the adults in the camps, men and women. Two questions were crucial: Do you swear allegiance to the United States and foreswear allegiance to the emperor? Do you agree to serve in the Armed Forces?

Of course, the *issei*, my grandparents' generation, were forbidden by law from becoming citizens (they couldn't even own property in the U.S.). So if they said Yes-Yes, they'd be without citizenship in any country. But most signed Yes-Yes anyway. America was where their children were born, who their children were.

As for their kids, the *nisei*, or second generation, were citizens; they had always felt loyalty to this country, always felt Yes-Yes in their hearts.

But a few no longer felt that way, now that they were in prison, now that they were surrounded by barbed wire and armed guards. Some even protested having to foreswear allegiance to the emperor. Never had such allegiance in the first place, they said. Some were *kibei*, who'd been educated in Japan, their loyalties divided and entangled.

I've gone over the documents, the testimonies, the FBI files, the personal accounts. In the camps many felt that the *inu*—the dogs—were the informers, the ones who worked with the camp authorities, the JACL. After the war the *inu* were the resisters. Those who had answered No-No. Pariahs. Black sheep. Whom no one wanted to talk about.

The real heroes, everyone said now, were the veterans like my uncle Elbert. The 442nd. The ones who showed that we were good patriots, who proved that the camps were clearly a mistake. The ones who gave their blood, limbs, lives. The ones who'd answered Yes-Yes.

The division was clear. Or, as I've often told myself, so it must have seemed to my father and mother, which is why they never mentioned any of this to Tommy and me.

But I was wrong. It's taken me years to see that despite all my reading, I still haven't understood their silence and what it held or held back. I had gotten it all wrong: Takeshi and Kimiko Ohara were not who I thought they were. And neither was I.

THE GYP JOINT

My mother always blamed it on the neighborhood. That was too easy, but she had a point. There were precedents. Bobby Jo's brother Jackie and the older boys used to hock—steal—things all the time from the Gyp Joint and, not surprisingly, we younger kids just tagged along. At any rate, it started out small, just petty crimes. How could I know where it was going to take me, how far I would eventually veer from the straight and narrow?

Our method was simple. You get a gang of kids and everyone crowds into the store at once. One guy buys a few things, some jawbreakers or baseball cards. Two other guys start arguing, then shoving each other. No full-fledged punches, just enough to rile the old man behind the counter. "Hey, you kids," he yells, and the two kids start arguing with him, as if he were the judge in their imaginary courtroom. Then the first guy rolls his coins on the counter so a couple fall off the glass behind the counter, and the old lady at the cash register bends down to pick them up. The other kids scoop what they can into their pockets, and the quarreling twosome start slapping or grabbing each other, making the old man yell louder. The kids who swiped the candy just slip out from the fray.

Sometimes Jackie and his friends let his younger brother Bobby Jo and us little kids come with. It made things more crazy in the store. One of the little kids would start saying, I want this, I want that, and pointing to things, and the other little kids could join in the swiping. The first time I did this, I pocketed Pez, a few coolers, and some chocolate malted milk balls. I liked those the best. I had to split my haul with Bobby Jo and Jimmy Pearson just like the big kids split their loot.

Afterwards I did feel guilty. Maybe it had something to do with religion. For a short while when I was younger, my mom sometimes took me and Tommy to the Christ Congregational Church on Buckingham; it was all Japanese (my dad was Buddhist, but we never went to the Buddhist temple, which was actually closer to our house). I learned the Ten Commandments and the Lord's Prayer. I even made a drawing that illustrated "lead us not into temptation but deliver us from evil" by showing a stick figure walking up one road and then turning back to the road toward good. I thought about how Charlton Heston as Moses brought the Ten Commandments down from the mountain and found the Israelites dancing and worshipping the Golden Calf. How he threatened them with the wrath of God. When I thought of what I'd done with Jackie Watkins and the gang, I knew I had sinned. I'd broken one of the commandments. I was as bad as Edward G. Robinson, the one who egged on the Israelites into pagan worship. I promised myself that I was never going to steal again.

Of course a couple weeks later I'd forgotten my promise. After all, as Jackie Watkins proclaimed, "It's the Gyp Joint. They're making a ton off of us. It's only right we steal a little back." Bobby Jo said that it was like Robin Hood, stealing from the rich to feed the poor.

But I didn't think of us as poor. It wasn't like any of us were starving. We were kids. We just wanted some candy.

Our bedroom at night. It was dark, but I wasn't tired. So, like any big brother, I told Tommy about my exploits at the Gyp

Joint, all the stuff we hocked—gumballs, baseball cards, coolers, jawbreakers, Pez—the list grew grander in my imagination. Part of me knew that it was stupid to tell him, but who else can you brag to if not to your little brother?

At first he acted like a goody-goody.

"That's wrong; that's stealing," he said. "I'm going to tell Mom."

I had to think quickly; he was young and dumb enough to do this.

"Yeah, you do, and I'll tell her you stole stuff too."

"She won't believe you."

"She will too. Remember I gave you that bubble gum yesterday. She saw you chewing it."

"You said you found a dime on the street."

"That doesn't matter. You squeal on me, I'll squeal on you."

Poor Tommy, I had him so confused, he almost thought he had stolen too. After all, he'd enjoyed some of the fruits of my thuggery. For a few moments, I could feel him thinking about all this. I thought that maybe he had fallen asleep. Then he piped up.

"Can you teach me to hock things? Can I go along?"

"Naw, you're too little."

"Am not. I'm in first grade."

"Yeah, well that's only because Ma lied about your age."

"That's 'cause I'm smart."

"Yeah, well she did the same thing for me. I started a year early too."

I could tell from his silence that he didn't know this. He'd thought he was special. And he was. Even then I knew that he was smarter than I was, but I wasn't going to let him know this.

"It's not right to lie," said Tommy Goody-Two-Shoes. "That's what Mrs. Matsuo says." Mrs. Matsuo was our Sunday school teacher.

"Grown-ups do it all the time," I said. "That's how they get things done. Mom lies, like to Aunt Satsu."

"Does Daddy lie?"

"Yeah, I suppose so."

"Did he lie about fighting in the war?"

A jolt ran through me, like I'd just wakened out of some nightmare. "Who told you that?"

"I heard Michael Nagata saying something to Billy Blevins."

"Nagata's a spazz. He doesn't know what he's talking about."

"He can beat you up."

"That's only 'cause he knows judo. If Dad would take me to judo class, I could take him."

Tommy seemed to think about this. "So Daddy fought in the war?"

"Yeah. Of course he did. Just like Uncle Elbert. They were both in the war."

Neither of us said anything for a while.

"I don't think Daddy lies like Mommy does," Tommy said.

"I told you: all grown-ups lie. You can do that when you're a grown-up."

"I don't want to grow up then."

"Don't worry, squirt. You'll always be smaller than me."

After a few moments, I could hear him sniffling.

"What is it now?"

"I'll always be smaller than you?"

"Yeah, you'll always be smaller." Let him sniffle. He was a skinny runt, always would be. Oh hell. "Heck, I don't know. Maybe you'll be bigger than me. Just shut up and go to sleep."

The sniffling gradually stopped.

"Ben?"

I pretended to be asleep. I had had enough lies for one night. I didn't need to make up any more.

"You ever think about what things were like when we weren't here?" he asked.

"You mean like before we were born? When Mom and Dad were younger?"

"No, like before there were human beings. Or anything living."

My brother. Always coming up with these strange thoughts.

"What does that have to do with anything?"

"It's just that I wonder. Where did living things come from? I mean, first there wasn't anything, and then there was. How did that happen?"

"How in the H-E-double hockey sticks do I know? Go to sleep."

"Those things were real, real small. So everything had to start off small. Just like me."

"Listen, I don't care. Go to sleep." He started to say something more, but I stopped him, "I said to shut up. Do you want me to pound you?"

Silence. But I could tell he was still thinking. Tommy could always get lost in his thoughts, transporting himself elsewhere, to another place, another time, another planet even. I couldn't. I was always too scared to go anywhere else. I lived on planet Earth. That was hard enough for me.

For a while my dad worked weekends at Yoshino's Camera Store down on Broadway. I don't remember either of my parents making a big thing of this. One weekend he just got up in the morning, shaved, and put on a white shirt and tie. Then he walked down to Broadway and took the bus a little south.

Once my mom and I visited him in the shop. He seemed busy and distracted, talking with a *hakujin* customer. Later he showed us the workbench in back where they worked on the cameras.

"Mits says he'll teach me how to repair them," he said.

"That will be nice," said my mom. "Maybe you can go to full time."

My dad snorted. "Maybe. But he's got all the help he needs now. I'm lucky to get this part-time work."

"Still, you never know," said my mom.

My dad didn't respond.

"Look, Ben. Look how tiny these parts are." He showed me the inside of the camera, the way the shutter worked, different lenses, screws, and gears. "They've got a dark room back there," he said, pointing to the far corner.

Just then Mr. Yoshino popped his head in the back room. "Tak, we need you out here."

"Sure, boss."

It seemed strange to see my father call Mr. Yoshino boss. He didn't bow to him or anything like that. But Mr. Yoshino was even shorter than my dad and may even have been younger. To me it would have made more sense if my dad had been Mr. Yoshino's boss.

My mom knew some of the people living in the building above the camera store. It was owned by Mr. Yoshino and his brother and sister. Other Japanese American families lived there too. In fact, there was only one white family. It seemed a bit strange to me, so many Japanese American families together.

We visited Mr. Yoshino's sister's family, the Tanakas. They had three daughters, Joanne, Susie, and Debby. I didn't know what to make of them. They were girls. Joanne was a year younger than me. She had bangs and a small pert nose and full lips. I supposed she was pretty, but I didn't want to think about that. She asked me if I wanted to play Monopoly. Sure, I said. This wasn't my neighborhood. None of the gang would ever know I'd played Monopoly with a girl.

I kept waiting to get Park Place and Boardwalk while Joanne gobbled up other choice properties on the board. I wanted to hoard my money in preparation for the time when I'd have the most expensive property and could build houses and then a hotel on them.

But then she landed on Park Place, and I knew it was over. I told her I wanted to quit. She accused me of being a bad sport. She was winning, that's why I wanted to quit. I said it was a stupid game—who cared about houses or hotels or property?

She turned up her pert nose and snorted. She told me I didn't know what I was talking about. Her mother and Mr. Yoshino and their brother Yaha owned the building they lived in. All the people there paid them rent.

"My mom says we're going to move to the suburbs next year," she said.

"So what's the good of owning a building if you're going to move?"

"Don't you understand? That's the reason why we're going to be able to move. My mom always says, 'You own some property, you'll never go broke.'"

I scrunched my face. "It doesn't make sense to me."

She gave me a disgusted look and seemed about to say something but then thought the better of it. Instead, she asked me if I wanted to watch TV. On the way to the living room, we passed a glass case with a Japanese doll inside it.

"That's my mom's."

I didn't say anything. I didn't want her to think I was interested in dolls. Especially Japanese dolls with their funny clothing and funny hair.

"Actually, it was my grandmother's, and before that it was my great-grandmother's. It's a family treasure. My mom says she's lucky she's got it."

"Why?"

She thought a second. "I don't know. She says her mom gave it to her after the war. Maybe it's got something to do with that."

"With what?"

"With the war."

"Oh."

I really didn't understand what she was saying. Besides, I wanted to see if *Popeye* was on, so I headed toward her living room.

On the bus ride home, I asked my mom why we didn't own our building like the Yoshinos and Tanakas. She was craning her head to look out the window for our stop.

"Mr. Johnson owns our building."

"But why couldn't we own it?"

She turned back to me. "Because Mr. Johnson does."

"But they're Japanese, and they own a building."

She gave an exasperated sigh.

"That's got nothing to do with it."

"We should own our own building, Ma."

"Ben, we don't . . . Oh, just forget about it," she said. "Just be glad you have a roof over your head." Then, as if she'd remembered something, she added, "Just be glad you aren't living in a barn."

I thought about that.

"It would be neat living in a barn," I piped. "With horses and stuff."

A sharpness came into her voice.

"You don't know what that's like. You don't know at all."

I was silent. I thought she was angry with me. I didn't know why. She looked at me. Then her face softened. She didn't smile, but I could tell she was no longer angry.

"Yes," she said, almost sighing, "I'm sure you'd like that."

Several weeks later my dad stopped going to Mr. Yoshino's store. He slept late on the weekends again. So did my mother. Sometimes I wondered if that was because they were up so late arguing. But then I told myself that they didn't argue every night. That was just the way grown-ups were. They liked to sleep late. The Saturday morning cartoons were just for kids.

NIHONJIN OR HAKUJIN?

I didn't understand family quarrels. I fought with my brother sometimes, but mostly I ignored him. I fought with Michael Nagata, but that was different: he wasn't family—he was just a bully. Family quarrels were more mysterious, their beginnings hidden somewhere back in time, before I was born. I didn't even know if there was a quarrel between my family and Auntie Satsu and Uncle Elbert. At some point we just stopped visiting them.

I do remember that when my mother's father came to visit us from Japan—he had returned there after my grandmother died—tensions arose between my Auntie Satsu and my mother. As the oldest, Auntie Satsu thought my grandfather should stay with her. I don't think that my mother really wanted my grandfather to stay with us so much as she resented Auntie Satsu presuming the right of the oldest sister. I recall her telling my Auntie Yo that Satsu was "always that way. She's so *nihonjin.*"

I wondered what it meant to be *nihonjin.* Whenever someone's name came up in family conversations, someone would always ask if they were *hakujin* or *nihonjin.* I understood that *hakujin* meant people not like us, and *nihonjin* meant us. But what did it mean that Auntie Satsu was "so *nihonjin,*" which seemed to imply she was "too *nihonjin?*" How could you be too much of what you already were?

Were the arguments over my grandfather the reason that we saw Auntie Satsu and Uncle Elbert less and less? We would still see Auntie Yo once and a while. My mother liked driving out to the suburbs.

On our visits to Aunt Yo's, after we slipped from the city, my mother always remarked how the air seemed cleaner. She cooed at the lawns and neatly trimmed hedges. "There's so much more room here," she said. I noticed too. Out in the suburbs, people didn't live right on top of each other, like in the city. No broken bottles and milk containers and newspapers cluttering the walks and alleys. Grass instead of dirt. People parked their cars in garages, not on the street. Kids played on baseball diamonds in a park rather than in ratty vacant lots.

Auntie Yo's house was a ranch. I liked the sound of that because it made me think of cowboys and Roy Rogers. But it was what was inside the house that mattered. My cousins Mark and Brian always nabbed the latest toys, things none of the kids around my neighborhood had—a Schwinn bike, a scooter, walkie-talkies, a crystal radio, a Lionel model train set, a Mr. Wizard chemistry set, a bumper pool table. Visiting their house was like visiting royalty.

There was one catch: almost always, when I picked up their latest toy, they'd inform me that they'd broken it. They managed to do this with almost everything they owned. (Or, with things like the bumper pool table, they'd lose a crucial piece, like the cue ball.)

My biggest disappointment was when I heard that Uncle Hank had built them a go-cart. A go-cart! Such a toy was absolutely unheard of in Uptown. When we got to Mark and Brian's house, I started to the garage. I'd gotten only a few steps when Mark yelled out, "It doesn't work. Something's broken. The belt."

When we visited, the grown-ups sat at the dining room table and smoked and talked while we boys played in the yard or took off for the park or went to Mark and Brian's room. On one visit, after trying to get one of the walkie-talkies to work, Mark gave up and showed me his coin collection. He opened a thick blue cardboard book and pointed out how many of the slots he'd filled already. A book of Lincoln Head pennies and one for Indian Head pennies, a book of Buffalo Head nickels. He only had two Indian Heads, they were so rare. He popped one out and held it forth as if it were some fabulous emerald or world-famous diamond.

"That's probably worth twenty-five dollars," he said. I didn't believe him.

"It's true," he said. He took out a book that listed the value of various coins. Man, all that for a penny.

Suddenly Brian piped up, "Dad said the next Indian Head we get is going to be mine."

Mark looked at him as if he were a speck of dog doo. He told Brian that he was nuts—he didn't even have a book for them.

"Dad's going to get one for me," said Brian.

"Liar, liar, pants on fire," said Mark.

"He is too," said Brian.

"Shut up, spazz," said Mark.

Brian started to sniffle. Then he got up and stiffened his back and yelled, "I'm going to tell Mom on you."

"Go ahead, tattletale," said Mark, as Brian left the room. "It's about time you left, the room was beginning to stink of B.O."

At this Brian turned, and I could see him think about running at Mark. But then he thought the better of it and slunk away. He was just like Tommy. Little brothers were all alike.

I don't recall what happened next very well. Certainly I couldn't tell my dad afterwards to his satisfaction.

Did I know what I was going to do right away? I must have popped an Indian Head out of its socket and held it in my palm, staring at its dull sheen and ancient date. To think a penny could be worth so much. Maybe I took out the second one then and compared the two, surprised that the older one seemed in better shape. I probably wedged out the nickels then, one Jefferson and one Buffalo and compared them. Just window shopping, I told myself. But the longer I held them in my palm . . .

Why did Brian and Mark get so many things? They never took care of them; they always broke them. If I had what they had, I'd always take care of it. I wouldn't leave things out for anyone to hock.

When Mark came back into the room, he was almost crying and was very angry. Apparently Brian had tattled and gotten him into trouble. Auntie Yo had pinched his cheek and told him that if he didn't behave, Uncle Hank was going to spank him. I felt sorry for Mark, but he was more angry than sad. He swore that he'd get back at that twerp of a brother . . .

He seemed to have forgotten all about his coins. But I hadn't. I told him that it turned out that I collected coins too. He gave me a look almost like the one he gave Brian. Sure, he said, I'll bet.

No, I told him, I really did have a coin collection. "My dad got some books like this at a hobby shop on Broadway. He collected coins as a kid. But he buried most of them one day in the backyard."

This wasn't a lie. My dad actually told me about this. I asked him why he did that. They had to move suddenly and he couldn't take them with. But why didn't you sell them? I asked. "Because I didn't want anyone else to have them," he said, "and I didn't know if I would get what they were worth. So I buried them." He told me that he buried his collection of marbles too, which only made things worse. If only he had kept them, I thought. Why didn't he take them with when he moved? "We could only take one suit-case," he said. "We didn't have time to take anything more." I never asked him why he had had to move so suddenly. That wasn't the part of the story I latched onto. It was those lost coins.

"But it turned out he did save a few coins," I told Mark, weaving truth with my lies. "I've got them with me. I carry them around all the time. Just for luck."

I reached into my pocket and showed him an Indian head penny, two Buffalo Head nickels, a Mercury Head dime, and a few other pennies and nickels.

He picked up the Indian Head penny.

"Man," he said, "these are real rare. I've only got a couple of these."

"Yeah. I was lucky my dad kept it."

"And this Buffalo Head, it's rare too," he said. "Are these all you have?"

"I've got more at home. I wish I had an Indian Head penny like you."

As we were talking Mark took the Buffalo Head nickel and was looking at it.

"I've got one just like this," he said.

"You do?"

"Yeah, I think. 1927. I think I do. Let me look."

The odd thing was when Mark opened his coin book I fully expected to see his Buffalo Head nickel there in that exact date, just like mine. Part of me felt as surprised as he did when his finger pointed to an empty slot.

First my dad took me to Brian and Mark's room alone. He made me give him the coins. He asked me if I stole them from Mark. I didn't answer. I stared at the floor. I kept hoping that if I didn't answer things would be o.k.

"Look at me," he shouted. "Did you steal Mark's coins?"

I looked back down at the floor.

"Don't lie to me. I know you did. Do you think I'm stupid? Did you steal them?"

I shook my head. He repeated the question. I nodded.

"Answer me," he said.

"Yeah. I guess so."

"You guess so?"

"Yeah."

"Why?"

Silence.

"Why?"

"I dunno."

"You don't know? How can you not know?"

But I didn't know. I didn't even remember stealing them. They just appeared in my pocket, I wanted to say. I just had them. But I knew he wouldn't believe me.

I looked up at his face, and he had a look I couldn't place. He suddenly seemed not angry, but confused and exasperated, like he didn't know what to do, like a man who's lost his wallet or has just stumbled out of his car after an accident.

"How can you steal?" he wailed. "We don't do that, Ben. We're *nihonjin.*"

He said it as if I had broken some ancient law or the Ten Commandments. I *had* broken one of the Ten Commandments, I knew that. But somehow my dad made it seem worse than that. Like I had done something not just to Mark but to him, to all of us.

A little later, in Auntie Yo's living room, he clamped a vice grip on my shoulder. He shoved me forward and made me apologize to Mark and hand over the coins. Even as I did, I didn't think about how I had stolen them. I kept wanting to think that they were still mine. Why did I have to give them to Mark?

At first I just mumbled something and handed them back. Then my dad squeezed harder. Apologize, he barked. I mumbled something more and he gripped me again.

At last I got the words out to his satisfaction.

Mark looked surprised, as if he didn't understand what had happened. Like he still too thought he'd lost his Buffalo Head nickel on his own.

On the ride home my parents didn't say anything to me or to each other. I didn't know whether I wanted them to talk. I knew I shouldn't say a word.

I wished I were dead. Then I wouldn't have to think about being punished. But then we passed the cemetery on Sheridan Road, and I thought about the worms that crawl in and out and play pinochle on your snout and I knew I didn't really want to be dead. But I felt sick. Maybe I would throw up. When we'd gotten in the car, Tommy had looked at me like I was a condemned man. Like he could hear the guard up the line yelling, dead man walking.

We were driving up Wilson from Lake Shore Drive. The skyscrapers stopped, and the buildings grew grimier and smaller. Bars and pawnshops. I could hear the El screech a few blocks away. We passed an empty lot littered with trash and a broken-down billboard. Behind that billboard I'd once watched Jackie Watkins and his friend build a fire and then make the fire leap up by dousing liquid onto it. They called the fire starters their "magic formulas." One liquid looked surprisingly like *shoyu*.

Then we were at Broadway near the currency exchange. Back in the neighborhood. Even to me it seemed a lot worse after our visit to the suburbs. Like the place had suddenly turned darker and dingier in just a few hours.

"You know what it is," said my mom. She said this as if she had been talking to my dad the whole way home. My dad didn't say a thing.

"Don't pretend you don't know, Tak."

"What are you talking about?"

"Decent people shouldn't live in a place like this."

My dad said nothing.

"Sometimes I swear . . ." she continued. "You just don't listen to me. He wouldn't do things like that if we didn't live here. With all these, these hillbillies . . ."

"What do you mean? Things aren't so bad here."

"They are too. Just look at the trash on these streets."

"So what's that got to do . . ."

"Everyone knows Johnny Watkins is a drunk."

"So people in the suburbs don't drink?"

"Do you want Ben to grow up on streetcorners with those Watkins boys? Do you want your boy to grow up in this filth?" She made a gesture of sweeping her hands in front of her as we turned the corner to our block. "Why can't we at least move down near Yoshino's Camera Store? At least there's some *nihonjin* there."

My dad's voice raised a bit then, though he never got as loud as my mom.

"Why do we have to be with *nihonjin*? I had enough of that back in camp. Besides, the Nagatas live up the block."

"And do you know what Michael Nagata tried to do a while ago? He tried to burn your son's hair with a magnifying glass."

"I don't think he did that. Ben, did he . . ."

"Don't bring him into this."

"You know we can't move now."

"Fine," she said. "Let your boy grow up to be a thief. If that's what you want."

My dad was looking for a parking spot. He halted the car and turned back to look at the spot as he backed up. I didn't want to look at his face, so I looked out the window. I could see the Puerto Rican kid who had the switchblade sitting as always in his window, staring down at us. My dad acted as if as long as he was parking the car he didn't have to answer my mother.

"Is that what you want for a son? A thief? God, I've never been so humiliated. I can't imagine what Yo thinks."

"She has her own boys. Boys . . ."

"All boys do not steal. No, no. Just ours. Just boys that grow up in places like this."

"Kimi, you know we can't afford . . ."

"And why is that? Why is that?"

My dad turned off the engine and looked straight ahead. "Hank's lucky. He's got a great job. Not everyone can get a job like that."

My mom turned and looked at him. He still was staring ahead. She had a look of disbelief, hesitation, and anger on her face.

"No? Well at least some men *have* a job."

That night I knew Tommy wanted to ask about what happened. I could tell that he didn't understand everything, only that I'd done something really bad. And that if he asked me about it, I'd pound him. I kept waiting for him to say something, but he knew better. Or maybe he was just tired.

Then he heard their voices. "Are Mommy and Daddy arguing?"

"No," I hissed. "Shut up and go to sleep."

He didn't say anything more this time. He knew I was in one of my moods.

After he fell asleep, I lay in my bed and pounded my stomach. A stupid thing to do, yes. But I was never very bright. Not like Tommy, who always seemed to manage to stay out of trouble.

Pretty soon my stomach hurt so much that I had to stop. It was worse then. I lay there and kept going over everything. Not just my punishment, but its aftereffects, the way my crime had darkened our whole apartment.

My dad had been quiet when we got home. And then furious. I was scared. I thought about what my mom had said. I didn't want to move from our neighborhood. I mean, I wanted to live in a ranch or a nice house, I wanted to have a go-cart like Mark and Brian. But I didn't want to leave my friends. Who cared if they were hillbillies? What did that mean anyway?

I think they argued more that night. I wanted to tell them to stop, but I knew better. I was the reason they were fighting in the first place. My dad would only punish me again. My mom would tell him to. And he did most everything she told him to do. Only never as fast as she wanted, never in the way she wanted.

Sometimes he seemed to me a little like the monster in *The Creature from the Black Lagoon*, as if he couldn't run that fast, as if he had webbed feet. Yes, he could catch me, he could put me over his knee. But other things outran him. Like my mother. I thought of what would happen if they raced together like we did on the schoolyard at recess.

I knew my mom would win that race. My dad didn't stand a chance.

THINGS THAT SCARED ME

The scariest movie back then was *The Incredible Shrinking Man*. It was much worse than *The Creature from the Black Lagoon*. There was *The Amazing Colossal Man*, where a guy got larger and larger, lost all his hair, and stomped around picking up trucks and yanking down telephone wires. It seemed that getting bigger made him cranky. He'd been exposed to atomic fallout. Eventually they had to shoot him down with bazookas and planes. But that wasn't so scary. Even if they did kill him, he was still bigger than everyone else. But the Incredible Shrinking Man kept getting smaller and smaller. At first he was like a midget, then like a kid, then like a baby. Finally his wife put him in a dollhouse. He got even crankier then.

At the start of the movie, he'd been out on a yacht and run into a mysterious fog. That's what made him shrink. His wife couldn't understand what he was going through. She kept telling him to keep calm. Then something happened—I think the cat came clawing after him—and he fled from his dollhouse. He ended up in the basement. He had to haul himself up to the windowsill to try to get out. Then a huge spider attacked him. It was utterly terrifying, the spider three times bigger than he was, and hairy with black beady eyes. At the last moment, he snatched up a sewing pin, skewered the spider, and all its innards came gushing out as the spider collapsed on top of him.

But what was even more terrifying was the end. Facing the basement screen, he discovered that he had shrunk enough to get through the holes in the screen. But where was he escaping to? I knew all the insects that were out there—ants, spiders, grasshoppers, worms, caterpillars, beetles—not to mention rats, squirrels, cats, and dogs. The music seemed both like he'd triumphed—he'd killed the spider, he'd gotten out of the basement—and like something else was now going to happen. Even if he'd be able to kill the next insect (he'd brought his needle with him), what would he do about his shrinking? Would he get smaller and smaller? What if he got so small that he fell between the spaces of atoms and just kept on falling? What would happen to him then?

That seemed to me the worst of fates: you escaped, you'd gotten past the bars, but everything was worse on the outside. You hadn't really escaped at all.

The movie reminded me of the story of Issunboshi, the finger-sized samurai, one of the Japanese tales my dad used to tell me before bed. Issunboshi killed a spider with a needle too. His sword was called *hari no ken*. He used it to fight off a bird and a frog. He sailed down the river in a rice bowl, steering with a chopstick, and he made it to the capital where he sought work as a warrior. One day he was hired by a *daimyo*—a great lord— to protect his daughter. The daughter and Issunboshi became friends. On a trip to a distant temple, demons—my dad called them *oni*—attacked the princess's procession. All the other samurai fled. Only Issunboshi stayed. He stuck one *oni* in its tongue with his sword and the other in the eye, and they both fled. They left behind a magic ring, and the ring granted Issunboshi one wish. Of course he wished to become a normal-sized man. When he turned normal size, he and the princess got married and lived happily ever after.

Even as a kid, I knew Issunboshi was a fairy tale. *The Incredible Shrinking Man*, on the other hand, was the real thing. Things never worked out if you were smaller than everyone else. That was how the world worked: the bigger kids picked on the smaller ones. Like sharks. Like lions or wolves. Like how the bigger fish ate the little fish. The way Jackie Watkins picked on Bobby Jo, or Michael Nagata picked on me, or my cousin Mark picked on his brother Brian. Someday you'd grow up and be a normal man; you didn't need a magic spell like Issunboshi. But my fear was that I'd never grow up, I'd always be small. I might even shrink like the Incredible Shrinking Man. It could happen. And Michael Nagata would always come after me.

When I asked my dad about what happened to the Incredible Shrinking Man, he told me that it was just a movie. I shouldn't think about things like that.

"The thing is, you've got to be brave like Issunboshi. Then good things will happen."

I didn't believe him. I knew he was just saying that because he was my dad. That's what he was supposed to say.

One day Michael Nagata was bragging about seeing this movie, *Go for Broke*. He said it was all about the *nisei* soldiers in the 442nd, the ones who'd fought in World War II. The best part was when the Buddhaheads—that's what the *nisei* called themselves—saved the Lost Battalion, the Texans surrounded by the Gerries. No one else had been able to get through, but the Buddhaheads wouldn't give up. I couldn't help but let everyone know that I knew about all that; my uncle had told me. Nagata looked at me as if he were going to say something, but then Bobby Jo Watkins came running up, yelling that he'd just seen a rat in the garbage cans out in the alley, and we all ran to look.

I told my mom about the film and asked if we could see it, but she said no. "Why?" I asked. "Michael Nagata said his whole family saw it. There were all these other *nihonjin* there."

"I don't care what other *nihonjin* do," she said. "We're just not going. We need to save money if we're going to move to the suburbs."

"Michael said there was even a soldier with our name. Ohara."

"No, Ben. We're not going. And that's that."

I knew from the tone of her voice not to argue anymore. I was so angry that I stormed to my room and slammed my door. When Tommy came in, I yelled at him to get out.

Why did she have to be so cheap? I thought. Why couldn't we be rich like Aunt Yo's family? Or the Yoshinos?

Later I tried asking my dad. He just shook his head no. When I asked why, he asked if my mom hadn't already said I couldn't go.

Something in the way he said this let me know that it was more than money. At any rate, I knew it was over. They were together in this. I wasn't going.

I used to hear them at night. It was her voice I heard loudest. In my mind's eye I saw him stammering, "But . . . but . . . but . . ."

"Tak, I swear . . ." "You don't know . . ." "I'm sick and tired . . ."

Sometimes I thought they were talking about me. I'd been bringing notes home from my teacher. I talked too much in class. Cracked jokes. Asked too many times to go to the bathroom. I got up and sharpened my pencil without asking. I rushed through my sums and subtraction and then sat around bothering the other kids. I called Johnny Gordon a fat pig. Everyone knew he didn't have a dad. I told him that he didn't deserve to have a dad. That got me into a heap of trouble when my teacher told my mother what I'd said.

One day I brought home a report card filled with checks for bad behavior. My mom yelled at me and pinched my cheek. When my dad punished me, he would pull down my pants and spank me with his open palm. Or a belt. I cried and screamed. But it didn't help.

And yet even as I heard them argue, some part of me knew they were not arguing about me. Even though I'd been bad. It was something else. I didn't know what.

Then one day my dad disappeared. I came home from school, and he wasn't on the couch.

When my mom came home, I asked her where he was. She said that he went away on a trip. Where? I asked. He just went on a trip, she said. Yeah but where? Don't ask so many questions, she said. I'm tired. Just let me be. Go out and play with your friends.

I could tell she really wanted me to leave her alone because it was getting dark. She never let me go out and play after dark.

Unlike me, Tommy wasn't scared of the Incredible Shrinking Man. In fact he liked horror films, though not as much as sci-fi. (*The Incredible Shrinking Man* was both.) Nor did Tommy seem as upset when our father went away. I suppose it just seemed normal to him. He was used to it. I could still remember a time when my father was working regularly at the CTA, when he returned with the other fathers at the end of the day. Unlike me, Tommy didn't pester mom about where Dad had gone. He seemed to live more in his own world, with his own view of things.

For instance, Tommy loved the world of Bizarro more than the regular Superman comics, which he thought were boring. He went around for a while talking in broken English like the characters in Bizarro. He thought Batman much more interesting than Superman. Both were orphans, but Superman had been raised by Ma and Pa Kent while Bruce Wayne grew up alone, except for Alfred, whom I always found a bit creepy. Tommy liked the dark shadows of the Bat Cave, that this superhero went out mostly at night, that he had chosen the bat as his totem because criminals were scared of the dark, fearing the evil inside their own hearts. "Batman's a good guy," said Tommy, "but he acts like a bad guy. And he doesn't have any superpowers like Superman. He's just like the rest of us."

"What about Robin?" I asked. "I hate Robin."

"Robin doesn't matter," said Tommy. "Neither does Alfred. They might as well be robots. In fact it'd be better if they *were* robots."

Tommy said that in the future robots would be more and more like humans. "One day they might even take over the planet." I found this prospect spooky, but Tommy liked it, the idea of a cool metallic perfection. Just like he loved how the dark of the night let him see the stars, the things that were hidden during the daytime.

"Do you know the sun's just like a big atomic bomb?" he told me once. We were sitting on the back steps. It was early morning; the rest of the gang hadn't shown up yet.

"Then why doesn't it blow up?"

"It's always blowing up. That's why it's so hot. It's just like what happened at Hiroshima."

"They can't be the same thing."

"Fine. Don't believe me then."

Tommy knew he knew more than me about these things. He didn't have to argue. I knew more about cool things, like baseball. Or grown-up things, like our mom and dad or family quarrels. He liked things that weren't quite human. Sometimes he seemed strange to me, even though we were brothers.

Tommy said he liked Japanese sci-fi films better than American ones. I thought that was stupid. And unpatriotic. The Japanese sci-fi films always looked goofy to me, like they were made by kids, with their cheap props and backdrops. Like Starman. You could see on the screen the strings that flew him over his enemies. And Godzilla knocking down those buildings that any little kid even could see were toys, just like Godzilla himself.

Tommy said that I didn't get it. Godzilla rose up out of an atomic blast. Like the one at Hiroshima. "He's atomic; he's a mutant."

"What the hell's a mutant?"

"They're like new creatures. It happens sometimes in nature. That's how we evolved from apes."

"Where'd you learn that?"

"A book."

"A book," I said mockingly.

Tommy was always getting science books from the library. The only books I got were about sports heroes. Or people like Daniel Boone or Davy Crockett (I made an exception with books about Abraham Lincoln, maybe because he was raised in a log cabin like Davy Crockett).

"If we were all alike," Tommy continued, unfazed, "like robots, that'd be cool, but we wouldn't change. But the atomic bomb makes things change faster. Like Godzilla. He's a lizard but a hundred times huger than other lizards."

Tommy said the Japanese understood the atomic age better than we Americans. After all, they'd had the atom bomb dropped on them. I thought that was idiotic. Japan lost the war. And they fought dirty, like the sneak attack on Pearl Harbor.

"Yeah, well what happened at Pearl Harbor?"

"That's not . . ."

"Sneak attack," I said and goosed him.

He might have been smarter than me, but he was still my little brother.

Down in the alley I could see Michael Nagata walking with Jimmy Pearson toward the Empty. I thought about how Michael always got me with his sneak attacks just like I got Tommy. Only I wasn't Nagata's little brother. Some day, I told myself, that was gonna change.

When my dad came back again, things were better for a while. He was even back working, at Yoshino's Camera Store, though only part time. Neither he nor my mom mentioned anything about where he'd been.

One night Tommy woke me up with his whimpering. He had wet his bed again. I told him to shut up, but he wouldn't stop whimpering. "You're such a baby," I said. But this made him cry even more. I looked at him and saw it wouldn't do any good to scold him. He was still half-asleep. Or maybe even all asleep (he was prone to sleepwalking).

Approaching their room, I could hear them arguing, so I made a lot of noise as I approached the door. My mom was sitting on the bed in her nightgown. My dad stood near the window, still in his khakis and sleeveless T-shirt. He'd returned home only a few days earlier. Somehow the T-shirt made him seem smaller. Both of them looked tired and drawn, as if they had just managed to crawl up on a beach, swimming to shore from a shipwreck.

"What is it?" asked my mom. A look of exasperation took over her face. She turned to my father. "Oh, Tak. You deal with this. I've had all I can take."

My dad stripped the sheets from Tommy's bed. Tommy sat on my bed, trying to stifle his whimpers. He was awake

now. My dad told him to get back in bed. I thought that
Tommy might say something about having no sheets, but he
didn't. He knew better. After Tommy got in, my dad sat down
beside him.

"You know you're too old for this."

Tommy nodded.

"You've got to get up at night and go *shi-shi*."

He nodded again.

"No more drinking before bedtime."

Something in me wanted to help Tommy save a little face. I
knew I shouldn't ask, but I couldn't help myself.

"Were you and Mom fighting?"

"No. Of course not." He turned and looked at me. "It's late.
Tommy, you get back to sleep. Ben, you pick up these sheets
while I say good-night to Tommy."

I bunched up the wet sheets in a clump, trying not to
breathe the smell. I was coming out of the bathroom when
my dad approached from down the hall. "Let's bring these
down to the basement. Your mom won't want them in the
hamper."

Out on the porch, the night air was cool. A single light on
the third-floor landing gave off a dim glow. I was surprised my
dad let me come with him. Just before we started down the
stairs he stopped.

"It's really not any of your business, Ben."

"Is it about me?"

"No, no, not at all." He paused. "It's complicated, *boichan*.
Grown-up stuff."

I didn't think I would get any more out of him. I knew what
grown-up stuff meant. It meant he wasn't going to tell me about
it. Like the grown-ups had their own secret club and wouldn't
let kids in on any of their secrets. He looked back toward our

kitchen door and seemed to be thinking. He rubbed his hand through his hair. "You're mother's angry at me."

"Why?"

"For being away so much, I guess. And other things."

"Are you angry at her?"

He looked at me. "Don't worry about it. It's not anything that concerns you. You get to sleep. You've got to get up in the morning. I can take things from here."

I told him that I wasn't tired, I couldn't get back to sleep.

"Well I'm tired, so go to sleep."

"Tell me a story," I said. "Maybe then I can go to sleep."

"Ben."

"Come on. Otherwise I want to go with you down to the basement. You said I could."

He sighed. "O.K., O.K." He sat down on the top step. I sat down next to him. He took a cigarette out of shirt pocket and a pack of matches. He flicked the match and it popped, and he drew in a drag and let it out. He took another puff and rested his arm on his knee. "Do you want to hear the one about Popeye?"

"That's a little kid's story."

"You used to like it."

"Tell me a story about when you were a kid. Like when you caught those guys trying to steal the grapes."

"That was a sad thing."

"But they were stealing."

"Why on earth do you want to hear about that?"

I'd only heard this story once before. It was still new to me. My dad grew up on a farm. Mostly they grew strawberries and grapes, some vegetables, mainly for their own use. But there used to be hobos that passed through the valley and they would try to steal fruit at night. Sometimes, my dad said, *ojii-san* and the hired hands would wait in the fields, hidden in a ditch or in back of the arbor and wait for these men.

My dad's story was about the first night his father let him come with them.

The night was cool and clear, and the stars so numerous you could not place a finger between them. Over in the arbor, the darkness was deeper, the vines thick with leaves, the grapes full and ripe, stretched to bursting. I crouched with my father and the other hands in the ravine at the side of the arbor. I placed my hand down to steady myself. The grass was moist, and the air smelled fetid, rich. I kept trying to hear a rustle, but all I could hear was my own breathing, and Okubo trying to force his cough back with his fist. My father looked at him, annoyed. I knew Okubo wanted to go back to bed, didn't want to be here in the dampness of this ditch, in the chill night air.

Up in the hills, the arbors were dryer—all the moisture there seeped into the grapes, and there was less leaf cover. It was easier for the thieves to sneak in there.

A whip-poor-will cooed in the grove on the other side of the ravine. My father gripped the stick in his fist. If they came back tonight, he was going to beat them.

It was hard to see anything in the arbor. It was all black leaves and shadows. Honda heard them first. He leaned forward, tense like a greyhound. My father grabbed Honda's arm, as if to leash him back. Charley was steady, calm, though there was a note of sadness on his face that never seemed to go away. I could barely breathe, and my stomach suddenly gurgled, like a small bullfrog. Okubo started to giggle, and my father slapped him. Okubo brought his sleeve to his mouth and bit it, and turned away, his body shaking. Footsteps, about fifty feet away. I could barely make out their shapes. I heard a whisper, caught a phrase, "Over here," and it took a second for it to hit me. The thieves must be white.

This shouldn't have surprised me. After all, there were as many poor whites—Okies, they called many of them—as there were Japanese, Mexicans, or Filipinos, but somehow the concept of white thieves raiding my father's arbor seemed improbable, absurd. And then I began to wonder what would happen when we caught them.

My father's lunge out of the ditch snapped me to, and I saw Honda uncoiling behind him. Charley and Okubo scrambled past, and I was behind them, trying to catch up. I heard a voice shout, "Jesus, let's get out of here," and then something falling against the leaves of the arbor, and a grunt, and footsteps, and all of us running, dodging the vines, trying to sort out which way to go, who was who. I heard Honda cry out in Japanese and Charley answer. They'd gotten one. I ran in the direction of their voices, and then Okubo was beside me, huffing and puffing like a sick dog.

My father and Charley gripped the man by his arms. Honda muttered something to Charley and bent down in the dirt to pick up my father's stick. He cut the stick across the man's face with a dull smack. The man moaned and spit out the words, "Dirty Jap." Honda hit him again at the temples, and the man's head snapped back.

Suddenly Okubo grabbed Honda's arm, and pulled him off. I thought Honda was going to strike Okubo, but he just glared at him and muttered, "Nandayo," and shook him off. Honda slashed the stick down again, but the man turned, and it glanced off his shoulder. Okubo placed himself between Honda and the thief, who was still trying to struggle away from my father and Charley, twisting like an eel in a net.

"This man is a thief; he's stealing my grapes," my father said.

"Let him go," said Okubo. "He's not going to come back."

"He needs to be taught a lesson. They all need to be taught a lesson. They think we're weak, that we won't fight back."

"He's just hungry," said Okubo.

"*Then let him work like the rest of us.*"

"*Let him go,* shacho-san. *Or bring him in to the police.*"

"*The police? What do you think they'll do? They'll probably arrest us instead, we're just* gaijin *to them. They might even lynch us.*"

"*So what do you think they'll do if you beat this man to death? What is going to happen to your boy?*"

My father turned to look at me, as if suddenly realizing I was there. I could see the anger draining from his face. He looked back at the thief, his bearded face, his eyes shining in the dark. The man had stopped struggling. His overalls were tattered, one strap was broken, a hole in the front of his T-shirt. His body was even skinnier than Honda's. The man glanced about nervously. All the Japanese words would have been gibberish to him, frightening in their incomprehensibility.

"*Drop the stick, Honda-san,*" *my father said.* "*Let him go.*"

Charley immediately let the man drop. I thought my father would too, but instead he slapped the man hard with the back of his hand. The slap somehow seemed even more violent than Honda's blows with the stick—colder, harder. As if he were challenging the man to a duel. The man looked dazed, like a punch-drunk fighter.

"*Don't ever come back,*" *my father said in English.* "*The next time, we'll kill you.*"

My father turned and looked at me, as the man lit out toward the far end of the arbor, running as fast as he could. I wondered where his companion had gone.

As my father told me the story, sitting in the dark, I wished we could have been out in the fields, waiting to scare away some thieves. All I had for a view was an alley of cinders, glass shards, and garbage. The wooden back steps of three-story walk-ups falling into neglect. The Empty with its gnarly weeds and broken sidewalk.

My dad said that was the night his father told him he was the real owner of the farm.

"I didn't understand what he was saying," said my dad. Then *ojii-san* explained that the deed to the farm was in my father's name. My dad was born in America, he was a citizen, he could own land. My *ojii-san* couldn't.

"Did the hobo ever come back? I'll bet Honda wished he would come back."

"Probably," said my dad. "But the moral is, Ben, you shouldn't steal. Japanese, *hakujin*, it doesn't matter. But especially Japanese. You shouldn't steal."

I knew he was talking about my cousin Mark's coins, but I wondered if he was talking about the Gyp Joint too. Part of me recognized that it was my own conscience that was bothering me. My dad didn't know. I vowed not to steal from the Gyp Joint again. I almost believed my promise.

"Now there's your story," he said. "You get to bed."

I opened the screen door and turned. He was still sitting there, smoking, the urine-soaked sheets beside him.

"Good-night, Dad," I said to his back. He didn't turn.

"Good-night, Ben."

The next day Tommy and I went out late in the afternoon. We shuffled to the Empty and headed for the fort Jimmy and I had dug there the week before. The fort was almost five feet deep with a cardboard refrigerator box on top. I was about to slide into the hole we used as our entrance when I saw an old man walking his dog nearby. I didn't like that. Who wanted to play ball in a bunch of dog doo? This was our lot. Let him find his own.

The old man wore a brown gabardine coat and a brown plaid hat, shaped like a hunter's hat or the one Sherlock Holmes wears. He had a fat jowly face and red skin. When he came up to me I could see the veins in his cheeks. His dog didn't bark, just stood there at his side.

"Would you like to pet him?"

His dog was a beagle. Not a cool dog, not a collie like Lassie. Or a German Shepherd like Rin Tin Tin.

"Sure," said Tommy, before I could say anything. He adored animals. He climbed up out of the fort and scampered over to pet the beagle. It had large ears and sad-sack eyes. It was motley white with large brown spots. It sniffed his hand.

"He likes you," said the man.

"What's his name?"

"Mr. Henry."

It seemed an odd name for a dog.

"What's your name?" he asked.

"Tommy. This is my brother Ben."

The man looked around. "Where are your friends?"

"I don't know," I said. "Supper, probably."

"What about you two?"

"We should get going too," I said. "Our mom's probably calling us."

"Are you hungry?"

"Yeah," said Tommy. "Sort of," I said, almost at the same time.

"I've got some gum. Would you like a stick?"

He groped in his pocket and fingered up a green pack of Doublemint. Tommy immediately grabbed a stick. The man then turned to me. I looked at him. I looked at the dog. I looked back at him. I would have preferred Juicy Fruit.

"Yeah. Sure."

I jammed the wrapper and foil into my pocket. Normally I would just have tossed it on the ground, but I thought that the old guy might say something. With his long coat, he looked like a butler or an Englishman or something. Plump, though not as fat as my uncle Elbert. He looked like he might be someone's uncle. Only he smelled sour and pungent like the Old Spice my dad used, but stronger.

"You boys speak English so well. Where are you from?" he asked.

"We live over there," said Tommy.

"But where are you really from?"

I never liked it when people asked me this. And I didn't want Tommy to answer again. He'd probably tell the guy we were visitors form another planet.

"My dad's from California. My mom's from Seattle."

"We're Japanese," said Tommy.

"Ahh, the Japanese. They're a delightful people."

"Well, I'm not really Japanese," I corrected. "I'm American."

The beagle tugged at its leash. Maybe it smelled a squirrel. Or he had to go *shi-shi.*

"Your dog wants to go."

He yanked the leash. "Mr. Henry. Sit. Sit." The dog squatted. Tommy began petting him again.

"We have to go," I said. "I hear my mom calling us."

The man looked around. He seemed distracted by something. "I didn't hear anything."

I looked at the ground, then kicked a few pebbles into the hole with my Keds.

"Yeah. Well, it's probably time for supper."

The man smiled. "Sure. You kids go on home. Say good-bye to Ben, Mr. Henry."

I turned to go. I nudged Tommy.

"Bye," Tommy said. "Thanks for the gum."

The man made a vague wave of his hand. "You're welcome. You want another stick?"

"No," I said. "It's time for supper."

We started to trot back to the alley.

"Maybe I'll see you some other time. I'll save a stick for both of you."

When I got to the fence I looked back. His dog was going *shi-shi* in the bushes. At least he wasn't going near home plate. I wondered if he would come back again, the man in the funny hat. Maybe he'd give us something else.

I was hungry. I hoped we weren't having *budda-budda* hamburger. That was hamburger in soy sauce. I liked real hamburgers. Or spaghetti. Or fried chicken. I hoped my mom had made chocolate pudding instead of Jell-O. But it was probably Jell-O or no dessert at all. Jell-O was o.k. It just wasn't chocolate pudding. Like Doublemint wasn't the same as Juicy Fruit.

The next time that I saw the man with the funny hat, Tommy wasn't there. The man had Juicy Fruit this time. I told him that that was my favorite, and he nodded his head slowly.

"Well," he said, "I'll remember that."

THE BOMB

Everyone in my childhood was afraid of the bomb. What could you expect when every couple weeks a buzzer blared in school and all the kids scrambled beneath their desks because an A-bomb or a guided missile might be soaring down on them? As a kid you don't realize it's ludicrous to suppose a wooden desk could protect you against a nuclear warhead. You can't imagine such a weapon, the destruction it causes. Oh, you've seen bombs dropped in World War II movies—*blockbusters*, they called them, the ones that they dropped on the Nazis. Maybe you might survive one of those, if they dropped it on the block next to you. You can't conceive of a bomb that could wipe out an entire city, block after block after block.

About the nuclear age, though, Tommy was right. Despite the air-raid drills of our childhoods, the Japanese knew more than us about the A-bomb. It had seeped into their unconscious, into their dream life at an entirely different level. Mutants, Godzilla, a giant pterodactyl named Rodan, sea monsters, all hell-bent on destroying whole cities, all born from a nuclear nightmare. Some say that even the spiky skin of Godzilla resembled keloids—the burns of the *hibakusha*, their raw scaly skin.

I remember first seeing these keloids as an adult, watching *Hiroshima, Mon Amour*. A French film written by a French woman: nothing an American could have directed or scripted. The film also features a love affair between a French woman and

86

a Japanese man, each carrying the troubled history of their respective countries. In the film, the flesh of the Japanese man and French woman as they make love is juxtaposed with clips showing the skin of the *hibakusha*.

As a child, Tommy suffered from eczema. His skin would parch dry and scaly, and he'd scratch the crook of each of arm incessantly, even at night; in the morning, there'd be scrapes and scabs and blood spots on the sheets. When he was really young, it got so bad that my parents tied his arms to the slats of his crib. Every night he'd lie in bed and stretch out his arms to be roped down, as if there was nothing as natural as being tied down to your bed at night. Even when we got older, I heard him scratching in his bed, trying to shave away his skin. When I first saw the opening scenes of *Hiroshima, Mon Amour*, I was reminded of the scaly skin on his forearms, how it resembled a cracked riverbed or the shedding scales of a reptile. The transformation into something other, a brittle outer carapace.

As we got older, Tommy got odder. He'd start talking at night in our room about Godzilla or Rodan. Then he'd tell me about the primal ooze from which life first emerged on our planet and how the first creatures crawled up out of the ocean just like the monsters in Japanese sci-fi. How, if aliens alighted on our planet, one of the first questions they should ask would be, have they discovered evolution yet? Because that would mean that we understood the reasons for mutation, that living creatures need to change.

Half the time I didn't understand what he was talking about. Sometimes he'd tried to explain it to me.

"Think of rolling a pair of dice, O.K.?"

"Yeah."

"So there are only so many pairs of dots you can have, right? Snake eyes, two and one, three and one, four and one, and so on."

"Yeah, sure I get that." I wasn't in Tommy's league, but I understood math. I always got my homework done before everyone else in class and had free time to draw pictures of Dick Tracy characters or cool cars.

"Well, suppose you threw the dice, but once in a while a new number combination would come up. Like seven and one. Or eight and one."

"That's impossible."

"But not in evolution. Things happen and new combinations pop up and something new gets born."

"Like Godzilla."

"Yeah. Or like us. Humans. There were only apes before us, and somehow the dice got thrown, and we came up instead of apes."

I still didn't understand what he was talking about, but I wasn't going to say so. After all, he was my younger brother.

"Maybe that's why we were supposed to create the atomic bomb," Tommy continued. "To make things change faster."

"That's crazy. We wanted to kill the Japs."

"Ben. We're Japs."

"No, we're not. We're Americans, dummy." He was so smart in some things, so stupid in others.

"That's what you think."

"That's what Mom and Dad think too."

"Maybe Mom."

I could tell that he wanted to say something more about our parents, but wasn't going to. He didn't want to risk making me angry enough to pound him.

"You remember how that little boy got to be friends with Godzilla?" he asked. "Well, he was Japanese like us."

"Of course, numbskull. It's a Japanese movie. Just like the guy in *The Incredible Shrinking Man* is an American."

"He's a *hakujin,* Ben. He's not like us."

"Sure he is. That's why it was so scary. Like if you were really shrinking and got to be that small."

Silence. Maybe I'd shut him up. No such luck.

"Yeah, maybe you're right." He paused. "I mean that's the way I think about Dad sometimes."

"That's nuts."

"No, it's not. It's like the more time goes on, the less there is of him. Someday, I think, he's just going to disappear for good."

"Listen, spazz. That's not going to happen. He always comes back, doesn't he?" I hoped that line would hold him. To my surprise it did.

"Yeah. I guess so."

It was a thin thread for both of us to hang onto, but it was all we had. I knew I needed to distract Tommy, otherwise he wouldn't let go—he'd find a way back to this place. So I asked him what it would be like if Godzilla were a giant frog rather than a creeping lizard. Wouldn't that be neat? The boy could climb up on the frog's back and hop all over the place. It wouldn't quite be like Rodan, the flying pterodactyl, but almost as good.

"Yeah," said Tommy, "and what if the frog could talk? What if the atomic blast had given it the power to see the future? How we should prepare for aliens that are going to come. The kind of questions they're going to ask us."

"But of course the army wants to the destroy the frog."

This got Tommy really sad. He kept trying to come up with a way to save the frog, and I kept trying to come up with ways the army would blast the frog to smithereens. I liked the argument better like this, him trying to save the creature, me trying to destroy it.

I sometimes think that if I could have kept up that argument with him, maybe things would have turned out differently.

But that was impossible. In the end, the real argument is with ourselves. And only one side wins.

No, that's too easy. I should have saved him, him and his damn frog.

One afternoon, my mom nabbed me coming out of the Gyp Joint with some coolers and Juicy Fruit with the man with the funny hat and the dog Mr. Henry. She was just coming home from work. Of course I hadn't expected to see her, and I had a vaguely guilty feeling. But I told myself that I wasn't stealing, like I did sometimes with Bobby Jo and his older brother. Why should she be mad?

But she was furious. She yelled at me to come to her. She told me that I should give the candy back. I asked her why. Because I told you to, she said. I didn't understand. What was wrong with letting him buy me candy? It wasn't like I stole it or anything. He was just trying to be nice.

My mom didn't say much to the man. She just said that I was her son. She would buy me candy if I needed it, which I didn't. No one else should be buying candy for me.

On the way home, she asked if the man with the funny hat had bought candy for me before. I lied and told her, just once. I didn't tell her he'd bought candy for Tommy too. I knew that would only get us into more trouble.

"Well," she said. "I don't want you to talk to him anymore. Or go anywhere with him. You hear me, Ben Ohara?"

I nodded.

"You hear me?"

A couple times later I saw the man with the funny hat walking Mr. Henry. He waved to me. I didn't wave back.

With that supply gone I went back to stealing from the Gyp Joint. But I didn't stop there. Soon I was filching quarters from my mother's purse. I spaced out these forays so she wouldn't notice. I told myself that I deserved it. She would have given me money during the day if she'd been home. At night she was too tired, she didn't want to be bothered. Besides, it wasn't like hocking from the Gyp Joint. You couldn't get arrested for stealing from your own mother.

And yet somehow I knew. This was worse.

Awhile after this, I too found a way to leave our family, though not like my father.

For a time, there was only the two of them left, just Tommy and mother, in that Uptown apartment. There was a day during this time that I've imagined over the years, one that I know about only because Mom told me long after it really mattered, when it was too late. It's strange. I seem to see every detail of that day, though I wasn't present. It's burned in my mind deeper than any memory.

It's Saturday, and Mom has slept later than usual. She knows that she has a lot to clean up, since today she is free from ordering the small cadre of workers at the post office, free from stepping in for this one or that at the counter, handing out stamps, weighing packages. She's good at her job, orderly, precise, with a good memory. The workers respect her, though they do not like her especially. She doesn't joke with them; she doesn't know how to joke. It's work, and she's always known how to work. *Gambare.* Work hard. That familiar Japanese motto for good luck.

In the kitchen, she sips her coffee and glances at the book on the formica table. She's been trying to finish it for ages. Out the window she sees the back porches of the three-story walkups, telephone poles and wires. The alley below, where a young boy is walking, like one of her boys, only white. Tommy said he was going out to the Empty. She looks for him and finds him digging a small hole with another boy. What are they digging for? China?

She smiles and recalls how she once told him, no, you can't dig all the way to China—it isn't possible, no one can. But why? he asked. It's too far, she said. But that hardly seemed to dissuade him. Then she remembered that the center of the planet was filled with lava. It's too hot, way too hot, at the core of the Earth, it's molten metal. This seemed finally to satisfy him, the scientific explanation. He gets certain ideas in his head and will just not let go. This morning he woke her wanting to tell her his dream. "Mom, I had a dream last night where the Lizard of Nature grabs the boy with his tongue and licks him and licks him until he's poisonous and takes him into the water. Then the Lizard rises up and then he holds the boy up to the sun until he's taken up by the sun." She laughed and told him he should stop watching horror films on TV.

"They're not horror films," he said. "They're science fiction films. Like *Science Fiction Theater.*"

Such distinctions, what do they mean to him? How does he see so much that she does not? Yesterday, as the sun began to set over the city, he pointed out the window and told her, "Look at the saffron sun." Then he explained why the color of the sun changed as it went down, how the light refracted through the atmosphere and why the sky was blue most of the time—something about how blue consisted of the shortest light waves, the most frequent.

Where did his odd brilliance come from? Not from her, not from Takeshi. Some throwback, generations ago. Rare and dormant. Not like Ben. She knows where he came from, from both of them, though perhaps more from Takeshi. But she tries not to think about him in reform school. *Shoganai.* It can't be helped.

She picks up the book. It's about a couple in the suburbs of New York, an executive stealing an affair with his secretary. The wife doesn't know, of course. Are there any other plots than this? My husband, she thinks to herself ruefully, is not having an affair. An affair would be normal. She tries to recall what he was like before the illnesses started, before the energy seemed to drain from him like a battery going bad on a transistor radio, the sound fainter and fainter, filled with scratches and static.

An image from a *nisei* dance pops up, like a hand waving for the last time in the ocean, just before going down. Or a dark fin gliding through the swells, hinting of the hulk beneath.

But no, it's not that mysterious. It's his stubbornness, his refusal to see how things are. I should have seen that from the beginning, she thinks. From the moment I learned his history, what he had done. But he hid it so well. I thought it was like the war, something to be put away, something in the past. What's done is done. I thought he believed that too.

No, she can't go there. That's forbidden territory. There is work to be done. She needs to clean the house, starting with the kitchen floor.

I fear I have not done my mother justice. Perhaps because she is a survivor, because she didn't give up, and oh, how many times have I wanted to give up. On my family, on myself, on this book and my scholarly tome, on America, on whatever road I am traveling on, lost and almost out of gas. Looking for the last-chance Texaco, the man with the star. I often wanted to think of my dad like that, as if he were the one who would save us. Like the reluctant sheriff, some Jimmy Stewart character who abhors violence but harbors it inside himself and lets it loose once, just once, to save the town. But it was my mother who always saved us, who held on, who fought and fought and would not let go. Who possessed that violence.

But there must have been times when she wanted to give up, needed to give up and couldn't. I think I know most of them. Or at least the ones I caused.

It wasn't simply the stealing. She caught me soon enough, my petty larcenies from her purse. Punished me as best she knew how, shouting, How could you; What kind of boy does this; Who told you you could do this; What am I supposed to do with you; What would your father think; How can you do this with him gone; You think I don't have to work for this money; Why, Ben, why; Don't you get enough to eat, clothes on your back; You think you're like all those other boys, all those, those hillbillies; well, you've got another thought coming to you, young man; you're just not going to play with them anymore . . .

Fine, I thought, they don't like me anyway (I was fighting at the time with Jimmy Pearson).

And then when she seemed to run out of invectives. She pinched my cheek hard. I started to cry and resented the hell out of her for that. If my dad hit me and I cried, that was o.k. But if your mother pinches your cheek and you cry, you can't do that. Only little kids like Tommy did that.

But she never had to pinch Tommy. She yelled at him once in a while, yes, but not like with me, who confronted her with more and more reasons for punishment, duties that should more properly have been passed on to my father.

And so the cycle took off. When the owners at the Gyp Joint finally got wise and caught me, my mother had a look of both exasperation and resignation, as if she knew this was going to happen. As if the police who stood at the back door with me in tow were something she had seen before. I got off with a warning then.

The second time there was talk of sending me to reform school. I thought it was all talk. I didn't think I would get caught a third time.

She was losing control of me, and she knew it. She knew there was nothing she could do.

When it happened the third time, she hardly got angry. Resignation. *Shoganai.* Can't be helped.

But back to my memory of my mother, the time both my father and I were away, when she was the only one there to look after things.

She's hanging the laundry now, in the late afternoon light. It's fall, the air growing cool. She wonders if the clothes will dry enough before the sun goes down. It would be nice to live in a place where she didn't have to share a laundry room, like her sister Yo, who lives in the suburbs. Yo has a whole room—a utility room—of her own to wash her clothes, and she owns a dryer too. Yo is a nurse, and it's her income that enabled her family to move to the suburbs. If only my parents had been working at the same time, they too might have been able to do that.

She looks down at the Empty. There are no children there. Tommy should be coming home soon, it's getting near time for supper. She wishes my father were here, he could put his two fingers in the corners of his mouth and send that shrill whistle like a spear out over the neighborhood, piercing every eardrum on the block, retrieving the boys. But he's not here, and Ben's not here, and Tommy should be back soon. She thinks about going to look for him, but then she remembers that she has to go to IGA to pick up some milk and frozen peas for dinner (there needs to be vegetables—she grew up on vegetables, though they were always so fresh in her father's produce store back in Seattle before the war).

She'll go to the store, and if Tommy's not back when she gets home, she'll go out looking for him. But he should be back by then. No need to worry.

It's funny how fate works in families. One child may seem totally fucked up while another is perfectly normal. Or even gifted, brilliant. And then something happens, and those places are reversed. Sometimes they're reversed again. And even again. It makes things difficult for a parent. How are you to know if you've succeeded? At age twelve? Sixteen? Twenty? Twenty-five? Thirty-eight?

One turning point, I see now, started with Luis Rodriguez. I don't quite remember how we got to be friends. I think it was after the fight I had with Jimmy Pearson. I recall one of the first things Luis and I did together was to team up and hock something at the Gyp Joint. That was what probably cemented our friendship.

Luis told me he couldn't remember anything about Puerto Rico. They left when he was two. His dad worked two jobs, one as a janitor, one as a busboy. He had black gnarly hair like Luis, with a few croppings of gray. When he was feeling good, he went around the house singing songs in Spanish. His voice was brown, deep and rich, like the color of the cigars he smoked. At other times he drank too much, especially when the pain in his back got to him.

Luis said that his older brother had been sent to reform school. I knew what that was. The cop that nabbed me at the Gyp Joint had told me all about it. Luis was surprised at this, how cool I seemed to be about the prospect of going to j.d., juvenile detention.

At his house, Luis and I spent a lot of time wrestling, imitating the pro wrestlers from TV. We'd jump from his bed onto each other as if leaping from the ropes of the ring. One of us would play the villain, the other the hero. It was always more fun to play the villain. You got to sneak up on the hero when he was arguing with the ref and go for illegal things like rabbit punches or throwing a chair or pulling hair. When you lost, you pounded the ground with your feet and fists, crying like a little baby. I loved these bouts. My mom would never let us do anything like that at our apartment.

Still, I didn't want to stay friends with Luis for long. I knew I belonged with the gang, that I had to somehow make up with Jimmy Pearson.

Luis's mom and dad used to argue a lot. They weren't like the arguments at my house, where my parents tried to whisper and not let us hear them. These were real ten-round affairs with screaming and throwing things. One time Luis's mom launched his dad's clothes out the window. His white T-shirts floated down awkwardly like pelicans, and Luis and I both thought this was so funny, even though both of us had gotten scared and left the apartment. Then we heard something crash and his mother scream, and we started walking back down the alley, trying to get away as fast as we could.

That's when the gang showed up, Jimmy Pearson, Bobby Jo Watkins, Billy Blevins, and Michael Nagata. Billy said something about me being with a spic and Jimmy laughed.

"So that's your new buddy," he said.

"Hey, look," said Michael Nagata, "Spic and Spam."

"Better watch it," said Bobby. "The spic's got a switchblade."

Luis said nothing. I knew he didn't have a switchblade. I could feel the fear rising inside me like always whenever Michael Nagata came after me. Only this time I felt different. Maybe it was all the times stealing things at the Gyp Joint, stealing from my mom's purse. Or maybe it was getting caught by the cops; what was Michael Nagata compared to the police? But some other energy began to bubble up within me. I looked at Nagata's face, his tortoiseshell glasses and black crew cut and rounded cheeks and cocky grin, and I wanted to smash his face, cut that grin out, the way you'd carve a smile out from a pumpkin and leave only this gaping hole.

Everyone was looking at Luis, so they didn't see me pull out the switchblade. It had been easy enough to hock. It wasn't Luis's. It was his older brother's. And Luis had shown me where his brother kept it.

I didn't say anything; I just flicked it open. Jimmy heard it and turned. "Look out, Harry's got a switchblade."

Michael Nagata's face suddenly looked to me like a terrified rabbit, some squirrelly rodent. Still, he wasn't going to give in. Maybe he thought his judo would save him.

"Who cares? Harry's a spazz. It don't matter."

"That's what you think."

I knew my response wasn't strong enough. This only made Michael bolder.

"He's not going to use it, he's a scaredy-cat," he laughed and turned to the rest of the guys. "Whaddaya expect? His old man's a No-No Boy. That's why he hangs out with spics."

There was that name again, the thing I didn't quite understand but sensed just the same. I took a step forward, pulled by a force beyond me. I lunged and swiped the blade across Michael Nagata's arm. Like an animal with a will all its own, the blade cut him at the bicep just below the edge of his T-shirt.

He screamed and leapt back, as if he'd touched a live wire. All the gang jumped back in turn like dancers in synchronized motion. Nagata stared at his wound and then at me as if he couldn't quite take in what had happened. I swung the blade again, and he jumped back. I swung again. The third time he couldn't leap back fast enough, and I caught his forearm. I started swinging wildly then, howling from somewhere in my belly, some force hurtling me forward, flicking my arm back and forth like a mad mechanical saw. To this day I don't know if I was just trying just to scare him or if I really wanted the blade to find a more permanent home.

And then they were all running back down the alley.

Luis turned to me. "Hey, that's my brother's." He looked at the gang scramble around the corner and started laughing. "I can't believe you did that," he said. "That was something. You're loco, man. Really loco."

I still felt agitated from the fight, disoriented, as if I didn't quite know how it had happened. Gradually I calmed down a bit, but as I did, the fear began to rise again inside me, only now it was different. What was going to happen? I'd probably go to j.d. for sure. And my mom would kill me. So would my dad.

I couldn't let Luis see my fear.

"Well, he had it coming."

"Sure. They started it," he said, as if trying to convince himself. He seemed younger to me now, not the kid I saw hanging out the window when everyone told me he was the Puerto Rican kid who had a switchblade.

"Let's get going, Ben. They might come back."

We turned and went back to his house. As we approached his back stairs, he said, "Maybe my mom and dad have stopped fighting."

We both stopped. We couldn't hear anything. Yeah, the coast was clear.

Budda-budda hamburger, rice, peas, a salad. A simple meal, it's just Tommy and her. My mother thinks of that as she leaves the apartment and circles around the fountain in the center of the two flank buildings. The fountain is dry and has never worked since they have lived here. Weeds sprout from its cracks, like tufts of gnarly hair. A wire fence, battered and twisted, surrounds the fountain. Someone should simply tear it down. It serves no use now. There's no water.

The sky is charcoal, the air cooler. She takes out her pink kerchief and ties it around her head. She thinks about going back inside for an umbrella but it's just a short walk to Broadway and the IGA. She tries not to notice the stray bits of newspaper and broken glass in the yard, in the gutters. She passes the tan brick building where the Puerto Rican boy used to live, the one who gave the knife to Ben.

Perhaps she should have watched Ben better, kept a closer eye on him. But she has to work, doesn't she? She has to feed the family. She has to perform the duties that Tak can't any longer. Will he ever again? She tries not to think of that possibility. She tells herself he'll get better, Ben will come back, things will return to normal. For a brief moment, she allows herself to imagine moving from this neighborhood, the type of house they might buy out in the suburbs. Wouldn't it be nice to have a bi-level? In one of those new tracts up north?

A flock of pigeons sweeps down from the girders of the El. A train roars overhead. She passes the vacant lot, thinks about how vagrants might hang out there. How the neighborhood kids light fires in an old trash can near the alley, heaping stray newspapers, sticks, anything they can find. There's a ratty ancient couch against the fence, its hide shredded in tatters as if attacked by a wild animal.

What a neighborhood, with its decaying tenements and boarded up buildings. Where apartments are broken into for almost nothing, for small amounts of petty cash. Where the laundry hangs between the buildings and gathers up the bituminous air, coal and car fumes and alley dirt. Birds the color of exhaust. Sidewalks cracked and split. Where there are no restaurants, only bars, long dark corridors, dimly lit, where men sit on into late evening, the amber light encasing them like insects trapped in prehistoric stone.

She rounds the corner and approaches the Chinese hand laundry. She recalls how there was a Chinese family near where she lived in Seattle who ran a laundry. How one day they put up a sign saying, "Chinese, not Japanese."

She glances inside and sees the steam rising from the ironing table. The husband and wife and children all working. Hot, hot, how hot the husband looks at his ironing table, sweat beading his brow, his T-shirt dark with sweat stains. He's balding and looks a bit like her father, tall and skinny with gold glasses and a beak nose. A small mustache, just like her father's. He's gone now, buried back in Japan where he returned a few years ago. America no longer his home. Was it ever?

It starts to rain, a slight drizzle. She could go back to get her umbrella, but she's almost to the grocery store. She thinks of the woman pining for her dead lover in a story she once read in college. Of the husband with his clumsy thoughtless lust. When was the last time she felt anything resembling lust?

She feels the wetness on her arms. The drops darkening the pavement before her, tiny pools beginning to appear. She recalls the mud in camp, how the streets became nearly impassable, swamps. More suitable for frogs than humans. Even the *geta* of the old people got stuck. How she hated that, the mud. And the dust and dirt in the summer. Nothing ever stayed clean. Ever. No matter how much she and her mother tried. We are not living like *nihonjin*, said her mother, and it could have been anything around them she was condemning: their imprisonment, the lack of work, the guards, and barbed wire. But what she meant most was that they were living like animals, unclean, maybe not as bad as the horse stalls back in Pullayup, but a nightmare nonetheless. She recalls the sound the rain made on the galvanized tin roof, plunk after plunk, and the lines of dripping water that fell here and there in the room, like bars, each of them with a cup or bucket beneath. How she would watch the cups to see which one was overflowing so she could pick it up and dump it out the door. How she read her schoolwork while watching. How bored she felt.

She's nearing the Gyp Joint. She remembers Tommy and hopes he went in when it started raining. But the thought passes. When she looks in the Gyp Joint, her chest buckles and adrenalin rushes through her. She feels nausea rise in her stomach as she sees the *hakujin* with the dog and the deerstalker hat handing a piece of candy to Tommy. Just like with Ben.

She will rush in, she will confront the man, she will yell at Tommy, she will tell him never to talk to that man with the funny hat, to go away from him every time he gets near, to tell her if he ever tries to talk to him again. She will tell him this over and over as she drags him home, him crying, crying so hard that he's incoherent, she can't understand a word he's saying.

But it doesn't matter. She knows what he's saying. She knows her luck has run out. That Tommy is not me. She has not rescued him in time.

3

THE NOBLE *SEPPUKU* OF DR. SERIZAWA

Though I've sometimes sported a cavalier attitude toward my academic calling, it hasn't been easy being such a scholarly no-show. It hardly fits the Asian stereotypes. Or the silent voices of community and family, chiding me for my incompletes.

Over the years, I've collected hundreds of pages of drafts for *Famous Suicides of the Japanese Empire*, endless ruminations on the meaning of the act, the similarities and divagations between Western and Japanese psychologies.* At times, confronted with all this material, I hardly know where to start. Perhaps that's one of the reasons I've never finished. So many sources, stories, notes, quotations. Scholarly bits (Lifton: "We suggest that death in Japan is less an individual event than an occurrence within the group or community, and that death and dead people have a certain familiarity in daily life"). Pensive aubades, like this one from the renowned author Akutagawa Ryunosuke, so

---

* It's amazing the mounds of Orientalism one needs to clear away. E.g., Emile Durkheim: "The readiness of the Japanese to disembowel themselves for the slightest reason is well known"—this despite the fact that premodern and modern rates of Nipponese suicide are not significantly higher than in the West; currently not only do economically debilitated European countries like Lithuania and Belarus sport higher rates of offing oneself, so do France and Austria. Ah, the Lithuanians, such a death-obsessed people. And the Austrians, copycat Nazis, great skiers, and proficient practitioners of *die Selbstmord.*

closely mirroring a certain voice in my own head that when I came upon it this spring I wondered at first who wrote it:

> We humans, being human animals, do have an animal fear of death. The so-called vitality is but another name for animal strength. I myself am one of these human animals. And this animal strength, it seems, has gradually drained out of my system . . . The world I am now in is one of diseased nerves, lucid as ice. Such voluntary death must give us peace, if not happiness.

Still, it's not always the obvious choices that I've been drawn to, the likes of Akutagawa or Misao Fujimura, the young man whose leap from Kegon Falls inspired so many copycat suicides by other troubled youths at the turn of the century. And sometimes it hasn't even been the lesser-known suicides, like the minor intellectual and writer Arishima Takeo. Often those that have stuck in my mind are quirkier, laced with some inner message whose significance perhaps only I can fathom.

When I peruse some of the places that my mind has wandered while researching this project, I can only wonder either at my sanity or my seriousness in approaching it. Or perhaps both. Here's one such example:

> In the original Gojira—a.k.a. Godzilla—Dr. Yamane, the scientist who discovers the monster, refuses at first to search for a way to destroy it. "Gojira," he says, "presents us scientists with a unique opportunity, one that only those of us in Japan can study." After all, Gojira arises in the aftermath of an atomic blast, a mutant marinated in fission, and who would have more interest in such effects than the Japanese? The movie even alludes to an incident where fallout from a U.S. test atomic blast drifted down upon a Japanese fishing boat. The boat's

tuna was then sold at the Tsukiji fish market to restaurants all over Japan. In the movie, as Gojira *approaches Japan, one Tokyo commuter turns to another and says, "It's terrible, huh? Radioactive tuna, atomic fallout, and now this* Gojira *to top it all off."*

Eventually even Dr. Yamane is forced to admit Gojira *must be destroyed. But no conventional weapon has any effect on the creature. In an ironic twist, the solution comes from the story's love triangle: Dr. Yamane's daughter Emiko is engaged to a mad scientist, Dr. Serizawa (we know he's mad because he's strapped with an eye patch and wild thrashing Einsteinean bristles). But Emiko is really in love with Lieutenant Nagata, who is also trying to destroy the monster.*

Turns out, though, that Dr. Serizawa has concocted an "oxygen destroyer" that disintegrates the oxygen in water and asphyxiates all living organisms in the vicinity. He claims that it's more powerful than a nuclear bomb. Indeed, it possesses the potential to destroy all of humanity, so he's reluctant to use it, lest the governments of the world find out and mass annihilation ensues. He falls into a fisticuffs with the lieutenant over whether to use the O.D. or not, a fight whose subliminal raison d'etre is the struggle for Emiko. Serizawa's a scientist, so he loses the fight, but it's only when he hears a bunch of schoolgirls singing "Oh Peace, Oh Light, Return" on television that he finally decides to use the formula. He declares that he will burn his papers so that the formula is destroyed: "This will be the first and last time that I will ever allow the oxygen destroyer to be used."

The opportunity comes when Gojira's *napping at the bottom of a bay. Serizawa and the lieutenant both work together to plant the O.D. device near the monster. The lieutenant then surfaces, but Serizawa remains. He radios Emiko, tells her the device has worked, and asks her and the lieutenant to be happy. Then, with a knife, he cuts his own oxygen supply, a grand* seppuku *that ensures his horrible weapon of destruction will never be used again.*

Thus, the world is saved and love triumphs, all through the cut of a blade. Not quite Yukio Mishima, but a suicide nonetheless. Who cares if this suicide is fictitious? In 1985, a New York Times/CBS News *poll asked fifteen hundred Americans to name a famous Japanese person. The three top answers? Emperor Hirohito. Bruce Lee. Godzilla. Dr. Serizawa's seppuku saved humankind and offed the third most famous Japanese we Americans know.*

This winter, when I first received that long-lost postcard from Tommy, I wondered whether I should head out to Japan to search for him. Looking for clues, I rummaged through his letters, just to check the handwriting. They're all there in a box in a closet in my office, his letters, his scientific papers and notebooks he left behind in his apartment.

I found a box of letters from when he was away at this posh private school Oakbrook, which he'd won a scholarship to. (For me, the ordinary nongenius brother, public school was good enough, though when Mom remarried, she and Marv moved us out to a Jewish suburb where the academic competition was as fierce as any private institution). In the end, Oakbrook was not such a good idea, filled as it was with spoiled rich kids with access to too much ready cash and a vast quantity and array of drugs. Tommy spent his spare time getting stoned and tripping, though he was still smart enough to keep up his G.P.A.

As I gazed at that box, it suddenly struck me as odd, the fact of my little brother writing me letters when we should have been talking and haggling with each other at night in our room. How did that happen? How did the two of us become separated like that? Who decided that was the way to go? Was it Marv or our mom? Or did Tommy ask to go? And how is it our mom ended up married again to a man who seemed so unlike our father, not just ethnically and racially but of an entirely different temperament and tone and with an entirely different attitude toward her? I remember that there was a time when she started dating various men, all of them white, some mousy and tenuous, some brassy and blustery, and some in-between, like Marv. Too cold, too hot, just right. Is that how she chose him? Practical, even-keeled, down to earth, no darkness in his past, no darkness in his future. Steady and steadfast, stirring up nothing.

At random I picked up one of Tommy's letters. It was filled with critiques of various sci-fi writers, along with a plot summary of a story he himself was working on. In the story, he was trying to combine the elements of time travel and aliens with his adolescent notions, fueled by acid trips, of alternative dimensions of the universe. Along the way, he threw in little tidbits about relativity, the speed of light, and the elasticity of time, how time would differ between someone who was stationary and someone who was traveling at the speed of light. Back in the day, when I received the letter, I probably didn't pay much attention to what he was saying. At the time I was going through my own readjustments. We all were.

I was a teenager by then, buried in my own solipsistic world. But even before certain bonds had been severed, the boundaries of my world had been drastically altered. I think for me it had started when I was sent off to a juvie center right after I got through taking my swipe at revenge against Michael Nagata. Suddenly I was cut off from all those I knew, from the neighborhood and friends, from anything familiar. I had to make my way into a new world, find out how to survive among the other delinquents and malcontents. I seem to remember that that was also the year my body changed; I shot up six or seven inches in a few months, my voice deepened and cracked, and suddenly certain things about boys and girls—even though there were no girls seemingly within miles of juvie—took on new import. But did I realize what was happening to me? And then, amid all this, there was what happened to my father, another drastic change I had to absorb on the fly.

So much of those years seems to me blurry and off-kilter, like some bad experimental film: all odd cuts and juxtapositions with no narrative flow. Back in Chicago, when we all lived in that apartment in Uptown, things were tough for all of us, what with my parents struggling with each other and their own separate secrets and dark recesses. There, their past selves spoke to them in admonishing tones about the life they had come to live. And of course the whole neighborhood around us, well, it possessed its own fierce trials and tribunals. A tough section in a tough city.

But somehow for Tommy and me—no, I won't speak for him—for me anyway, things made sense then. There was a slowness to that time, things unfolding, uneasily perhaps, but unfolding, not hitting me out of the blue. I always woke up in the same bed in the same bedroom, and even when my father was gone, he would still return; we hadn't been severed forever. We were the Oharas, the four of us, and that meant something. And even though through the years I've read and learned more and more about who our people were, where they came from, and what happened to them and why, I don't think I ever had a firmer grasp of what the grown-ups meant when they referred to our own kind as *nihonjin*. Of course it never meant to them that we were Japanese, because we clearly weren't. What it meant was something else.

Or maybe I just paid more attention in those days; maybe time was slower. Back in college, when I got into my own drug use, mostly grass, and one or two acid trips, the thing I liked was how time seemed to slow down, how every moment possessed a density and myriad bouquet of fresh details. Yeah, yeah, I know. Adolescent drug days and bullshit. But of course that sense of time's always available to us. We feel it when we travel, when we move ourselves out of our old routines into some unfamiliar place, among people and things we've never seen before, things we're seeing for the first time and so we absorb those experiences more deeply and slowly than those things we see every day where we pass on by as if we've really seen it all before.

I remember that evening after I had sunk into Tommy's letters, I came down to dinner, the words of my brother still filtering through my consciousness. "It's not that difficult, bro, really. It starts with the fact that the speed of light is constant, no matter where you are, no matter how fast you're traveling, it's always the same. Which of course is a paradox because you would think if you were stationary and I were traveling faster and faster I would be able to gain ground on a beam of light while you wouldn't. But that's not what happens . . ."

I stood in the hallway by the kitchen and felt this longing to talk to him, to see him again, my long-lost brother, and I wanted to believe that I could, that it was still possible. I knew it wasn't. There was only what was before me, Grace scooping up the sizzling bacon for the spaghetti carbonara, brushing her hair from her face, little beads of perspiration on her brow. I was looking at the pattern of freckles on her face, the pattern I'd seen day after day for how-many years, and I noticed how they formed their own little constellations, little designs that had somehow escaped me. Or had they appeared through the years as age and sunlight had brought out new flecks of darkness on her skin, and I was only now noticing them?

She was shouting at the boys to set the table. I moved into the kitchen and began to pitch in, telling them to set water glasses out, and no, we didn't need spoons. Kengo and Takeshi started bickering about who should do what.

"That's your job."

"I did it last night."

"Just quit it, you two," I said. "Kengo, you put out the water glasses; Takeshi, you do the utensils."

"Why do I always have to do the water glasses?"

"Just do it."

"It's not fair."

"Ha, see, I told you."

"Dad, it's not fair."

Raising my voice a little: "What does fair have to do with it? It's just water glasses."

Kengo shut up then, but I could see that he was still simmering about something. And I realized that I didn't know what it was. First he accused Takeshi of taking the big water glass when it was for Grace. Then he pointed out how Takeshi had given himself a larger bowl and that that was because Takeshi ate too much.

"See, Dad, he's calling me fat. You little punk. You wanna see who's fat? You wanna a fat lip?"

"Sure, you want some of this?" said Kengo, not backing down.

At this point I would have normally brought out the dad voice, telling them both to shut up and do what they'd been told, that I was tired of their squabbling, that their mother was tired of their squabbling. They needed to learn to get along. They were just egging each other on.

But instead I simply said to Kengo, "Yeah, I want some of that."

He turned to me, his face still scowling.

"Yeah?"

He raised his fists slightly, and I moved forward. A sly smile appeared on his face.

"You think you can take me?"

"I know I can take you."

"Come on, old man."

"o.k., Mr. Tough Ass, bring it on."

He took a mock swing. I dodged, feinted, and then he took another, and Grace said, "Ben," and I said, "What?"

"Watch your language!"

I said, "What?" again, just as Kengo smacked me across the face.

"Shit, that really hurt."

He laughed.

"You just got me because Mom distracted me."

At that point Grace stepped in. "o.k., o.k., stop beating up your dad, Kengo, and get the water glasses. And Ben, you really shouldn't swear like that."

"Yeah," said Kengo, sticking his tongue out as he went to the refrigerator to fill the glasses. "Watch your language, old man."

I often step in when I sense Kengo and Takeshi getting into things. Sometimes I just yell at them to stop, but other times I pull one of them aside, sometimes distracting them; other times I'll talk to them more about what it means to be brothers, how they're going to have each other longer than anybody they know, how they're always going to be in each other's life. I remind them how much better they get along than a lot of brothers, how Takeshi has never hauled ass and really wailed on Kengo the way almost all older brothers do to their younger rivals.

But what I saw that night was that distracting or lecturing them wasn't the only way. There was simply listening, observing, taking in the actual words that they were saying and trying to hear the meaning behind it. I saw how each time Kengo interrupted or tried to insult Takeshi, Takeshi only got angrier and complained harder to us, the parental judges, about how Kengo was bugging him. But the more I watched Kengo, the less annoyed I got at his obnoxious behavior, the more I understood it. At one point, I saw how Kengo asked two times for someone to pass the rolls and no one responded. I took one of the crescent rolls and said, "Forty-two, thirty-six, hup-hup, hike," and tossed one over to him, but he was on to something else.

"Takeshi, that's my water."

"I just want a sip."

"Hey, Kengo," I said, "stop giving him lip."

He looked up at me, not quite sure.

"Yeah, what you want, you big old Nip?"

"Well, look at you, you squeaky pip."

"At least my mouth's not leaky and crusty and old. Like bread mold."

"Hey, who threw you the roll?"

"Yeah, all out of control."

So we continued like that, for a couple more lines, and finally he quieted down and began to eat and stopped interrupting and bothering his brother. I saw then what he'd been saying, what he'd be asking for. And isn't that what we all want? Just a little attention.

After dinner, even when he finished his part of the clean-up, Kengo stayed with me and helped, our banter continuing back and forth. I saw how easy it was to keep up the flow between us as long as I took cues from him, as long as I listened.

Well, we do learn things, I thought. Though sometimes a little late. And I guess it was then that I knew Tommy and I still weren't finished.

When I was away at my first juvie institution, my father was also away again at a different sort of institution. So it was just my mother and Tommy back at home. As Halloween approached, Tommy started to pester my mother about making him a Godzilla costume. Did my mother protest that he should simply buy a costume from the store or choose something simpler to put together—a ghost, a pirate, a hobo? Or did she delight in Tommy's unique persistence, in the ways he was constantly pushing the envelope, some brilliant letter demanding to be read?

Making the costume couldn't have been easy. It wasn't like cutting out a cape or dyeing a pair of pajamas. Tommy later told me that she even used a pair of white gloves, which she'd gotten from her mother, that must have been worn at festivals and at the Buddhist church back in Seattle. Dyeing those green was bad enough, but dyeing one of his good white shirts? My mother couldn't go that far. It would be a waste of money. She got some green felt cloth and jerry-rigged the costume together. As for the shoes, she said that Godzilla would just have to wear black Keds for one time in his life. Tommy knew that she was reaching her limit, so he relented. Getting the snout correct was a problem, though. My mother came up with the idea of using a tin measuring cup and gluing its bottom and sides against the felt hood. Tommy was really pleased about the snout. He hadn't thought that she'd be able to do it.

He didn't tell any of his school buddies about the costume. He wanted to surprise them. But when they showed up to pick him up, none of them said anything. He kept waiting for them to mention his costume, but there was nothing. Nothing. Nor did any parent in the building or down the block who handed him candy say anything about the scary monster. He tried roaring, but this only made his friends laugh. He tried roaring at the adults, and they only laughed louder. When Godzilla roared, everyone ran in terror. But no one even said the word *Godzilla*.

He could have been an alligator for all they knew, and indeed, Jimmy Pearson said to him, "Hey, Ohara, nice alligator suit." He meant this to be nice, but Tommy took it as an insult and said he was never going to speak to Jimmy again (Tommy had this way of taking on grudges and holding them for all they were worth).

And then he and his friends turned the corner, and there was Michael Nagata. Michael Nagata, whom I had knifed in fear and fury and who was longing to wreak vengeance upon the Ohara clan. He took one look at Tommy and, with the sixth sense of a fellow *sansei*, surmised who Tommy was trying to be.

"Oh, isn't this cute," he said. "Ohara's a little baby Godzilla. Come here, Godzilly. Come here, little Godzilly."

Tommy burst into tears and stomped off. But Nagata rushed up behind him and stomped on the rope of cloth attached to Tommy's behind, ripping Godzilla's tail off and revealing his cowboy underpants. "Look," said Nagata, "Godzilly has cowboy underpants. Root 'em, toot 'em, six guns on his butt."

Tommy ran off. Even now thinking about it, I want to knife Nagata all over.

Tommy told my mom that he never wanted to go out for Halloween again. And he didn't. He was a stubborn kid.

There are the things you remember and the things that are a blur. Sometimes even the most important things are just a blur. And other things, like Tommy's costume, even though I never saw it, are the things that stick.

Perhaps it was inevitable. That's how I looked at my father's death for a long time. It made it easier to accept. He'd been gone often enough so that it didn't seem that unexpected when at last he didn't come back.

When it happened, I don't think any of us were surprised. My father had been in the institution just a few days that time.

He must have smuggled the razor blade in. They found him in the morning in his bed, the blood drained through his wrists. I like to think that he didn't want my mom to be the one who found him.

My father killed himself when I was twelve and Tommy nine. Just before Tommy's birthday.

Does our difference in ages explain in part the difference in what happened to us? I had, literally, already left home, out on my own in reform school. Tommy was used to a life where our father would be there for a while and then be gone and then return. But then he left and never came back. What did that mean to Tommy? He knew cognitively—as Tommy would say—that our father was dead. But in that primitive reptilian part of his brain, did he believe that Dad would magically return?

As for me, I knew my father was dead, and it wasn't just cognitive knowledge. I saw him in his casket. My mother didn't want Tommy to see him like that. She had him stay with a neighbor during the funeral.

Later, she wondered if that had been a mistake. But to be fair, she was trying to do what seemed best. Tommy was her odd, sensitive one. Who knew how he would react seeing his father laid out, pale, almost blue, against the white silk of the casket? It was hard enough to keep him inside reality. "You were my earthly one," she said to me years later. "Tommy, Tommy was from some place else."

ST. JUDE'S

I am the son of internees. Two young people whom the government jailed because it believed that they might be spies for old Nippon. Not quite Julius and Ethel Rosenberg, nothing as specific as that. No, everyone in my parents' entire community was rounded up. It was easier that way. And most went along with the government, followed their orders to the letter, wanting to prove it was all a big mistake. And some, at a certain point, did not go along. Among these was my father.

After all these years, this history seems no more real to me than nineteenth-century Polish politics or a list of the maharajahs of some Indian province. A handful of obscure documents, a sidelight to the major, real events of history. No one knows about it anymore; no one cares. And what it all has to do with my father sinking afternoons into the dark folds of our living room couch, I still can't fathom.

Perhaps, as the psychologists tend to view things these days, it was all chemical. A few tabs of Zoloft or Prozac would have saved him; it would have all melted away. And there'd be no past, no shame, no stigma from raising his hand in protest rather than bowing his head in patriotic obedience. Perhaps politics had nothing to do with it all. Perhaps it lay buried deep inside my father long before Pearl Harbor, before the war, before everything changed. Merely biochemical fault lines, bad synapses, something in his genes. Our genes.

Too many questions without answers. So why ask them? my mother would say. *Gambatte.* Work hard. Move on. *Shoganai.* It can't be helped.

A few months after my father died, I was transferred from the state's juvie institution to a place called St. Jude's. The authorities told my mother that it was a promotion for good behavior. In a way, it was almost like winning a scholarship, they said, given the quality of the teachers there, mostly Jesuits and Catholic brothers. If I did well, I'd be let out at the end of the year. Though there had been classes at the state's reform school, they were mostly a waste. It was more a holding pen than anything else. I didn't know what St. Jude's would be like, but I figured it couldn't be any worse than the grim facilities of the state.

St. Jude's Home for Boys. Wayward and otherwise. A sheaf of buildings way out in the sticks, somewhere past Half Day Road. Corn fields all around. Nowhere to escape to. A chapel and rectory, a two-story classroom building, a dormitory and gym, all in red brick and looking more like a prison than anything else. When I saw *Shawshank Redemption*, the prison seemed a doppelgänger for St. Jude's, a certain chilly darkness and rigidity to the structures, as if rectitude and recrimination could be embalmed within each brick. There were red brick walls around the grounds, which did include a football field, and a locked gate.

When I'd first arrived at St. Jude's, I was warned about Father Boland. Perhaps a wiser kid would've taken heed of these warnings. Father Boland, who'd once broken his paddle against an unfortunate boy's backside. Father Boland, dubbed Captain Bligh after the infamous British sea captain whose cat-o'-nine-tails slashed seamen's backs to bloody mesh. Father Boland, who'd persuaded authorities to send juvenile delinquents to St.

Jude's, asserting that the discipline at his institution was far stricter and more edifying than the state's other facilities. Father Boland, who showed up in classes asking the instructors if there were any boys that day who needed a proper thrashing. Father Boland, who stalked the halls of St. Jude's like an alpha wolf keeping the rest of the pack in line. Whose office was his court and dungeon, seat of judgment and all-too-earthly punishment.

But somehow I passed all this off as exaggeration, a Catholic boy's fear of the clergy and threats of damnation. I was the son of a Buddhist and a Congregationalist, free of their silly schoolboy rumors. What could Father Boland do to me?

Where Father Boland stood was at least clear to me. I was more confused by Brother McConnell, the English teacher. Brother McConnell was neither feared nor denigrated by the boys. In a way, this troubled me more. Like all schoolboys, I liked things clear-cut, bad guys and good guys—and I could hardly imagine St. Jude's containing any good guys—and no in-between.

In retrospect, I wonder how Brother McConnell felt about the institution. In all likelihood, he couldn't help but feel himself as banished to a far colony of the empire, some isolated Pacific island or dark remote armpit of Africa. Far from the gleaming capitals of civilization, he needed to shout louder than any of his brethren in order to be heard. As much marine drill sergeant as religious brother. Or given his bent for the classics, a chiseled Roman senator.

Perhaps this was because he knew *he* had been fed to the lions. Forced to teach orphans and malcontents, the abandoned and the unruly. Faced with such a population, he must have found it difficult to separate those who had suffered irreparable loss from those who would wreak irreparable loss, perhaps because they were often one and the same. At any rate, we were a volatile mixture: part orphanage, part reform school. And poor Brother McConnell's impossible job at this quasi-prison was to teach the classics to a bunch of young miscreants. Or, as he called them, cretins.

"Do you know, Mr. Slade, what a cretin is?"

"No."

"No, what?"

"No, sir."

"Then indeed you must be one."

Charlie Williams raised his hand. "Isn't a cretin a dummy?" Charlie was one of the orphans, not a true j.d.

"Yes, indeed. And I see by your answer, Mr. Williams, that you are not a cretin. But is this the only meaning of the word?"

To my surprise a strange impulse raised my hand.

"Somebody from Crete?"

"Ahh, Mr. Ohara. Are you making a joke?"

"No, sir."

"And how is it that you know about the island of Crete, which I can assume no one else in this class knows anything about."

"Well, isn't that where the monitor comes from?"

"Minotaur," he corrected. "But what is a Minotaur?"

"It's a guy with the head of a bull, and he lives in this maze, and he eats people who get trapped in the maze."

"But you have not answered my first question. Can I assume that you have actually done the reading for this class? A wild assumption, I must admit, since it seems no one else in the class has."

I didn't want to appear to be a suck-up. Well, not too much of a suck-up. After all, I'd already raised my hand. That was enough.

"I saw it in a movie once. A horror movie." Actually Tommy had told me all about the Minotaur. Greek and Roman mythology was where the names of the constellations came from. And perhaps because of him, I picked up some interest too, and I had actually read the assignment. After all, reading never was that hard for me.

"And whom—or what—pray tell, killed the Minotaur?"

For some reason I raised my hand again. "Thesis?"

"Theseus," he corrected. "But what was the difficulty in killing this beast with the body of a man and the head of a bull? Was it simply its ferocity?"

"He was in a thing called a labyrinth or something like that."

"A labyrinth. And what is that?"

I knew I'd already crossed the line. I was a suck-up. No two ways around it. I might as well go with it.

"Like a maze. And no one wanted to go into the maze 'cause they would get lost and never come out, even if they did kill the monster. But that Theseus guy figured out that if he took a ball of yarn and unwound it as he went into the maze, he'd be able to follow it back. Sort of like Hansel and Gretel, when they dropped breadcrumbs behind them. Only this was yarn, so I guess the birds couldn't eat it up. So Theseus got out."

"Excellent, Mr. Ohara. I see, though you seem loathe to admit it, that you have actually read the assignment. So what sort of punishment should I devise for these cretins who have not?"

I realized that I'd fallen in way over my head. Like he'd sprung a trap around me. Any punishment I devised would only cement my fate. I'd probably have to fight more than one fight. (I already knew Slade and I were probably going to get into it.)

"Well, I think it's really a neat story."

"Neat?"

"An excellent story. And it would be a shame for them not to read it. So maybe we should all read it in class. Like we did with the story of Jason and the Argonauts."

McConnell looked at me. Something like a smile slipped across his face and quickly vanished, as if never there at all.

"Class, I am loathe to give up on the idea of punishment. It clears the brain cells far faster than anything else. But since Mr. Ohara seems to have actually read the assignment, and since I have given him this fine opportunity to punish the rest of the class, and since he deems this the proper punishment, we shall take him up on it. Everyone open their books to page sixty-three . . ."

At the end of class, I hoped everyone had gotten into the stories of Daedalus and Icarus and Theseus and forgotten how I had sucked up.

But just in case they had forgotten, McConnell made sure to remind them.

"Boys, what are the lessons of these myths? Are they merely stories from ancient times? Or do they have a deeper meaning for us? I referred to Mr. Slade here as a wayward son. But the rest of you should not gloat. Many of you are wayward sons. Sons who have tempted God and the law. And so you have fallen and now find yourselves here. And if you do not change your wayward ways, in years to come you will find yourselves in a place far harsher and more desolate than St. Jude's. Indeed, the prisons toward which you may be headed contain horrors you cannot imagine. And yet you think your youth one glorious carefree ride, like Icarus did. But if you proceed like this, I can assure you you will fall. Plummet into a wine-dark sea, never to be seen or heard from again.

"Far better that you learn from the lesson of Theseus, who knew that bravery and strength are not all. That a man must have cunning. That if you enter the darkness, you best have a plan to leave. A thread to help you out of the maze. Right now many of you are lost in mazes of your own making, and yet you have no way out. That is why you have come here, why I am teaching you. To help you find that thread and devise a way out.

"The Lord provides for those who provide for themselves. Mr. Ohara has proven that today. I only hope the rest of you can follow his example."

I should have hated McConnell after that speech. I should have resolved never to speak up in class again. Being a suck-up would only get me pounded.

But for some reason I didn't quite feel this way. And that only confused me more.

I didn't relish the prospect of some face-off with Slade. Having hit puberty a bit earlier than the other kids, Slade carried a couple inches and pounds on me, though I was starting to flesh out too. He had the budding muscles and bulk of a middle line-backer, like Ray Nitschke or Dick Butkus, or some future gang-land thug. And from the way he carried himself as he barked in the hall that he was going to get me, I knew this wouldn't be the first of his fights.

Like a voice from the sidelines, some part of me kept say-ing I shouldn't be afraid, I should stand and fight. But I knew the difference between my boyhood worshipping of the 442nd or warriors like Issunboshi, and the real thing. My time in the state reformatory had undercut those illusions, and it wasn't just the fights there. Yes, I'd finally gotten the better of Michael Nagata, but only by wielding a knife and wildly swinging for the fences, as if possessed by some demon with nothing to lose. But there *was* something to lose, and I had lost it. I'd been taken from home and placed in juvie; after that, St. Jude's wasn't half bad. If I wanted to stay, I couldn't go after Slade with a knife or anything like that. Besides, I didn't want to get back at him the way I'd wanted to get back at Michael Nagata; indeed, it was Slade who wanted to get back at me. But how could I refuse him? That would be even worse. I'd seen what happened at the state reformatory to kids who backed down; that just invited not only the lions, but any lesser jackal. There'd be no end to it.

But what if I got in trouble? Slade was nothing compared to Father Boland, if I could believe all the stories. I'd heard Boland really had it in for kids who'd gotten caught fighting. If they were willing to pummel someone else, he proclaimed, they should be prepared to receive a proper and righteous punishment. The paddle he kept in his study was broad and heavy, like some dark, medieval instrument.

I puzzled on these choices for the rest of the day. In the hall between classes, some kids asked me when the fight was, as if it were already a done deal, the contracts signed and only the final arrangements to be made. At lunch hour, I could see Slade staring at me, inviting me to stare back. I just kept my head down and ate, as if I didn't see him. In our afternoon math class, I did my equations quickly as usual, but this only left me more time to brood. Brother Clarke thought that I wasn't doing my work and threatened me with detention until I offered to come up and show him my worksheet. As I passed Slade, he stuck his foot out and tripped me, and everyone laughed. I turned and looked at him; he just smiled. Part of me wanted to go after him right there, but I thought the better of it and continued on toward Brother Clarke's desk. Slade kept staring at me as I walked all the way back to my seat.

In the end, it was as unfudgeable as math equations, with space for just one answer: there was no way I could back down. And if Slade outweighed me literally and in terms of experience, well, there was nothing I could do about that. I was the new kid; sooner or later I had to take whatever this cretin threw at me, and it was probably better sooner. Probably.

As for Father Boland, I'd worry about him later.

The fight took place behind the gymnasium, just before supper. October, a gray evening with the sun going down early, making everything darker. A fitful wind stirred up the leaves in little whirls as Slade and I, followed by a ragtag group of onlookers, made our way to that unofficial site of most such altercations at St. Jude's. A shadow filled the corner between the buildings. In a way I felt comforted by that. I reasoned it better for me if it was harder to see; I probably had Slade on quickness. Or so I thought.

For a few moments, we circled each other, trying to spy an opening. Slade managed to catch me once on the face, more a slap than a punch. He laughed and told me that it was just a taste, that he was going to send me back to China with all the other chinks. I tried not to pay attention to either his lucky shot or his slurs. Then he hit me with another, a jab to my ear that truly stung, and I wondered if I'd underestimated him. He was quicker than I had thought.

I told myself that I was just lulling him, letting him think that he had a chance. Like most guys, Slade was looking for some knockout roundhouse punch and paid almost no attention to protecting his lower body. When he took a couple wild swings, spurred on by his two successful jabs, I knew I had him. I faked a punch toward his head and quickly stomped on his right shin. He howled and bent to address the pain. After that I didn't even have to go after his windpipe. The solar plexus was fair game. Two swift punches there and poor Slade crumpled to the floor. One rabbit punch to his neck in case he was even thinking of getting up. I walked away, hearing his groans behind me.

But then I heard someone shout behind me. Slade had gotten up. Oh Christ, I thought. As he righted himself, I could hear him sputtering out more insults, half swear words, half *chink* and *Jap* and *slant eyes*. I'd underestimated him. He was crazier than I'd thought.

The windpipe, I said to myself. You've got to shut this lunatic up.

It took me longer than I thought. At one point Slade came at me full bore, like a member of the kickoff team. As he hurtled toward me, some signal went off, and I grabbed him with one of the judo moves I'd learned almost by osmosis from Michael Nagata, back in our bouts in his living room, where he'd used me as his training dummy. Slade flipped on his back, taking the wind out of him. Before he could get up, I kicked him in the windpipe. That finally settled it.

But I couldn't stop. I kept kicking him, two or three more times, before this kid Brian, one of two black guys at the school, came up from behind me and pulled me away. I kept grappling to get back to Slade, but Brian gripped me tighter, muttering something about the boy ain't worth it. I stopped struggling then, and he let me go. I looked at Slade, who was still lying there, groaning and gurgling softly, like an infant on the bridge between crying out and falling back to sleep. I turned and started walking away, aware of the way the onlookers parted before me.

It was only later that I thought about what might have happened if I hadn't been stopped.

If I'd underestimated Slade, he'd also underestimated me. What Slade and the other kids didn't know was that at the juvie back in Chicago, I'd run into much tougher cases. This one kid, Bonnetti, had an old man rumored to be Mafia. Bonnetti showed me certain useful professional moves. One was a swift kick to your opponent's shin, the other a jab or kick to the solar plexus or better yet, the windpipe. Slade might have thought it was jujutsu that did him in, but mostly it was All-American Mafia knowhow.

At first I hoped that I might have gotten away with the fight and been spared a summons to Father Boland. Only a few kids had been there, and Slade was not the most popular guy. All through supper I waited to be called out and collared. With each moment I felt more relieved. I even managed to down the spaghetti, which unlike most of the swill at St. Jude's, wasn't half bad. Someone asked where I'd learned that move on Slade's shin. Was it jujitsu? Nah, nothing like that. I don't know any of that stuff, I said (blocking out those years I'd envied Michael Nagata's judo classes at the Buddhist temple or that final maneuver that tumbled Slade on his back). Instead, I told them about Bonnetti, elaborating his background. Bonnetti's father was a higher-up in the Cosa Nostra; an underling thug had taught Bonnetti that maneuver, useful in collecting from deadbeats who wanted to rat out of their gambling debts. I was elaborating here, but I'd reached that familiar point where I'd begun to believe my own j.d. blarney.

Just as I was explaining that this was how a loan shark collected his debts, I looked up and saw a familiar black cloak marching toward our table.

It didn't take me long to discover that what I had taken to be rumors, exaggerations about the big bad wolf, Father Boland, were not rumors. If anything, the rumors didn't do him justice.

When Father Boland finished with me, he was sweating, like a jungle explorer at the end of a long trek. Beads popping from his red briny brow, coughing hard, trying to catch his breath. There was a faraway look in his eyes, like he was coming out of a trance or a daydream. I could hear myself whimpering, like a beaten mutt. I can't remember the pain. I know I must have felt it, my skin burning and bruised, I must have still been terrified, but none of that comes back to me. All I see is Father Boland, his gray eyes riddled with pink. The veins on his nose and cheeks and forehead pulsating. His dingy yellow teeth. Wiry arms hanging down like ropes, their tension released.

"And Ohara?"

I was at the door already, slipping out as quickly as I could. I turned and saw the look cross his face, half smile, half sneer.

"You come back here again, I swear, by the grace of Our Lord's Mother Mary, you'll rue the day you were born." He paused. "And if you ever want to get out of here, you'll see that doesn't happen."

I closed the door and stood a moment in the hall, wondering when the pain would go away. A chilly breeze hit me when I left the rectory and stepped into the late fall air, the odor of burning leaves from the far end of the compound. Leaves scattered down from the giant oaks that guarded the grounds like giant sentinels.

I could see the gate farther up the road. I had a brief thought of running for it, but I knew where we were, in the middle of farm fields; there was nowhere to escape to. I'd never make it back to the city.

I rubbed my behind, the pain dulled a bit but still alive, like an animal that would not let go. I wondered if I would have to fight anyone else besides Slade, how soon I might make my way back to Father Boland's study. And in some dark corner of my brain I caught a glimmer of what lay in store for me, and not just with Father Boland. Michael Nagata, Slade. I was getting close to the edge, to taking myself out.

At that moment I flashed back on the image at the end of *The Incredible Shrinking Man*, the fury of the fight over, the thought of what was coming next looming, the moment teetering between triumph and terror.

What am I doing here? I thought. How in the hell am I going to get out?

CRY HAVOC

Sometimes at the end of class Brother McConnell would try to read us poetry. Poor man. It was a useless cause, given who we were. Even the famed go-for-glory of Henry the Fifth at the battle at Agincourt failed to rouse us. If the king himself had been strutting before our bored mugs, barking out his silver-tongued oratory, old Hank Five would have found himself storming the French alone. Cry havoc, and let slip the dogs of war indeed.

But at least Harry, the warrior king, was almost in our ballpark. Why on earth Brother McConnell would read us the poems of Yeats seemed a complete mystery to me. I chalked it up to his being Irish. McConnell did love spouting on about the Irish mythology, Cuchulain and Aengus and all those guys. He tried appealing to the Irish blood in some of the students. And of course he made a joke about my name, saying that this mythology should appeal to a member of the Ohara clan. I felt for the guy. He was really trying. But the best he got was a few giggles rather than outright guffaws. It was a sign of respect really, those giggles. Somehow we understood that Brother McConnell had a concern for us that went beyond most of the rest of the faculty, who saw themselves more as jailers and wardens than teachers and molders of boys.

One thing he talked about did pique my interest. Often he'd invoke the history of Ireland and how the British had put their foot upon the neck of the Irish people for centuries, taking their lands, suppressing their religion, banning their language and replacing it with their own. But the Irish, he said, never forgot their ancient heroes, their myths. They never gave up their religion. And if many, including him, no longer spoke the tongue of their forefathers? Well, that was indeed a shame. But it did not stop the Irish from rebelling, from trying to kick out the British.

"And who, pray tell, also kicked the British out of their country?"

Silence. I didn't want to suck up again, but I was tired of the silence. Didn't these cretins know the answer?

"The United States."

"Precisely, Mr. Ohara. It is a dreadful shame, gentlemen, that the rest of you did not recognize this resemblance. Our great country started through an act of rebellion. Throwing off the yoke of tyranny. And do you know what the British called these patriots? Traitors. Scoundrels. And that is what happened to the Irish and, indeed, is still happening to this day back in Ireland."

Brother McConnell went on and on like this. No one had the least idea what he was talking about. A man making a speech to his own head.

Then he paused for a moment, as if catching his breath, and as he did, he looked at me, as if there were some connection between us, some secret we shared. But the look quickly passed. Before he could continue, the bell rang.

I got up with the others to go on to the next class, but he called me back.

"Mr. Ohara, you are Japanese, are you not?"

"Japanese American."

"Yes." He seemed to think a bit. "I know why you are so angry."

What was he was talking about? My fight with Slade? Did he know what happened to suck-ups?

"What they did to your people. It was a dirty shame. We Irish know something about that. Unfair treatment."

"Thank you, sir." I didn't know what else to say. I still didn't get his point.

"Any time you want to talk about it, you let me know. All right?"

Talk about what? What was he getting at? But I nodded. "Yes, sir."

He waved his hand toward the door. "Now run off to your next class before you are late."

I turned and left. In the hall Slade muttered something as I passed. I knew it was an insult, but I didn't react. I was too unsettled by what Brother McConnell had said. How, somewhere inside, I did know what he was referring to, even if I couldn't say exactly what that was.

A few days later, in orotund tones, Brother McConnell recited to our class this poem by Yeats: "Easter, 1916." He explained that it was about those who took part in an attack on a post office in Dublin, part of the rebellion against the English rule over Ireland. Someone wondered why they attacked a post office. McConnell said they chose it because it was an institution of the British government, but the target wasn't important. Then what was? He said that it wasn't just that these people stood up against the British. Not that Yeats agreed with them exactly. He was a man who appreciated chivalry and the way of the old warriors. He thought the attackers on the post office were off the mark, too caught up in their own arguments and way of thinking.

"So why did he write a poem about these people?" Brother McConnell asked. "Does he praise them?"

"I think so," said Charlie Williams tentatively. He was often the first besides me to venture an answer.

"And why does he praise them?"

"Because they gave their lives for something?" Williams responded.

"Yes, but Yeats says here that the British may keep the faith. That is, they may eventually give the Irish their independence. So what does it matter that these people died? Did they die in vain?"

No one answered. I wasn't sure what McConnell was getting at, but I raised my hand anyway. "But he calls one of the men a drunken, vainglorious lout."

"Yes, excellent point, Mr. Ohara. And what, pray tell, is a lout?"

"Some sort of bum?"

"So why would he praise a bum? Did he believe in what they did? Does he endorse it? Come, come, Mr. Ohara, give us an answer."

I looked at him. He had this slight smirk on his face, and I wondered why he seemed to be picking on me.

"I really don't know, Brother McConnell. I guess, well, I guess he feels both ways."

"So the answer to my question is . . ."

"Yes. And no."

"Yes and no."

"That don't make no sense," someone from the back spouted out.

"Precisely," said Brother McConnell. "What Yeats is saying is that things aren't always clearly right or wrong, black or white. Sometimes a man can be both wrong and right, sometimes he can be both a vainglorious lout and some sort of hero. Life isn't so simple, gentlemen, as some might lead you to believe."

He looked around at the class, half pleased with himself, and half in resignation. Probably he sensed that most of this was going over our heads. Everyone stared at him in blank silence.

He looked out the window as if to tell by the sun what time it was. Then he turned to us. "Well, I suppose you've had enough poetry for today, haven't you? Go, gentlemen, I can see Mr. Murphy is already out on the field ready for your gym class."

As we all filed out, I couldn't help but feel McConnell might pull me aside again. But he didn't, and when I looked back, he was simply arranging the papers on his desk.

Late that night, in the dormitory dark, I kept thinking about what McConnell had said. It wasn't that I was entranced by Yeats's poetry. But it was better thinking about that than where my thoughts often wandered at the end of the day—back to our apartment and my mother and Tommy and my old neighborhood. And of course that only brought on thoughts about my father and an ache I couldn't contemplate without an unsettling nausea rising up within me. What did it mean that the Irish rebelled against the British just like the Americans had? And what did that have to do with me being Japanese American? Brother McConnell didn't even know about my father.

Afterwards, it wasn't as if I felt better or even relieved. Or that I even understood what connected the Easter Rebellion with my family, other than the fact that the world was a confusing place, and who might be a hero and who a coward or a vainglorious lout wasn't always clear. And yet something lay there unsaid on the tip of my tongue, murmuring along with Yeats: Sacrifices might come in many different forms. Too long a sacrifice makes a stone of the heart. All changed, changed utterly. A terrible beauty is born.

There were a couple black guys at St. Jude's. Gabe and Brian, both orphans. They were both good at sports and were small enough in number so no one made too big deal about them. A couple of the kids would call them nigger from time to time, and fights would ensue, but kids were always fighting there. It was a dog-eat-dog, beat-or-get-beaten, world.

When I first got there, I saw two white kids going at it, thrashing with the fury of Dobermans, and I thought, what the hell are they going to do with me? But if you couldn't fight your way to safety or respectability, you could manage a certain uneasy truce with the others. The real venom was toward the teachers and especially Father Boland, whom Jack O'Toole called the Irish Hitler. (How about the Irish Mussolini? said Bobby Smith. Nah, said O'Toole, Mussolini was a sissy. I just hoped no one came up with the Irish Tojo.) As for me, I was helped too by the presence of Gabe and Brian. With two black guys in our midst, I was somehow more like the rest of the white boys.

By chance we all three ended up on the same intramural football team. We played every afternoon after school was done. Brian was incredibly quick; Gabe was a tall, rangy tight end, while I had a strong arm. The three of us constituted a formidable team. We would run a quarterback option from the wishbone, and Brian and I worked it to perfection, me holding onto the ball as long as possible, drawing the defenders, and then tossing the ball out to Brian, who zipped toward the sidelines for huge chunks of yardage, if not a touchdown. Gabe was my other option—a quick flick to his sure hands, and he'd be off like the Bears' Galloping Willie Gallimore.

But our easy ways on the football field never seemed to translate to off the field. I went my way, and they went theirs. If fights did come up, I never stepped in to help them nor they with me. We were in two separate spheres, overlapping only on the football field.

One weekend afternoon I was walking around the grounds, still mulling over how I might get out of this place. As I neared the machine barn I picked up the faint murmur of voices and then

a bit of laughter. The barn was set off far from the other buildings; it held a truck, a tractor, and some mowing machines. I
peered around the door and thought I heard Gabe's voice saying shut up—someone's coming. I tired to appear nonchalant. If
it was Gabe and Brian, I didn't want them to think I was spy-
ing on them. There was no way I could have withstood a beating by those two.

I entered the dark, weathered structure. Coming in out of
the bright sunlight, my eyes were blinded for a second. A
flapping of pigeon wings in the rafters. The air musty and
smelling of gasoline and oil.

In the back, behind the tractor, I could make out two bodies.

"Hey," I said. They said nothing. Part of me said that I
should just back right out of there. "Gabe? Brian?" Nothing.
"Guys. I know it's you. It's just me, Ben."

I circled around the tractor and came into view.

"Oh shit," said Brian.

"Who invited you?" said Gabe.

I could see that Brian had clutched something to his chest.

"What you got there?"

"Nothing," said Gabe.

"Oh man, let's just show him, Gabe."

"It's none of his business."

"He's here—he ain't going nowhere now. You might as well
show him."

Gabe looked at me.

"Come on," I said, encouraged by Brian. "I'll make sure I'll
look for you next game."

"You better look for me, you yellow Mick. Or we'll never
score." The Yellow Mick was what Gabe had started to call me. "I
save your sorry ass every time," he continued. "All you throw out
there are those dying quails. Got no wings. Quack, quack, quack."

Suddenly Brian leaped up, unclenching the clump of paper at his chest. "Holy shit! Did you see that?"

"See what?" Gabe asked and we looked to where he was pointing.

In the corner of the barn was a rat. A large rat. A very large Mighty Mouse Godzilla of a rat. The size of a cat or a small dog. It reared on its hind legs, hissing at us. We just stood there staring at it, blocking its way. I saw a rusty rake lying against the wall next to me. I grabbed it and slowly brought it up over my head. Brian started to say something, and I shushed him. I edged forward.

The rat arched up, hissing, trying to decide whether to fight or run for it.

As I brought the rake down he seemed to hesitate a second and then leapt for it, guessing wrong, for the first and last time in his ratty life. The rake forked right into his back, two of the skewers spearing his hide. The rat gave out an unearthly screech. His body struggled at the end of the rake, like some huge walleye on the line, and I smashed down hard, trying not to let him up. Gabe grabbed a shovel and smashed its head.

Suddenly, from the corner, behind some buckets, came a zillion rats. They were everywhere, scurrying past us in a mad dash for freedom. I didn't want to let the big one up, and Gabe kept smashing it again and again. Motherfucker, he was yelling. Mo-ther-fuck-her. The rest of the rats scurried out the shed door behind us.

At last the king rat was silent. Gabe put down his shovel. I let go of the rake. A collective sigh issued from the three of us.

"I never seen a rat like that before," said Brian. "Even back in Cabrini Green."

"Man, Ohara, you sure speared that bastard. Like John Wayne with his ba-yo-net," said Gabe.

"Did you see that?" I asked. "All those other rats. Jesus, where did they come from?"

"Yeah," said Brian. "He came after us like some kamikaze rat. Trying to protect his gang."

We all sat down again on the gravelly floor of the shed. Pondering what we had just done. Part of me had the silly thought, this is what it must feel like after battle. This is what my uncle Elbert must have felt.

A few moments passed. Brian snorted, and started laughing, Gabe too, and then me, until we were all rocking back and forth with laughter.

Gradually we quieted down again.

"So what you got there?" I asked again, nodding to the magazine Brian had dropped when he pointed out the rat.

"Show him," Gabe said. Brian picked the magazine up, came over to us, and opened its pages as if he were opening the Bible, about to read from one of its holiest passages.

And that is how I encountered my first *Playboy* centerfold.

After we'd finished looking at the magazine, Gabe put it back on the shelf at the rear of the barn. Gabe took out a pack of Luckies and handed Brian one. He looked at me.

"Sure," I said, not really wanting it but knowing the offer was an honor, and I shouldn't refuse. When I took a first drag, I coughed and almost spit out the cigarette. Both laughed.

"This your first cigarette?" Brian asked.

"Yeah."

"So," said Gabe, "we popped your cherry twice today."

I didn't quite know what he meant by this, but I smiled stupidly.

After a few minutes, Gabe stubbed out his butt and looked toward the corner, toward the rat carcass. He said that we should take it out and burn it.

We took some straw from a corner of the shed, got one of the gas tanks, and went to a far edge of the grounds, where the walls came to a corner. I was carrying the rat on the end of the rake. Hairy and bloody and lifeless. It took two arms for me to hold up its dead weight. I heaved it onto the pile of sticks and straw and dry leaves that Gabe and Brian had gathered. Gabe doused it with gas as if performing rites of ablution. Gabe nodded to me. "You do the honors, bayonet man."

Gabe handed me his matches, and I snapped one against the carbon, once, twice. Nothing. The third time it popped and flared, and I dropped it onto the gas-soaked straw. A flame shot up, translucent and white, an audible gasp. In seconds the whole pyre was jumping and the flames blackened the rat's fur. The smell of its burning meat was oily yet oddly familiar. Smoke seared our eyes.

I suddenly felt sorry for the rat. I didn't quite know why. Part of me wished that we had simply let it go. He seemed like some great warrior, an Achilles, someone we could only beat because we were bigger and stronger, and not because we were more courageous or boasted larger hearts. I thought of that Viking movie where that great warrior—was it Kirk Douglas or Victor Mature?—is set on a boat of logs and they light the bier and then the funeral raft is launched out to sea, the body to be burnt and drowned, befitting a people whose notorious long boats traversed the globe. A king rat. A kamikaze rat. A warrior rat. Going down for his tribe. Feeling welled up inside me; I didn't know where it came from. I only knew I should tap it back down before my companions saw it.

The fire crackled before us. The smoke rose. The rat burned.

"Don't they eat rats in China?" asked Brian.

"I'm Japanese," I said. "Japanese American."

"Yeah, you cretin," said Gabe, slapping Brian. "Don't you know the difference?"

By the time the rat was engulfed in flames, Gabe and Brian grew bored and headed back to the dorm. But there was still the good *sansei* boy inside me. I thought one of us should make sure the fire didn't flare up and get out of control. And since I'd speared the rat, I felt some obligation to witness his funeral pyre down to the ashes. It seemed the least I could do.

I watched the fire for a long time, mesmerized. The flames seemed to take forever to expire; perhaps it was the gas. Eventually I decided to go back to the barn and look for a bucket and some water to put it out.

I was in the back of the barn when the workman found me. I tried to explain that I'd seen this fire out back and I was looking for something to put it out. But he seemed certain that I was back there for something else; nothing I said could dissuade him. He went to where I was standing and immediately noticed the magazine Gabe had put back in the shelf. Father Boland, the workman said, would know what to do with me. As he hauled me off, he muttered beneath his breath something about the foul sins of the flesh.

At one point he stopped and asked me how I had found the magazine, if anyone had told me about it. But I didn't fink on Gabe and Brian. No use in the three of us going down when one would do. After all, I needed to keep all the friends I could.

But none of them would do me any good with Father Boland.

When the workman dragged me into Father Boland's office, the secretary said that Father Boland was away at a conference. He should bring me to Brother McConnell.

"Do you know what this boy was doing?" the workman muttered. "I can't even say it. This is something Father Boland should hear about."

But the secretary, a young seminarian, said that it couldn't be helped.

"Father Boland isn't here," he repeated. "You'll have to see Brother McConnell. He's in charge of these things when Father Boland is gone."

A sigh of relief exhaled from my body, and I said a small prayer of thanks. I didn't know what McConnell would do to me, but it couldn't be worse than what Father Boland would have done.

We went down a dark hall toward Father Boland's office, way down at the far end. I was no longer a dead man walking, but what exactly lay in store for me I didn't know. The workman told me to wait. I thought of bolting, but really, there was nowhere to go, they'd catch me eventually. Besides, this was Brother McConnell. He knew that I was a good student, smart, at the top of my class. The workman shut the door behind him. Seconds later I could hear his voice getting more and more agitated as he told Brother McConnell what I had been doing. But it wasn't so much the description of my crime, which he passed through as quickly as possible, given its embarrassing nature, but more the need for punishment that he emphasized. I'd been caught in a place I wasn't supposed to be, sneaking into belongings that weren't mine, committing a foul and unholy act in complete disregard of God and all that St. Jude's stood for.

"But whom, pray tell, did this magazine belong to?" asked Brother McConnell.

"I don't know, Brother. That's not the point . . ."

"It must have been one of your workmen, Mr. Clarke."

"Yes, I suppose so. I have a suspicion who it might be. If I find out for sure, I'll fire him immediately."

"You'll have to talk to Father Boland about that."

"But the boy . . ."

"The boy would not have discovered the magazine if one of your workmen had not hid it in the machine shed."

"Yes, that's true, but the boy shouldn't have been in there in the first place."

"I agree with you. And he will be sufficiently punished for it."

"Father Boland would give him the paddle. You know that. Twenty whacks. At the very least."

"I'm not sure twenty whacks . . ."

"I'll leave the number up to you, Brother. But remember, spare the rod and spoil the child."

"Yes, I am perfectly aware of that homily."

The workman still didn't seem satisfied. He ranted a bit more. Then he left.

"Get in there," he said to me. "Brother McConnell's really going to give it to you." He tried to make this threat sound convincing, but he couldn't hide the disappointment in his voice.

I wasn't surprised that Brother McConnell didn't take up the workman's enthusiasm for corporal punishment. He was younger than some of the other brothers, who looked as if they'd been exiled to St. Jude's in the nineteenth century, ancient as Yeats's bald scholars. He lacked their jaded attitude toward the orphans and delinquents in their charge. He still believed there was something in us worth saving.

He was darker in complexion than some of the other brothers, especially the ones with red hair and freckled faces, with their cadaverous pallor. His hair was black, almost as black as mine, though a few strands of silver were starting to appear. In class he often swiped a strand that fell down his forehead, touching his wire-rim glasses.

If you listened you could hear a faint trace of Ireland in his voice; he had told us that he had come over as a young boy, just before the beginning of World War II. This is a great country, he told us. Where even an Irishman can become the President of the United States. We were a shining city on a hill for the rest of the world to see and learn from. And we students had to be worthy of that charge, had to appreciate the sacrifice of those who came before us. We were future citizens of that city on a hill.

He looked up as I came in. "Sit down, Mr. Ohara," he said, motioning to a chair next to his desk. He moved his chair closer to me.

"I'm very disappointed in you, Ben." His voice held just a hint of anger. "You're one of my best students. Why, pray tell, would you do a thing like this?"

"I dunno."

"Have you done this before?"

I shrugged. "Not really."

"What do you mean not really?"

"No. Sir. It was the first time."

"There were no others with you?"

"No. The janitor found me alone."

"You mean the groundskeeper, Mr. Clarke."

"Yeah, him."

"But other times, Ben. Did you do this with any others? Look at those magazines?"

I tried to look him in the eyes. "No sir."

"If you're lying to me, Ben, that just makes it worse."

"It was just me, Brother McConnell." I knew I had to make it sound convincing. "Why would I do, well, why would I do what I did with anyone else?"

He scrutinized me, trying to decide. "Well no, I suppose that makes sense." He paused as if thinking about what to say next. I wondered if he was going to get angry at me; I feared my punishment. The waiting made it seem worse. Just whack me, I thought. I can take it. You can't do anything worse to me than Father Boland could, that's for sure.

"How many blows, pray tell, do you think you deserve for a sin like this?"

"I don't know, Brother." What if I guessed higher than he had in mind? That might add to my punishment. I glanced at Father Boland's paddle leaning in the far corner, like an executioner about to be called forth.

But Brother McConnnell did not tell me to get Father Boland's paddle. Instead he started in about how hard it must be for me here. In a new place, far from home. How lonely I must feel. "I was sent away to school myself," he said. "Back in Dublin. I know how it is to be a schoolboy far from home. From his parents, family, and friends."

He said that it was hard to live a righteous life under any circumstances, much less the one I was in. All these other delinquent boys. Any one of them might lead me astray. And I was doing so well. Why even last week he was telling Father Boland about how bright I was, about my latest essay in class. He said

that there was a *nisei* he knew back in the army, before he went
to seminary. That's how he knew about my people. How fer-
vently American we were, how badly we'd been mistreated.
How hard we worked. His friend Lou Nakajima was even a
Catholic, like me. I reminded him a bit of Lou, who played on
the base softball team, a good athlete but also very smart.

"This is no place for a boy like you, Ben. You're not like
these other boys. Yet the temptations of the flesh are difficult,
even for a boy like you. To look at such pictures, such filth. Oh,
I know you're lonely. That's part of what it is to be special. So
intelligent, so bright." He moved his chair a bit closer then,
looking me in the eyes. I looked away, down at my lap. I could
smell something on his breath, sweetly sour, like the way Luis's
father or Jackie Watkins's father used to smell. "But I can help
you, son. Do you believe that, that I'm here to help you?"

I nodded.

"You trust me?"

He put his hand on my knee.

"Yes."

"You believe in the redeeming power of Christ, do you not?"

What was he asking? His hand started to knead my thigh, just
gently. I wondered if he was going to squeeze it harder or pinch
me, in punishment, the way my mom used to squeeze my cheeks.

"Ben?" He moved his hand a little higher, gently stroking
the bottom of my thigh. I felt a vague sense of unease. "You
know I want what's best for you? That what happens between
us can be kept secret? That if we swear an oath to Christ we are
both bound to keep it?"

I tried to nod, though I didn't understand what I was assent-
ing to.

"You believe in Christ?"

Did I believe in Christ? Was that why he was testing me? I

knew what I should answer. Yes, yes, Brother, I believe. But when I looked deep inside I couldn't find it, it wasn't there. True, my mom was a Christian, but I never really paid much attention when she took me to church, and that was only for a couple years; it all seemed sort of fake to me. I could never really see why we were supposed to be worshipping this white guy when we weren't white. It didn't make sense. But Brother McConnell was trying to help me; he wasn't Father Boland— he didn't want to thrash me till I cried out like an infidel. And I didn't want to disappoint him, I truly didn't.

His blue eyes gazed intently at me, lemur-like in their sincerity, waiting for an answer. I turned away, as if somehow ashamed, trying to think my way past his question.

Perhaps there was some other way of answering that might deflect him, other than a simple no.

"Well, my father was a Buddhist, sir."

"What?"

I knew I'd answered the question wrong. He took his hand off my knee. I was sure he was going to slap or hit me for this blasphemy.

"You . . . you're not a Christian?"

"My mom's sort of Christian, I guess. She goes to Christ Congregational sometimes. But my dad was a Buddhist. I don't know what that makes me." I hoped my answer was ambiguous enough, though I sensed it wasn't.

"I thought you were Catholic."

"Because of my name? That's a Japanese name too." I felt a slight sense of relief. Perhaps this was some other sort of mix-up, perhaps it didn't have to do with my belief—or rather, disbelief—in Christ.

"No, no," said Brother McConnell, "because most of the boys they send here are Catholic. I just assumed . . ."

"Maybe they assumed because of my name too."

"But how . . ." He paused. "So you've never been confirmed? Or taken confession?"

"No, no," I answered. In fact I really didn't even know what those things meant.

Brother McConnell looked at me, his forehead furrowed.

"Well, we need to talk about this."

Oh crap, I thought. I've blown it. I should have simply said I was a Christian. A Catholic. Even an Irish Catholic. But now I was going to be passed off onto Father Boland, just when it looked like I was going to get off easy.

"Do you understand, Ben, the concept of original sin?"

I shook my head, as if signaling for him to continue. I couldn't tell if he wanted to convert me or not. I figured I should just sit there and nod my head when appropriate. It had to be better than whatever I would have received from Father Boland.

Yet deep in my heart I knew that I would never be converted. I just didn't have it in me.

Despite his efforts Brother McConnell finally gave up on me. I can't say he then paddled me with the gusto of Father Boland. I don't think Brother McConnell relished such punishment; he wasn't strapped with the same stern stuff as his superior. Still, he clearly seemed angry at me, almost insulted, as if I had personally affronted him. Or perhaps his God.

After that it soon became clear to me that I was no longer Brother McConnell's favorite. That spot now went to Charlie Williams, the second in the class. In a way that made me feel more comfortable, not being the nail that sticks out.

And it wasn't exactly that McConnell turned on me. He continued to note my academic excellence, and he never singled me out for punishment. It was more like I'd become a neutral site in his eyes. Or even someone he felt a bit uncomfortable with. He talked to me occasionally about what I needed to get out of there and back home. I couldn't tell exactly why this became his focus, but I suspect that he did put in a good word about me from time to time to Father Boland. Because a few months later, I was informed that I would not be staying at St. Jude's. I'd done my time. I suppose, too, my father's recent death also had something to do with their willingness to set me free.

THE PROMISED LAND

By the time I got back from St. Jude's, things had clearly changed. My mom had been promoted at the post office and she'd moved us to a new apartment a little further north, in Rogers Park, just a couple blocks from the lake and the beach. The neighborhood felt cleaner and more settled, a couple notches above the gritty toughness of Uptown. Tommy and I were going to a new school.

I didn't particularly like this new neighborhood. But I couldn't see going back to the old one, after what I'd done to Michael Nagata. I didn't fancy facing my old gang. Freed from juvie, like an ex-con vowing reform, I wanted to get away from my past.

But I wasn't ready for the fact that my mother was also moving on, that she too wanted a new life, and not just a better job or apartment. After all, what son, Hamlet or otherwise, is prepared for his mom to date?

During this brief period, a number of suitors came calling, almost all of them white. The one exception, a cousin of Uncle Hank's, was short and squat and worked as a mechanic and always smelled like his garage. Even I could see why he wouldn't have worked with my mom. But I couldn't see her with any of the white guys either, including Marv, who appeared a few months after I got back. They all felt strangely foreign, either tall and gangly or a little too fleshy and large and pale. They tended to approach Tommy and me as if we were wild animals,

speaking to us slowly as if they didn't want to scare us or perhaps as if English weren't our native tongue. Most of them
spoke to my mom a little like this, or else they tried to pour on
the charm, acting like gallants out of some high society or an
English movie. Only Marv seemed to talk to her as if she were
a normal person. He worked for Allstate and drove a gold Buick
LeSabre, and I had to admit that that impressed me.

Tommy wasn't impressed. He always disappeared when
Marv came around and had to be coaxed to come and say hello.
Sometimes Mom elicited my help.

"Just go out and say hi. Then you can come back," I told
Tommy.

"No."

"Why?"

"I don't want to. That's all."

"Tommy, it's the polite thing to do."

"Who are you to care about politeness all of a sudden, Mr.
Juvenile Delinquent?"

"Hey, I did my time. Paid my debt to society"—thinking I
could joke him out of his foul mood—"Besides, you don't want
to end up like me, do you? Didn't I tell you all about mad Father
Boland and his paddle?"

"I'm not going out there. And that's that."

When I went back to the living room, I told my mom and
Marv that Tommy wasn't feeling well. Marv was polite enough
not to mention that Tommy never seemed to feel well when
Marv came calling.

"Well, just make sure you both get to bed early."

"Ma."

"O.K., make sure Tommy gets to bed."

I nodded and watched them go out the front door. As Marv
opened the door, I noticed him put his hand on Mom's back as

if guiding her through, and I knew that there was nothing either Tommy or I could do.

I tried to tell Tommy this, but he wouldn't listen. He was stubborn in that way. I said he was acting like a baby, but that only made him madder.

After that I pretty much gave up talking to him about our mom and Marv. If he wanted to go the ostrich route against the inevitable, that was his choice. I didn't really want to get into it with him. This was more than just our mom's dating. After I got back from doing time at St. Jude's, the relationship between us changed. He seemed moodier and more volatile, more prone to take things the wrong way. I felt suddenly much older than him, and the things that interested him, his sci-fi and crazy scientific theories, struck me as childish, unrelated to a more grown-up world I was now entering.

Besides, I had my own things I didn't want to talk about. It was better for the two of us to brood separately, alone in our own worlds, neither of us knowing how the years would stretch the space between us in ways that would become unbreachable.

And so, as they say, time passed, with the speed of light constant and yet our own individual versions ticking off at separate irreconcilable rates.

It was November, a cold fall rain, the droplets smacking the windowpane of the kitchen. Quite late, probably past twelve. I was studying in the kitchen. I sometimes did this after everyone went to bed, ambling down from my room for a snack. I'd plop down beneath the cone of light above the kitchen table, lay my books out. A sandwich, a cup of coffee to keep me going. I was seventeen. The house asleep so that I had the room all to my own, the only time of day I could wander the rest of the house freely. I would come home after school and football practice, eat dinner with Mom and Marv, and then go to my bedroom to sleep a couple hours, dead tired, the food making me more so. Then I'd wake and study till past midnight. No need to worry about me anymore—I'd buckled down as my mother had implored. Football kept me busy after school (I was starting nose guard), my studies the rest of the time. We lived among Jewish kids now, with a smattering of middle-class Irish Catholics, in Skokie, across town from my cousins Mark and Brian. Modest bi-levels and ranches, assembly-line suburbs from the postwar boom. The dark and begrimed walk-ups of Uptown were light years behind us. No hillbillies or Puerto Ricans here.

But maybe this night I wasn't studying. Maybe this was the time I came back after riding around with Cohen and Gillespie and Kermit, four nerds with no dates, even though Gillispie and Kermit were on the football team with me. They were always fighting, like a married couple. One of them would do something stupid with the car, like speed through a stoplight or careen around a corner or go down to Dempster and loop the cloverleaf onto Edens over and over. The other would say, "A car is not a toy." And the one driving would slow down and say, "You wanna get out? You wanna get out?" Cohen and I would sigh and burst into laughter.

One night after these ridiculous antics I came home and was walking around the garage to the back door when I spied two dark hulks on the grass. It was a pair of bodies. A guy and girl. They were making out. They looked up. I didn't want to startle them—I just walked quickly past, muttering, "Have fun." I felt like a dork. I wondered if I'd ever be with a girl like that, lying in the grass, making out. It seemed a distant possibility, as remote as Tommy's fabled travels to some other planet.

But no, it wasn't one of the nights with the guys. I must have been studying, because that's why my mom came down and told me I should go to bed, I had school the next day. She sometimes did this even though she knew I always studied late, that was why I slept after dinner.

"You're such a night owl," she said, sliding into a kitchen chair, rearranging her flannel nightgown. Fuzzy slippers, curlers in her hair, in a state of dishabille she'd never let a soul outside the family witness—and then only late at night, like this.

The last of her beauty was still there, though—its faint but still captivating glimmers, whatever drew in my father and later Marv Richards and a few other white guys she dated. Diminutive in stature but possessing the sharp aristocratic cheekbones and elongated nose of some Utamaro pinup (if I may be permitted such a reference, given its geisha connotations), she resembled the old Japanese movie star, Shirley Yamaguchi, the one who took on an American name. Yes, I could see what men spied in her, as much as any son can of his mother. Not that I thought of such matters much back then. She was just my mom, I didn't want to consider her existence as a sexual creature. Of course I know now her being Japanese helped: she looked younger, exotic, all that Orientalist fantasy fandango—that was probably there for old Marv. He was a G.I., he'd been stationed in Japan. He'd acquired those tastes, part of the bounty of being the conqueror, the occupying army.

But no, that's a little too harsh. He was a decent guy, my stepdad. He tried, god knows he tried. It wasn't like he'd married into the Brady Bunch or anything. He was beyond his depths with us, and to his credit, I think he appreciated how much she protected him, kept him in a zone of comfort (like sending her more recalcitrant son, Tommy, the one who'd had trouble adjusting to her new marital status, away to school).

She looked at me across the oval formica table. I was in the booth semicircle, my books spread out before me: calculus,

American history, *Portrait of the Artist as a Young Man.* She picked up *Portrait.*

"I read something of his, a long time ago. Back when I was in college."

"Yeah, I think you still have that book. It's in the bookcase downstairs." I took a sip of coffee. "I can't believe you read anything of his. I can't understand a word."

"Isn't this one supposed to be harder?"

"Yeah, and our teacher says there's even a harder one, and a harder one after that. It makes calculus seem easy." Of course I didn't tell my mom that the only part I enjoyed of *Portrait* was when Stephen Dedalus goes to the whorehouse. I read that passage over and over, thinking of what it would be like to have a woman undress before you, to say those things.

"Sometimes I wish I could have stayed longer in school. Did you know I was on the basketball team?"

Boy, that seemed strange to me. My diminutive *nisei* mother on the basketball team. But I suppose it was no different than me at five-nine going around with guys like Kermit and Gillespie, both of them about six-four. I looked like a midget next to them.

She looked around at the books. "You really have come a long way, haven't you." She sighed. "I guess we all have."

I didn't know exactly what she meant by this, though I could guess. There were so many things she could have been referring too. Probably my stealing from the Gyp Joint or even my knifing Michael Nagata, at the very least.

"I'm proud of you, Ben. I really am."

Where is this coming from? I thought. I suddenly wanted her to go back to bed. To be alone again. She didn't say anything for a few seconds. I hoped she was gathering herself up to leave. No chance. She sighed and tried to compose herself.

"Marv tells me he saw you out on the lawn the other night with a girl."

"Ma . . ."

She raised her hand as if to stop me. "Now, I'm not saying . . ."

"It wasn't me. Jesus, I wish it was, but it wasn't. All I did that night was go around cruising with Kermit and Gillespie. And then when I came home, I just stumbled on this guy and girl on the lawn."

She thought about this for a second. I felt embarrassed. Partly it was the accusation and the subject matter it brought up. But probably even more it was that the accusation was false and that my lack of anything resembling such a coupling should come up with my mother. But then it only got worse.

"Well, I don't know," she continued. "In a way it doesn't matter. He said he'd talk to you, but I told him he didn't have to. It was my job."

She folded her hands together, then looked up at me. "So if you have any questions you'd like to ask me . . ."

Christ, of course I had no questions. This was my mom. Not that I'd have wanted to talk to Marv either.

"We went over all that in health class, Mom."

"I know. I'm sure you did. But there are other things . . ."

"No, Mom. Really. We covered it all."

She stopped. Thank god, maybe it was over. She slumped back, as if defeated. A different line of thought seemed to take over her.

"Do you remember that man I dated before Marv? Philip? He was an odd duck."

Then why did she date him? I asked, glad the subject had seemed to have shifted.

"He kept taking me to Chinese restaurants. I mean I like *China-meishi*, but not for every meal. Then I realized he didn't seem to make a difference between Chinese and Japanese. For him it was all the same. That's when I stopped seeing him. How can you make a mistake like that? I couldn't be with anyone so stupid."

Why was she telling me this? I wanted to change the subject only I was afraid that she'd focus back on me.

"Do you know what I worried about when I first started dating? Oh, aside from whether men would find me pretty or not. It was that I was *nihonjin*. And I didn't want to be with another *nihonjin* man. I couldn't. So I wondered what a *hakujin* man would think of me."

I remembered that time. She was always buying dresses then, more expensive than she could afford and then worrying constantly about the expense. She seemed so frantic, so unnerved. She'd put on dresses before her dates and then change them, talking to herself the whole time. It seemed so unlike her.

"But Marv's a good man. He's a good man, don't you think?"

"Yeah, sure, Ma." I tried not to make that sound sarcastic but didn't know if I succeeded. I really meant it in a way, if only because I was glad she'd gotten off the topic of her dating white guys.

"It was so nice of him to pay to send Tommy away to school."

Yeah, the little genius. Sometimes I wished I could have gotten away like him. Only I wasn't smart enough. I was smart, but not one of those geniuses, not one of those guys who light up a 1600 on their SATs using half of his brain, left-handed. Not one of those guys like Barry Levine, whose brain was so large and whose looks so strange, almost like a Down's kid, as if the low and high end of the IQ scale merged at some strange vanishing point beyond the rest of us. But Tommy didn't look like that. He looked normal. That was the strange thing. In fact, he was clearly better looking than me, the rat, and taller. And he was smart enough to get a scholarship, so Marv didn't have to pay all his tuition, which made it affordable. And whether the fact that Tommy seemed less willing than me to accept Marv's presence in our midst had much to do with their sending him away, I still don't know for certain, though I have my suspicions.

Thinking of my mother and me in that suburban kitchen, I see now that she viewed me as her last link to the past, some-one she could confide in in a way she couldn't with her sisters. Her sisters who hadn't gone outside the race. Who hadn't had a crazy husband. Who weren't disgraced by a kid who went to reform school. Who weren't unnerved and even afraid of a strange, younger, brilliant son who only seemed to get stranger as the years went on (and who had already been caught at Oakbrook taking drugs and who the following year would be caught with another boy in some sort of compromising position that was never quite explained).

And something inside me did pity her, did realize, whatever isolation my nerdiness and J.A. status gave me, I would never be as alone as she was, as out to sea. I would never bear the burdens she had. All I could do was make sure that I wasn't one burden more. It was the least I could do, after all the shit I'd given her.

Not that I would have told her all this then. I simply looked up from my calculus and said, "I've really got to study, Ma. I've got a big test tomorrow."

I knew that would shut her up, make her go back to bed. I didn't think then that maybe she didn't want to go back to bed. That the thoughts that circled her head as she lay there in the dark next to Marv were what kept her up, what made her want to go downstairs and find someone to talk to, anyone to talk to, even if it was her taciturn and truculent adolescent son. That the November rain snapping at her window only let her know how difficult it was to really fall asleep.

FALLING BODIES

A couple days ago, in the UCLA library, just before I decided to make my divagation to Sin City, I was skimming through my notebooks for *Famous Suicides of the Japanese Empire*. All the years I've struggled with this book, the wasted efforts, the false starts, the structure that never seemed to arrive, much less any hope of finding the end—I kept looking for a spark, something that might propel me back into the project. Nothing. *Nada. Nani mo . . . nai.*

Then I came upon another of my wayward entries. And somehow its modest farce spoke to me, energized me more than any of my intricate explanations of the group psyche in Japanese life or *bushido* and the way of the warrior. Manic scribblings drawing me in different direction. From notebook No. 12:

In August, in Nishinomiya, Hyogo, Japan, Toshio Fujimoto leapt out of a building and landed on a pedestrian below. Not quite a double suicide like Romeo and Juliet. Or even a suicide-homicide, one of the many examples of lovers or husbands gone berserk. No, this was that rare beast, the suicide-manslaughter.

The thing is, if Mr. Fujimoto had not died in his fall, he would have then had to commit seppuku *to atone for offending his pedestrian victim. (If only the pedestrian had heeded the sign: watch out for falling bodies.) Unfortunately, not steering any vehicle, Fujimoto-san could not be ticketed or fined for reckless driving. Look! Up in the sky! Is it a bird? A plane? No, it's . . . splat!!! No*

*Superman, poor Fujimoto-san couldn't take the heights. Weighted
down by his troubles. Couldn't stick around for the elevator, much less
take the stairs.*

*And yet isn't Fujimoto the concrete embodiment of a well-known
principle—one suicide often begets another? Certainly a suicide
plummets through families, from generation to generation. Though
the second death may not follow immediately after, surely the weight
of the first falls up those who come later. Every time you look up, there
it is, descending like a bad angel. A shadow dropping down, looming
larger and larger.*

*Perhaps the trick is to avoid memory. Avoid memory and you
avoid those ghostly bodies. That, I think, was my mother's way.
Maybe that was why she was so much stronger than the rest of us,
why she survived, and in the end, flourished.*

*For isn't that what it means to be a true-blue American?
Elsewhere in the world, people vividly recall battles and massacres,
pillagings and rapes five centuries past as if they were yesterday. The
air thickens with ghosts, with falling bodies, popping into consciousness at every moment, calling people back to the deaths of the past,
suicide or otherwise. Asking the quick for their proper revenge.*

*But here in America, nothing is recalled. Our atmosphere may be
increasingly polluted, but it's ghost-free. We head out for new territories, we begin all over, without a past. If we are wise and cunning
enough, we escape into the future, that far-more-promising and free-
falling dimension.*

About the time Tommy was finishing up his graduate work at
Berkeley, I went to visit him. I was thinking about leaving the
Midwest then, moving to a place where there might be more of
my yellow brethren, where I wouldn't feel so lonely and alien,
so detached and uncounted. Grace said that if that was what I
wanted . . . But I could tell that she wasn't really buying it. She

liked her job and the four seasons of our windy city, where being Irish Catholic was almost as easy as in Boston. Still, ever reasonable, she was willing to entertain the idea, so I was out looking to see what my prospects might be in the Bay Area. (It turns out they weren't much. I was a high-school history teacher then, hardly a hot commodity.)

Tommy was living in a room above a garage in a more fashionable section of town up in the hills. The house sported a pool and gleamed like something out of a Hockney print. The recently divorced owner had decided to rent the guesthouse for the added cash and to have someone around when she wasn't there (she traveled a lot during the summer). Gail wore long flowing robes and grew her dazzling blond hair past her shoulders. She'd never quite left the flower child's sense of fashion, even though Reagan, the oil embargoes, coke, and punk rock had hit everyone else with a vengeance. Her husband had been some rich tax attorney. Alimony set her free to pursue such typical Bay clichés as yoga and Buddhism and poetry. It was only later that I learned about her and Tommy. But back then I didn't even think about that because she was ten years older than him. (You could fill a book with the things I don't know. Blame it all on my Midwestern J.A. upbringing.)

All I knew was that she was cool about Tommy smoking weed or doing whatever he felt like doing up in his garage apartment. Tommy was doing coke then too, but he knew I wasn't too cool about that, so we just toked up together. Toked and talked. And one night he told me some things about our childhood that on some unconscious level I knew but never wanted to know. In that way, as hard as it is to admit, I guess I was like my mother.

Earlier that night we'd taken the BART over to the East Bay. He asked me if I wanted to go to the Mitchell Brother's nightclub. I demurred. A peep show wasn't my idea of brotherly bonding. We hit a nightclub near Chinatown instead. He said he liked to go there and just soak in the atmosphere, hardly a *hakujin* in the place. We slid into that club like a pair of homeboys. Or so we thought. Who really knew what the locals saw. They might have spent the whole evening guffawing in Cantonese over the two geeky J.A.s in the corner. Well, one geeky J.A., Tommy, lean and lanky, three inches taller than me, looked the part. Black pants, black leather jacket, shades. Like he was trying out for a role in *Year of the Dragon*. Who would have guessed that he'd gotten through Cal Tech in three years (not quite super-genius speed but fast enough).

I kept waiting for one of the Chinatown punks to come up and challenge our showing on their turf, but nothing like that came up. We didn't really do much, just drank at the bar and looked around. Tommy asked this one girl to dance, long and willowy in a glittering slinky dress. Someone I would have been afraid to approach. I watched as he chatted and danced with her. "Got her number," he said as we left. "Told her I was a tax lawyer with a house in the East Bay. She didn't believe me, so I showed her this picture of me in front of Gail's house. I could tell she bought it then. That's when I asked her for her number. I said I'd show her the other side of the Bay." He said this in a way that meant she was just part of the hunt, perhaps a little game he was playing to show off. I didn't like the way he said this. It didn't make me like the man he'd become.

Maybe he saw it in my face.

"Hey, man, I'm not all shackled up like you. I'm yellow, free, and twenty-one."

"Thanks, Tommy. I'll tell Grace that."

"That's the point. There's nothing to tell her. Jesus, Ben, you were like a nun in there. Why not have a little fun? Go off the reservation. Or maybe you only like white girls . . ."

I swung my arm at him playfully, and he backed away, so I only grazed the leather. We both laughed.

We were hungry, so we walked up to North Beach. Tommy said he knew an all-night pizza joint there. We passed the Condor, famous for the double-ds of Carol Doda, with a blond in a miniskirt outside cooing at us to come on in. I looked at her and then back up the street toward the next strip joint. Three white guys were approaching, gesturing and barking with an amped-up volume that shouted to me, move over a bit, let 'em pass.

But Tommy just kept on ahead like he didn't see them at all. Bumped right into one.

"Hey, asshole," the guy jabbed. "Watch where you're going." Tommy just kept walking. I kept up with him. I could sense the guy turning back toward us, saw his arm reach out to Tommy's shoulder. "I said, 'Hey, asshole' . . ."

Tommy wheeled. "Yeah," he said in a voice so calm it startled both the guy and me. "You want something?"

"I said, you better watch where you're going."

"Is that so?"

"Yeah, asshole," and he slapped the flat of his hand against Tommy's shoulder as if getting him back. But just as his palm hit Tommy's jacket, Tommy's left hand flashed up, grabbed the guy's wrist and his right suddenly appeared at the guy's throat. It took me a second to register the switchblade's edge pressed against the guy's carotid artery.

"You want to say anything else, asshole?"

The guy shook his head.

"I thought so. I thought so."

The guy's eyes registered the rest of his answer. He slunk off like a gelded greyhound, all sleek and polished but no fight inside him. We watched him go back to his buddies, who both looked like they wanted to say something but thought the better of it. I turned to Tommy.

"What the hell do you think you were doing?"

"Oh Jesus, Ben. You did the same thing with Michael Nagata. I didn't even cut the guy like you did."

"That was years ago. I was a kid then."

"Well, maybe I just haven't grown up." He gazed at me, this cold, hard look I'd never seen before. "Fuck you, man. Who are you to judge me?"

He had me there, but I wasn't going to let him know it. "What if he'd had a gun?"

"A white boy like that? Give me a fucking break. I wasn't born yesterday, even if I am your younger brother."

"This doesn't have anything to do with you being my younger brother."

"Oh, doesn't it? You always think you're so fucking high and mighty—you do something like cut up some guy, it's cool, it's part of the family lore, it's part of the good old days . . ."

"Those were hardly the good old days."

"Oh, bullshit. I've heard you tell that Michael Nagata story a hundred times."

"Not recently."

"Yeah, now you're the responsible married man. The high-school teacher. *To Sir, With Love.* Fuck that. These white motherfuckers think they still own the city. I'm just ridding them of their delusions. You saw that club tonight. That's what's happening. We Asians are taking back this fucking city. You think that was just me being crazy? Well, hell, maybe I am crazy. Maybe I just need to be a little crazy. Maybe we all need to be a little crazy. You ever think that? Jesus, Ben, what happened to you? You used to be a tough cat. You used to have a rep."

"I was never tough, Tommy. Just scared."

"Whatever. You live your life, I live mine. You wanna be the good *sansei* son, fine. Be that. Don't cross against the light. Don't cheat on your taxes. Don't bump into white guys on the street. Just kowtow and everything will be fine. But that's a fuckin' delusion man. That's just what the *nisei* did, and where did it get them? In a concentration camp. No way, no way, I ain't going. You wanna be a Boy Scout? Fine, maybe that sells back in Chi-Town. But this is Chinatown, here. J-Town. This is our fuckin' city. This is where *ojii-chan* first landed probably way before that motherfucker's ancestors ever got here. So it's *my* fuckin' sidewalk. Mine. And no honky asshole like that is going to take it away."

I looked at him almost as if I were seeing him for the first time. Which perhaps I was.

By the time we finished our pizza, it was late. We'd have to wait a half hour for the next BART. Tommy said we should just take a taxi. I protested the cost.

"Hey, Gail and I hit it big last weekend in Reno."

"Gail and you?" I caught on to his grin. "You sleeping with her?" For some reason this bothered me, only I knew I couldn't say so.

"It's cool, man. Nothing serious. She just got out of her marriage. She's not looking for anything steady."

"And what about you?"

"Neither am I. It's loose, no ties. We're just two peas in a pod."

"And what if one of you wants more than just a pod?"

He looked at me. "Christ, Ben, are you that bourgeois?" he muttered, like I'd just joined the Young Republicans. He slid into the cab then, and I let it go.

The cab driver was a Chinese American in his thirties, starting to bald, though his thinning hair was still hippy length. A little soul patch beneath his lip. Faded army jacket. Puka shells hanging from the rearview. He asked if we were Chinese.

"But you're ABCs?"

"ABJs," said Tommy.

"*Sansei*, right?"

"Yeah," said Tommy.

He asked what we did. "Isn't that something," he said. "A history teacher and an astrophysicist. Of all the people I could have picked up. You wanna hear a story? You're a history teacher, you'll like this. It's the history they never teach, those things the government never lets out. And you, Mr. Scientist, this is right up your alley."

"Go for it, brother," said Tommy, laughing at the cabbie's manic enthusiasm.

The cabbie announced that he'd been in the army, in a special experimental unit, working on high-tech spy equipment. "Now maybe you're thinking James Bond shit," he said. "Miniature cameras, tracking devices, and the like. But that's not what we were examining. It was more chemical stuff. Mind-altering drugs."

"Like truth serums?" I ventured.

"That was part of it," he said. "But also chemicals that could induce certain moods or mental states. Fear. Sadness. Happiness or euphoria. One problem was that the brain was not designed to stick entirely within one emotional state. It's designed to register variety, a panoply of shades and combinations. Some states are easier to maintain than others. If blue were depression, that's a color you can maintain for long periods. A less chaotic, less organized, less energized state. More static. Whereas happiness or joy isn't really just one color, it's more like white light, a combination of colors in a way but also the absence of others. Fear, that's almost a third category. Like flashing from red to yellow back and forth again and again . . ."

I passed the cabbie off as some former hippy who'd done one-too-many trips.

Tommy felt differently. "O.K., I get all that," he said. "Use them on your enemies on the battlefield, get them in full retreat. But there's more to it than that, isn't there? Like what about the government using these drugs on its own citizens?"

"You're one step ahead of me, my friend." The cabbie said contentment might seem at first what you wanted to induce in the populace. But perhaps not. Perhaps you wanted some parts of the population to feel paranoid, to live inside a state of permanent fear. They'd want some stronger power, the government, to come in and make them safe, let the government do whatever it wanted to. But then with other parts of the population, you might want them to be depressed, willing to settle for less.

"The problem then," said Tommy, "would be one of distribution. You couldn't just drug the water supply—that would affect everyone equally."

"Precisely, my friend. That's the problem we were working on. Distribution. Just like any drug dealer," he laughed. Then his mood changed. "But you know, ever since I left, I've begun to feel that they've figured out a way around that problem."

Tommy seemed fascinated with the spiel, even as the cabbie clearly drifted off into la-la land, telling us about how he'd been followed by agents from the government. "I'm sure you're thinking, this guy's O.D.-ed one-too-many times," the cabbie said to me. "Ha, maybe I swallowed too many paranoia pills? Fair enough. But your brother's the scientist, he's the one who knows about shit like this. Why doesn't he think I'm nuts?"

He's just too polite to say so, I thought.

"But I know you're thinking, how the hell does a cabbie know this shit? Well, I went to Berkeley. I studied math, physics, chemistry, just like any other nerd. Does Professor Brockman still teach there?"

Tommy looked startled. "Yeah. I took a class from him last semester."

We were nearing the end of our ride, gliding through downtown Berkeley. He glanced back at us.

"Since you think I'm crazy anyway, I'll tell you one more thing. The army, they're working on this invisibility suit. Now that's some real weird sci-fi shit. An invisibility suit. They don't have the technology for it yet. You've got to have a certain material and miniature electronic transmitters, things so small they haven't been invented. But everything in technology keeps getting smaller. You remember those tube radios, how huge they were. And then came transistors. And now they're using these electronic chips. Each stage getting smaller and smaller. That's what's going to happen and once they get small enough: wham, the army's going to have its own invisibility suit. James Bond will be able to go anywhere," he laughed. "H. G. Wells come to life."

As the cab pulled away, I smiled at Tommy.

"You can't have it both ways, Ben," he said. "You either believe in God or you believe in science. Or rather, you either don't believe in God or you don't believe in science."

"How about a healthy skepticism toward both? And besides, he wasn't a scientist. He was a fucking cab driver."

Tommy slapped my back in a patronizing manner.

"Sure. And you're the one who knows a scientist when he sees one. Mr. Chips. All you know about is what Grant proffered to gallant Lee at Appomattox. Who are you to talk?"

He had me there.

"Well, I know a voodoo cabbie when I see one."

"All science is voodoo, Ben, before it happens. That's what they said to Galileo."

"Great, so now I'm a member of the Inquisition?"

Back at his apartment, though, Tommy wouldn't let it go, as if my skepticism were some affront, or a failure to take him seriously because he was my younger brother. He said we should smoke this dynamite hash he'd gotten from Gail. Open up my mind. I told him that it would just make me stupid.

"Sometimes you got to get stupid to get smarter."

"My brother, the boy genius."

"Hey, somebody in the family had to be a nerd. You should just be glad it was me."

So I smoked the hash, which made my recollections of the rest of our conversation somewhat unclear, though it would haunt me as so many memories of Tommy do.

Last year, in the newspaper, I came upon this very brief article about how a Japanese inventor claimed to have developed a new invisibility cloak that uses a material composed of thousands of tiny beads called "retro-reflectum." I thought about Tommy then and wished he had been the one who invented such a cloak.

Or maybe he already had.

For various reasons, including their difference in ages, I feared my brother's fling with Gail wasn't the wisest of moves. I tried talking about her to Tommy once or twice. As always, I didn't get very far. He started in about how I'd gotten my white girl, so why shouldn't he? A quick shot from there to the gelding of Asian American men in general and the good J.A. boys, like me in particular. I knew enough of what he was talking about that I didn't want to listen anymore. It was his love life, let him screw with it as he wanted.

In terms of the color line, certainly Gail was a true WASP, with generations going all the way back to the Mayflower. Blond, well-off, sophisticated. She'd gone through the early days in the Haight and must have seemed to Tommy far more worldly, regaling him with stories of the parties with the Dead and Santana and other legendary Bay Area bands. She'd slept with a member of Moby Grape or some band like that, as well as one of the lesser Beat poets. She taught Tommy about Buddhism, proclaiming it was time that he learned something about his roots. "You know, Ben," he said to me once, "I feel like when I'm fucking her, I'm fucking America." No, with Gail, he was in way over his head. (I'd never felt that way about Grace. Well, not much.)

But what I'll never forgive her for are those trips to Reno she and my brother took. It's really a mistake to take a messed-up mathematical genius to a place like Reno. The genius sees all these numbers and thinks, hey, I'm a duck in water here. Perfectly adapted. Genetically programmed to succeed. But as De Niro declaimed in *Casino*, the house always cleans up, because the house always gets you to come back, and the longer you play, the more the odds turn toward the house. Steady as the laws of gravity, you'll just start rolling downhill. But if you've got a genius who thinks that he can outplay everyone else? He just knows he's the one who can defy the odds, because after all, his brain is one in a million, right?

It didn't help that three out of the first four times they traipsed off to Reno he came back a winner. Not huge, but a few thousand dollars, and that's no chump change for a graduate student. Especially one with a coke habit.

And where was our mother in all this? She had no clue. Or if she did, she kept it from herself. All she did was complain to me from time to time when Tommy hit her up for funds. "He keeps telling me it's only till he finishes his studies," she said to me. "But when is he going to finish?" I lied and told her that dissertations often take longer than expected.

I wasn't any better than my mother, though. Yes, from time to time, I'd tell him he really needed to cut out the drugs. Or the gambling. But I never got on him about both at the same time. And every time he shot back at me with that tone that said, you think you know it all, big brother, you think you have it all together? who are you to talk to me like that? why the fuck do I have to listen to you? you were never around when I was younger, you don't know me at all, you have no fucking idea who I am . . . and I backed down. He was right. I didn't know him. And I was treating him like a pain in the ass. Like my younger brother. Which he was.

Perhaps I've taken up not just the wrong project, but the wrong profession. At times I think my failures as a scholar stem less from matters of intellect than of temperament, some inner reluctance to perform what's expected, to assent to the obvious. For example, who could be a more logical choice for *Famous Suicides of the Japanese Empire* than Kimitake Hiraoka—the given name a schoolboy abandoned to protect his writings from the backlash of his fellow students? Yet with this renowned figure, my notes foist up a tone no serious historian would essay (though it still seems to me the only sane response to Kimitake's story). From notebook No. 4:

For the West, perhaps the most famous Japanese suicide is Yukio Mishima, the great author. Mishima believed that post-World War II Japan had gone soft and corrupt, strayed from the true path of bushido, *the code of the samurai. Certainly, Japan, after the war, had been defanged militarily. By the dictates of the U.S.-imposed constitution, the Japanese were allowed only the tiniest of armed forces, so small it had to rely on American forces for protection from any real threat. All that Nipponese warrior tradition shrunk to a toy army.*

Somehow, in this decline from glory, Mishima scried his own narrative. Or, rather, he projected his own dreams onto the nation. Sickly and skinny as a child, your classic runt of the litter, he became a body builder as an adult, cut himself into the cult of muscles and the way of the sword. The classic ninety-five-pound weakling who pumps himself into six-pack abs and iron pecs and biceps like Mount Fuji: if he could become Charles Atlas, why couldn't Japan do the same?

Part of his problem started when he was quite young. His convalescent grandmother snatched him almost at birth from his mother and kept him with her—a small boy imprisoned in a sickroom filled with the smells of ether and her decaying flesh. He wasn't permitted to play outside with other boys but only with three specially selected girls. In these years of captivity, obaa-san *forced him to hew to her autocratic aristocratic ways, to worship at the shrine of her family's glorious past.*

An American right winger might conclude that this was why young Yukio, né Kimitake, ended up a homosexual. At any rate, playing on the other side of the tracks is different in Japan. You can still be kosher if you do everything else you're supposed to do on the sunny side of the street. Mishima was married with children and lived a respectable bourgeois life, the life of a famous Japanese author with a variety of literary honors. Year after year, he was short-listed for the Nobel and expected, hoped, to win it like his mentor Yasunari Kawabata, another suicide.

Then, in the late 1960s, his military fantasies and martial philosophizing began to crowd out his literary and other artistic concerns.* He concocted his own private militia—partly because he

---

* Keep in mind that Mishima, in addition to his writing, was already one of the century's great performance artists. After a well-publicized exhibition, he published a glossy photo book featuring himself in various stages of undress and torture, sporting his muscles, his steely gaze. One of these poses put him up as St. Sebastian, wrapped only in a loincloth, arrows sprouting from his torso like a human pincushion or Toshiro Mifune at the end of *Throne of Blood*. St. Sebastian was one of Yukio's favorite icons. As an adolescent, he had his first conscious sexual emission while staring at a European

was past the proper age for the armed forces. He arranged for his
Tatenokai, *or Shield Society, to go on maneuvers with the* jieitai
(not the Luke Skywalker warriors, but the Japanese Defense Forces).

But for old Yukio, that wasn't enough. Like Yeats, that other literary fascist, also fascinated with swords and masculinity (remember his
transplant of monkey balls?), Yukio wanted a return to the good old
days and the samurai ways. He wanted to revert the Japanese tribe
and the emperor to their former numero uno status—even if that status happened to have caused catastrophes of death and destruction.

Yukio's grand scheme was to arrange for him and a few fellow
Shield Society members, including his lover, to meet with a Japanese
Defense Force general. They'd take the general hostage and threaten
to kill him unless the jieitai were assembled before the building.
Mishima would then give a speech, and his fierce rapturous words
would inspire the jieitai to revolt, take over the government, and
return Japan to its former military might.

O.K., the plan was a bit kichigai, as the Japanese might say. Loony.
Meshugganah. And it says something about Mishima that he even
thought a plan like this might have the slightest chance of succeeding.

When Mishima finally got up to speak, sporting a hachimaki
tied around his forehead, strutting on the roof of the jieitai head-
quarters, he believed himself at center stage, in the hushed spotlight.
But the young officers below could hardly hear him for the news hel-
icopters hovering overhead. Not that hearing his speech would have

---

print of the saint (at least if you take as autobiographical his novel *Confessions
of a Mask*).

Among his many art projects, Mishima also made a film of his short story
"Patriotism," which recounts the suicide of a young lieutenant in the twenties
who is part of a failed coup by a group who wanted to militarize Nippon to
the max. In the film, Mishima plays the young lieutenant and does the old *seppuku* sword dance. The blood gushes from his belly like a Texas oil geyser—
or, well, you know.

made a difference. They were quickly laughing and jeering at him.
Bakatare. Nan da yo. *Telling him what a putz he was. To go fuck himself. Shove it where the sun doesn't shine.*

But of course this latter instruction was just what Yukio wanted. Seeing his cause was fruitless, he shouted, tenno heka banzai—*Long live the emperor—three times, and retreated back into the general's office.*

The real tragicomedy occurred there. To his credit, Mishima shoved the short sword deep enough into his guts to make the correct geometrical incision, cutting across the belly. But in such ceremonial seppuku, *it's not the slit belly that brings death. No, a second comes up from behind and with a long sword, lops off your head. Only Mishima's lover was a callow, nervous young boy, not his match either as a fanatic or a swordsman. The scene quickly turned to farce, not Grand Guignol, as the lover-second banged on Yukio's neck without success.*

Fortunately, another young follower, Furukoga, stepped forward and zap, like in the old samurai films, the master's head plopped off.

Among other things, Mishima's death teaches us an important lesson: just as surgeons shouldn't sleep with patients, you shouldn't fuck around with your seppuku-second. *It clouds his cut.*

His fate also teaches us that the world, like the harshest of physicians, eventually cures us of our illusions, the impossible wishes and dreams we cling to despite evidence to the contrary. And sometimes the cure is more fatal than the disease.

Tommy's affair with Gail ended, as I half-prophesized, badly. Oh, they had their run of fun, trips to Reno and Big Sur and L.A., and I suppose she liked having this young, good-looking Asian boy genius on her arm; that was Berkeley, the Bay Area, where all things Far-Eastern are chic. She ran in a certain circle of women who prided themselves on the rainbow coalition they invited into their bedrooms, globetrotting between the sheets.

Eventually, though, she took up with an older white guy, some media magnate with holdings both here and overseas, and she started trotting off to Cannes and remote Pacific islands and leaving Tommy pining in the room above her garage. Soon she'd sold her place and kicked him out. Shortly after that, he dropped out of grad school. At the time I blamed her, but his plummeting was about more than just her. She was just a convenient target for me to direct my ire at.

Not that Tommy and I had much contact during this period. Grace and I had just had Takeshi, and we were preoccupied, as new parents are. Then, too, I found it difficult to talk with my brother without bringing up—perhaps it was just the Kimiko Ohara in me—his precipitous decline and the various reasons for it. He told me that I didn't know what he'd been going through, what he'd been doing. I had no right to make the inferences I was making, whether about Gail or gambling or whatever he might be imbibing strictly for recreational use. He was doing his own work now, he said; he didn't need a degree, and besides, who was I to talk about dropping out of PhD programs? He was just following the family tradition.

Of course that is just what I feared.

The last time I went to see Tommy, he was living with this Chicano girl named Anna over in Oakland in a low-rent apartment complex. I arrived in the early afternoon and rang the doorbell. No answer. I rang and rang. Then I went down the block and called his apartment from a payphone. No answer.

I was really pissed by then. He'd known I was coming. I'd talked with him the night before, back in Chicago. I'd come out because he'd told me Anna was pregnant and he needed money to help her out.

"Help her out?" I said. "Who got her pregnant? Some space alien?"

"Come on, bro. It's a tricky situation. I mean I like her, I really do. But I'm not gonna marry her or anything like that. And to tell you the truth, I don't even know if it's mine."

"Come on Tommy, don't bullshit me."

"No, man. I mean it probably is. I guess."

"You guess?"

"Well, what the fuck, if you're gonna be like that . . . Fuck it, don't help me out."

But of course I couldn't refuse him. He knew that.

I returned to the apartment complex that evening. He opened the door and stood there in his bathrobe, half-shaven. It looked like he'd just woken up. It seemed useless to say anything. He told me he'd been asleep, he hadn't heard me ringing the doorbell or calling on the phone. I could guess what sort of sleep that was, but I didn't say anything, didn't even tell him how pissed I was. I suddenly realized that I had no real notion of why I was there, that I should probably just give him the money and leave. There was nothing else I could do.

The one-bedroom apartment was a mess, clothes strewn about, a few boxes of Chinese food on the counter, dishes in the sink. The stereo was thumping out Boz Scaggs. A plateglass window opened onto a back parking lot. Tommy turned the stereo down.

At that moment, a woman walked out of the bedroom in a waitress outfit looking a little sleepy-eyed, brushing her long, wavy hair. Well, I thought, he always managed to pick out a fine one. I couldn't help but wonder if she was the reason Tommy hadn't responded to the doorbell. She was short and slim. The thought crossed my mind that perhaps she wasn't really pregnant at all. Tommy introduced us. Anna kissed him, shook my hand, told me it was good to meet me, and said good-bye.

"Listen, bro, I've got to take a shower," Tommy said after she'd left. "But I could really use some o.j. Got to get some v-c in me. Would you mind going down to the corner store and getting me some?"

Jesus, I thought. What do I look like, your delivery boy?

Walking up the street, I noticed a low yellow moon in the east, swollen and larger than usual. I wondered if that was a good or bad sign. I wished I knew more about Asian mythology.

The bodega at the corner looked a bit ragged, even for the neighborhood, like it had gone a couple-too-many rounds. A few aisles of necessities, cigarettes, and candy, and an old white guy behind the counter, who looked like he'd been there since v-j Day. After I entered and headed toward the refrigerated section in back, I heard a loud gabble of voices.

Four kids tumbled in, three Chicano, one white, and they were jostling with each other as if hot in argument.

"I paid the last time, man. It's your turn now."

"No way . . ."

The old guy behind the counter started yelling at them to get out unless they were going to buy something, but the kids paid him no mind. I knew immediately what they were up to; it was like the old routine we used play at the Gyp Joint, stealing penny candy.

I saw one of them slip toward the back as the three others went up to the counter and started arguing with the clerk. But the clerk kept zeroing back at the fourth kid lurking in the middle aisle. I grabbed my orange juice and started toward the counter. The clerk just looked past me. I plopped my orange juice down on the counter to get his attention, but he glanced at me and then back toward the stray kid.

"Excuse me," I said. "Ex-*cuse* me. I'd like a pack of Marlboros please. Filtered." The guy muttered something about wait just a second. "Listen, I haven't got all day. Can you just get me my cigarettes."

"O.K., O.K., hold your horses." The clerk took one more look back toward the aisles and then turned and searched for the cigarettes.

Just when he grabbed the pack of Marlboros, I said, "Actually could you make it a pack of Camels. Unfiltered."

He turned to me. "What is it you want? Marlboros or Camels? Filtered or unfiltered? Make up your mind."

"Marlboros. Filtered. Sorry. I just thought I'd try something new."

The clerk muttered to himself and reached up for the pack.

By then the fourth kid had slipped out behind us, and the rest of the kids, who were still shouting among themselves, turned and split. I glanced back at them and smiled, despite my anger at my brother. O.K., O.K., I thought. Just give him a chance.

Outside the bodega I tossed the Marlboros in a trashcan and walked back up the hill.

When I got back to the apartment, I could see Tommy was already high. I wondered on what. There was no mirror on the table; I couldn't smell any weed.

"Hey, Bro. What's up?" he practically shouted, waving to me from the couch, his face wan and pale, his eyes slitted like a lizard's. It was apparent that he wasn't going to get up. Or rather, couldn't.

All the anger that I'd lost back in the bodega came surging back. Forget it, I thought. I'm just getting out of here. I'm not going to even give him the money. But then I thought about

Anna, how she seemed nice enough during our brief encounter. I wondered if she had hurried out because she knew why I was there and was embarrassed; I told myself that she shouldn't suffer just because Tommy was a jerk, just because she'd made the wrong choice.

I gazed out the window and saw the huge yellow moon hanging just above the houses. It appeared almost as if it were hanging over the parking lot out back. Tommy looked too.

"Man, that's a fucking huge moon. Remember that *Science Fiction Theater* episode about those mice that went to the moon? Scared the shit out of me."

"Yeah."

"God, I loved that show. I wish they'd show it again. It'd be nice to see it on reruns late at night. Now all you get is some crappy televangelist ranting about the wrath of Christ and being born again."

"Well that wouldn't be such a bad idea."

"What? You going Christian on me, bro?"

"No, not really."

"Oh, I see. You were referring to my situation. I get it, I get it. You got me. I am a sinner, no bout adout that. A real genuine sinner. And now my righteous brother has come from the good, godly Midwest to save my soul."

"I'm sorry to disappoint you, but I don't have any such delusions."

"Oh, we're playing the guilt trip now, are we? You want me to beg for my coins of silver, is that it? Like some Biblical traitor? Judas sold Christ for what was it? Twenty talents of gold, wasn't it, not silver. Whatever. And whom do you suppose I'm betraying, dear brother?"

I'd had it. I didn't feel like giving him an answer, and Tommy barreled on as if he didn't expect one.

"Am I my brother's keeper? Isn't that a Biblical question? Only we never studied the Bible, did we, Ben? We were supposed to be Buddhists. Don't you find that strange? That Mom started going to the Congregationalist Church so regularly right after Dad offed himself? *Seppuku* to Christ, *seppuku* to Christ, come in, come in . . ."

He startled giggling then. I suddenly wanted to strangle him. But I couldn't. I told myself, that it was whatever was coursing through his veins, not my little brother Tommy. Whatever it was, he just kept talking.

"And then she goes out and meets old WASPY Marv and becomes an Episcopalian? And now, what is she? She doesn't go to church anymore. Does she still believe? Or was it all a show? I think it was a show, don't you? That's what we do, don't we, us *ni-hon-jin*? We put on shows."

"Maybe you do."

"Oh, yes. I forgot. You're the reformed one. You're the prodigal son that returned. You're the one who used the knife on old Michael Nagata and terrified the neighborhood and got locked up with crazy orphans and thugs. The one who came back and straightened himself up. Turned himself into a real nerd. But that's not a show, no. Ben's the genuine article, the only hundred percent true blue-blood among us."

I looked at him. "Just what are you on?"

"Me? High? God forbid. I forgot, you only do a little weed, and that's O.K., isn't it? Whatever little brother Tommy does, well, that has to be really nasty. What makes you think I'm high? Maybe this is just the way I normally talk. Maybe I'm just a jerk all the time. You ever think that?"

I wanted to hit him—I really did. Instead the best I could come up with was, "I bet you can't even get up from that couch."

He laughed. "Oh, really?" He started to get up, pushing up

from the couch with his right arm. "See?" he smiled, standing before me, throwing out his arms. "Look, Ma, no hands." He walked right up to me, his arms out as if he'd just been picked up by a cop and was walking a line to prove his sobriety. "See, officer, I'm stone-cold sober."

He was in front of me now. Then his right arm leapt up in a swinging roundhouse and stopped an inch in front of my face.

"I could have smashed your face, couldn't I? Could have knocked you stone cold. If I was *really* angry. If I was *really* high. But I didn't, did I? But go ahead, think what you want, think the worst of me, you always do."

Suddenly a shiver went through him, like a small seizure. He shook it off. "Man, it's cold in here. Christ, Anna left the sliding door open." He bumped into the coffee table with his shin, swore, and then continued across the room. Something in me wanted to tell him to stop. As he approached the door, he looked up. "Jesus, that moon is huge, fucking huge. Like you could grab it. Like you could punch that guy in the moon in the face."

He seemed to stand there for the longest moment, staring at the moon, as if he might start some conversation with it.

Suddenly he reared back his arm and smashed it into the plateglass window. The window was thick—it must have taken a great force to break through it—but he did it, his arm sticking right through the hole, as if he'd punched himself into another dimension. He stood there looking at his arm as if the window had somehow severed the half that now lay outside dripping blood.

"Fuck, man. What the fuck?"

And then he fell backwards as if the moon, not him, were the one who had struck the knockout blow.

THE LAST SOLDIER

I wrote this note last March, just after my trip to the Adler Planetarium and my decision to resume work on my book. Even as I wrote it, I could hear a voice in my head—and I knew just who it was—asking: what sort of history are you writing, Ben? From notebook No. 12:

One of the twentieth century's mythologies was the Japanese soldier holed up on some remote Pacific island long after World War II ended. Sometimes the soldier does not believe that the war has ended, that Japan's been defeated. Sometimes he knows Nippon has been vanquished but refuses to surrender himself. A soldier like this popped up more than once on Gilligan's Island, *terrifying Skipper and his Little Buddy (though I don't think the Jap ever threatened the thighs of Mary Ann or Ginger, despite Ginger's offstage reputation as a wailing slut). Back in the fifties and sixties, Japan was no longer the monstrous imperial threat of the Pacific (or in its next incarnation, the devourer of the American economy, the* gojira *rampaging through the American auto industry). No, the Japan of my childhood was cheap baseballs made of paper that would waffle apart the moment your Louisville Slugger got a hold of one. Or little windup toys that broke down by the fourth or fifth turn. Tinny transistor radios you hid beneath your pillow at night to listen to the top forty as you fell asleep.*

Behind the myth were real Japanese soldiers, a few of whom did hold out long after the war. Most of them eventually were found and surrendered. But three or four, faced with capture, answered their enemies with no white flag but self-annihilation by bullet, bayonet, or sword. Seppuku for an emperor who had long ago lost his divine status. (Whose voice in the surrender broadcast surprised so many Japanese by being tiny and squeaky, which caused them to ask, this is the voice of a god?)

Like Ishii, the last of his California tribe, these lone Japanese holdouts grip the imagination, whether comically or tragically or absurdly. Existential ghosts in a timeless landscape. Asking last questions about the meaning of their lives. About loyalty and courage. The faith or foolishness of fervent belief. The mortal and the divine.

I am no lone Japanese soldier, though I am the last of my family, my clan, the last of the pure bloods. Last year my mother contracted lung cancer, an ironic illness for a woman who never smoked or drank or lived in any way to excess. Who married into moderation and the American mainstream. Who seemed likely to outlast us all. But before the lung cancer progressed very far, a stroke took her instead. I had been planning on visiting her in some further stage of her cancer. But again, alas, I was too late.

At the funeral I was surprised and touched with how broken up Marv was. At one point I saw him caress my mother's cheek as she lay in the casket, and my heart went out to him. And yet I knew he was going to make it, to go on. He's just that sort of guy. Maybe not this year, but a couple years from now, I wouldn't be surprised to find an invitation or letter in my mail, announcing a new Mrs. Marv. Living single men are a hot commodity in those Sun City developments. And Marv was, is, a good man. He treated my mother well, loved her as if she were made of rice paper. Even though she was far tougher than that.

So I stood in the Arizona sun, with Marv and a few of their friends from Sun City and my aunt Yo, the only surviving sister, and watched them lower my mother into the desert dirt. The Episcopalian priest, sweating in his robes, said a brief prayer. For some reason, I felt a bit irritated at him. Partly his homily at the service seemed so bland and nondescript. But that wasn't his fault, he didn't know my mother, she wasn't a regular in his congregation. I couldn't put my finger on it, and then I realized that it was because he looked like the Republican Senator from Missouri, Danforth, the one who'd championed Clarence Thomas. The same gaunt gray face and pale dry cheeks and carefully groomed silver hair, a face filled with patrician airs and vanity. Such a man, I thought, wasn't worthy of saying grace over my mother's body. Even had he known her he wouldn't have understood who she was or known what she had gone through, he wouldn't have been able to see her. No, not at all.

For a moment, for that moment, all the misgivings and recriminations, all the accusations jammed up inside me, dissolved, the way a dust devil dervishing across the sands whirls upward and vanishes into the air that fevered it. And what I wanted to believe became briefly a small grain of truth—that she had tried as best she could, that she had done all that could be expected; there had been too much for any one person to deal with, and that was why she held back so, why she kept herself so tightly sealed and the world and us at bay. God knows she'd had her share of it, had suffered in her own silent way.

Yes, rest, Mother. Rest. You've certainly earned it.

The desert is where Tommy disappeared. There was some suspicion that it was connected to his gambling or some of his other illegal gambits, even perhaps back to his time in Japan and some Yakuza connections, but I don't know if I believe that. Tommy always managed to pay off his debts, one way or another. Sometimes through women, sometimes through dealing.

At one point he told me that he'd just begun working with a start-up computer company that was just about to take off. The money would have come in, and maybe he might have found a place for his gambler's instincts in what eventually became Silicon Valley. But perhaps that was simply a ruse concocted to hide his forays into the smuggling trade.

In the end, I brushed away all the questions about his end. I chalked it up to our family history and his drug habits. My mom, though, wouldn't believe he'd become a heroin addict and nothing I could say could dissuade her. I think that even if I'd had a picture of him with a belt strapped around his forearm and a needle piercing his veins, she'd tell me it was a gag or a Halloween stunt. Or maybe he was trying out for a movie. Or she'd simply say nothing, pretend ever-afterwards that she'd never seen the picture. At times she was like Cleopatra, the Queen of De Nile, as they say in the Twelve Steps.

My guess is that he was probably high when he wandered out into the Mojave. I'm sure it was at night, when the stars are myriad and the desert sky so clear you might reach up and grab a handful of them. He headed toward the mountains in the distance the way some lone survivor from a massacre would make his way back to the fort, bearing his disastrous news. But he was no soldier, he was an astrophysicist. He would have walked and walked—or stumbled—scrying various constellations, marking names, his encyclopedic knowledge of the heavens far superior to any astrologist. His knowledge of the future of the universe, the real future that counted in his mind, vaster than most mortals will ever comprehend. String theory and branes—the membranes between dimensions—still rattling about in his head. Twenty-first-century cosmologies.

All the authorities found was a rented silver BMW, a couple needles, traces of speed and smack. Stay up all night and watch the stars and somewhere near dawn crawl into a desert cave and shoot up and pass away. Not a bad end if you're going to go that way. If you were someone like my brother.

When they found his car, I asked if I should come out there to help them look. I was told not to—it was dangerous and a waste of time. But you found the car, I said over the phone to the investigator. "Yeah," he said, "but there were no tracks around it. It was windy, and his tracks might have vanished. Or he could have hitchhiked up or back down the road a hundred miles. We just don't know." What about foul play? "We're looking into it," he said. But they never came up with a thing, one way or the other. Just wrote it off as one more missing person. What did the police care if some addict teetered off into the desert all juiced-up on a speedball? One less fuck-up to worry about.

But back then, not that I wanted to acknowledge it, some part of me felt the same way.

Long after Tommy disappeared, when I wanted to think of him, I'd go back to that time in Berkeley, the night that we went to the Chinese disco. The night that we met that crazy Chinatown cabbie and then came back to Tommy's apartment and smoked and drank some of Gail's Rémy Martin. It's a better memory than the last time I saw him alive, that night he almost o.d.-ed.

At least he still had his brilliance that night up in Gail's garage apartment in Berkeley. Miles Davis on the stereo. *Bitches Brew.* His favorite more than mine, the electric phase. I preferred the modal *Kind of Blue.* Just as I preferred Herbie Hancock's *Maiden Voyage* to *Mwandishi.*

He was rapping on as usual about certain things I didn't understand. How our brains can only visualize three dimensions. "So that's a certain limit. We're just hardwired that way.

Oh maybe when computers get more sophisticated, they'll intuit a few more dimensions. But we're never going to comprehend more than that. And yet what if there are not just a dozen more dimensions, but millions?"

I just nodded my head.

"Now there's stuff about this you're probably not interested in."

"Oh, really?"

"But maybe since you're stoned . . ."

I raised my hand in a Vulcan salute. "o.k., o.k., warp speed ahead, Mr. Sulu."

"The problem is we look at computers now as mere extensions of us. Like a souped-up electron microscope or a prosthetic limb. But what happens if they get so far out beyond us they leave us in the dark. They'll seem to us more like oracles, like what was that Greek thing . . ."

"The Oracle at Delphi."

"Yeah."

"Well, at least I learned something from Brother McConnell back at St. Jude's."

"Whatever. Anyway, we'll just stand there, like monkeys, as these computers come up with mind-bending conclusions about the nature of the universe, and we won't understand it, not in the way they understand it. We'll just have to take it on trust."

I asked him what all this had to do with astrophysics.

"Other dimensions? Of course that's part of the field. Was there a big bang? Was there only one big bang? Could there have been others? And black holes. Is it possible that a black hole is simply a throughline to another big bang in another dimension? And if all this speculation about alternative dimensions is true, what would be the raison d'etre for other universes? You can take that one out to pasture theologically or mathematically. But it all comes, to my way of looking, like rolling dice, infinite possibilities in infinite succession."

In my stoned state, I felt like I understood not one bit of this. And yet I could feel what he was saying, like an undertow beneath the surface.

"Einstein was always asking," Tommy continued, "'Did God have any choice in the creation of the world?' And you know what he answered?"

"Wasn't it something like, God doesn't roll dice?"

"Yeah, yeah. But forget about Einstein. Let's get back to those alien beings and the possibilities of life elsewhere. More likely than not, whoever we encounter will be far more intelligent than we are. And they'll probably foresee how freaked we're gonna be so maybe they'll take some earthly form, like that cab driver tonight."

"Tommy, please . . ."

"Or maybe they won't even appear to us at all. Maybe they've gone beyond the whole notion of physical space travel, transporting their bodies. Of course they could do that *Star Trek* thing, teleporting, but that always seemed to me a little hokey. Mental travel, the mind goes but the body stays here, that seems more like what they'd be into."

I hauled myself up and got a drink of water. Cottonmouth. I thought my brief absence might slow Tommy down. Not a chance.

"That's not so far out, really, when you think about it," he called. "You know how you sometimes daydream and get so far into your daydream you feel like you've left your body?"

I yelled back at him. "Tommy, a mind is a terrible thing to waste . . ."

"No really, I'm serious. It happens all the time. To ordinary people."

"O.K., I'll grant you that," I said, sitting down again. "But they're still here on Earth, not anywhere else."

"Maybe. Maybe. But how do we know? I mean, I was sitting on this park bench in Berkeley, up in the hills last year, overlooking the bay. It was a sunny day, everything beautiful, the birds were singing, the sky was blue, I could see Oakland and San Francisco. And suddenly I had this feeling that I was in a different time. Or rather, not so much a different time as a different outcome. That something before hadn't happened as it had happened in the world as I knew it. You know, like Dad hadn't killed himself. Or, well, something larger, like they never put us in concentration camps. Or, I don't know, maybe Japan and Germany won the war. Something huge. A whole other world with a whole other history stemming from change like that. Like I'd wandered into this other dimension, parallel to ours—well, parallel's probably the wrong way of putting it, it's not a spatial relationship or anything like that."

It was only years later that by chance I discovered Tommy was just rehashing one of Philip K. Dick's novels, passing it off as his own vision. Was he conning me then or was he simply deluded? I still don't know. At the time all I could answer was "Drugs, Tommy. You're a walking ad for Nancy Reagan. Bro, just say no."

"I'm serious . . . Fuck you."

I could see that he was really upset. He was serious. Maybe even more serious than he was letting on. *Bitches Brew* had finished. I could hear a Sundowner wind blowing up the hill, a low howling sound, almost an audible moan. I shouldn't have smoked that last pipe, I thought. At least I wasn't drinking the Rémy Martin.

"O.K., suppose you did enter this other dimension, so what?"

"You don't get it, do you? You're just humoring me."

"Paranoia, Tommy. The hashish answer to Nirvana."

"Forget it."

"No, I am taking you seriously. So, what if there are other dimensions? What if we sometimes, for a brief moment, get misplaced or travel to some other universe? We still go back to our boring everyday lives, we still go back to the same old shit."

He looked at me in a way that made me sorry I'd said what I did, and I suddenly saw in him the young kid who used to bunk with me. Who made up crazy stories about aliens and astronauts, and who was always reading way beyond his grade level and even way beyond mine. Where had that kid gone? But he was there, right before me. And then that look vanished and the kid vanished, and I wondered if Tommy really did have a point.

He put Santana on, *Abraxas,* and smoked another bowl. I was getting tired. I told him I was going to crash. Sure, he said, go ahead. I crawled onto the couch and pulled the blanket over me. He was still sitting on the floor beside the stereo, humming to himself, his eyes closed. He opened his eyes and asked me if I remembered back in Chicago, when we lived in Uptown, that lot we used to call the Empty. Sure, I said. He said, you remember how we used to build fires there? Yeah, I said.

"Well one day Jimmy Pearson and I were building a fire back near the fence. And that guy with the funny hat, what was that, a homburg, yeah, a homburg, that was it, the guy in the homburg came up to us."

"Yeah," I said, closing my eyes, "he was a weird guy."

Tommy didn't answer. I thought he'd fallen asleep. I opened my eyes and saw him sitting there and then closed them again and the image of a frog popped up in my mind from some remote past, hidden in my brain.

"You know, Ben. I went home with that guy."

"Mom told us not to," I murmured.

"Yeah, but I went home with him."

I didn't answer. I was falling asleep. Tommy didn't say anything more. An image from my own past bubbled up, myself alone with Brother McConnell in his office, a series of questions I somehow managed to answer and elude. Was it all just luck, a throw of the dice? One escapes, one doesn't.

The next day I wondered if I'd heard him right, but I didn't ask him. I don't know why. I guess some part of me didn't want to know. Or maybe I thought that I'd just wandered into some other dimension, some other reality for a moment, just like Tommy had, and now I was back in this dimension, back in this real world.

PHOENIX

A month after Tommy disappeared in the desert, I went to see my mother. She was living with Marv in a Sun City development out in Phoenix. It felt odd to visit that place where the heat, like a barreling semi, smacked you the moment you stepped out of the airport. Blinding glare. The air so dry you wanted a drink every few minutes. The inside of the car was like that tin shed where they roasted Alex Guiness in *The Bridge Over the River Kwai* (didn't someone commit suicide at the end of that? was it Guiness or the Japanese commandant?). Driving through the city, we passed development after development, all set in a bowl between the mountains, making me feel claustrophobic, as if some wave of stone were soon going to wash over and bury me.

How could my mother move to a place like this? I wondered. I grew up in a city of seasons, of leaves turning gold and scarlet and vermilion in autumn, of sliding through thick snowfalls in the winter and rivers of slush and sewage in the spring. Weren't we people of the deep north? Didn't the Japanese composers of haiku always mark their imagery with a different season? Icicles on the eaves, cherry blossoms, crickets, the autumn moon.

But of course my mother wasn't Japanese, nor in the end, very Japanese American. Not surprisingly, there wasn't a J.A. in the whole division that she lived in, though there were a couple Chinese Americans. A few dots of yellow—few enough not to be remarked on—in a school of whites, into which my mother seemed to slip in like one of their own. She'd taken up tennis and golf, went on trips with Marv to Las Vegas. In her early sixties, she'd still shop for casual outfits that showed off her legs, legs that mirrored her looks, good enough to be mistaken for a woman ten, fifteen years younger. She always liked to regale me with stories from the golf course or tennis court, where she'd squashed some woman twenty years younger and the woman being completely bowled over when my mother revealed her true age. As she grew older, she seemed to grow younger, if only in comparison to Marv, who must have been pleased when his friends at the club or the local senior center remarked on his much younger—perhaps even trophy—wife.

But really, none of this had much to do with me. I was carting around other agendas. I wanted to talk to her about what we should do about Tommy, whether or when we should have some sort of funeral. I didn't care what it would be, Buddhist or Shinto, Congregationalist or even Episcopalian. I wanted some event to mark his going. I felt I owed him that. I knew I couldn't talk to her about it with Marv around. She'd say it wasn't the right time. Which meant it was private, family stuff. *Nihonjin* stuff. But she wasn't going to say anything like that to Marv.

So when we went out to eat that night at a steakhouse, I talked about Kengo, who was two then and his fascination with Thomas the Tank Engine and how he had taken to calling himself Sir Kengo the way Thomas called himself Sir Thomas.

"He can't get enough of those trains. We keeping buying them and he still wants more."

"You'll spoil him, Ben," said my mother.

"It's not his first," said Marv. "He knows what he's doing."

"I didn't do that, did I, Ben? Spoil you?"

"No, Mom, I guess not." I wondered if she caught the irony in my voice.

"Maybe you shouldn't let him watch so much TV."

"You're probably right. But it's not the TV so much as video. He has this Thomas the Tank Engine video that he watches over and over. He's obsessed." I thought a moment, then went on. "In a way he reminds me of Tommy when he was a kid."

"Tommy liked trains?" asked Marv. A look crossed my mother's face like a gust sweeping across the calm surface of a pond.

"No, not trains. Space, the stars. He was destined to be an astrophysicist. He couldn't stop talking about them."

"I don't think we need to talk about Tommy now," she said, not looking up as she cut her steak.

"Oh, sure," Marv said. "I'm sorry. I should have . . ."

"Just forget it," she said, lifting the piece of steak to her mouth. She stopped and held it up in the air. "Are you still working on your dissertation, Ben?"

One for me, one for you, I thought.

"Ma, really, that's over with."

"You've finished it?"

"No. What's the point in it? I've got a job—"

"Teaching high school."

"Yes, teaching high school. But I might be getting a job next year at a community college. Besides, it's not like I'm working at McDonald's."

"I didn't say that."

"No. Not in so many words."

"You've got children now."

"We're doing fine, Ma. Really."

"Yes, you're lucky. I'm sure Grace brings in enough from Hyatt." She turned to Marv. "She's so smart, that girl. I knew when she married Ben I wouldn't have to worry."

"So why are you so worried about my finishing the dissertation?"

She looked as if she was about to say something and stopped. She shrugged. "I don't know. If that's what you want, fine." I caught the irony in her voice.

Marv looked at her, then at me. "Could you hand me the A.1., Ben?" I picked up the bottle and passed it, waiting for my mother to start in again, but she didn't.

The rest of the meal, Marv and I talked about whether the Bears were ever going to make it back to the Super Bowl. My mom let us go on. I think both of us knew that the second round was coming.

Over the years I'd tried to bring up some of our messed-up J.A. history with my mother. She always cut the conversation short. It wasn't the right time to talk about it. It was all in the past, no sense in going over all that again. Why can't you just let things go, Ben? You don't understand, Ben. It's private. I'm entitled to my privacy. It's none of your business. Why would you want to bring that up? I'm not going to sit here and answer questions like that. I'm too tired, Ben. I don't have the energy. You don't understand what it's like to get old. I've got too much shopping to do now. It's Christmas, you know, it's not the right time to go into such things. I've got to think about Marv now. I'm his wife. His health isn't that great. He's not going to live forever. You have more important things to think about now, Grace and your children . . . Behind every defense I might penetrate she'd put up another, like an infinite labyrinth I'd never get through.

Still, in a way, she was right. I did have more important things to think about. Why wallow, why root around in the past, why dredge up things that can't be solved, that can't benefit anyone, shit over and done with, what good is that?

That night after we got back to her house I knew I'd have to wait to talk to her alone. I left her and Marv watching some tennis match on TV and went out walking.

After ending up in a couple cul-de-sacs, I set off in a different direction. I cut through the golf course, moving up and down through the hollows, the air temperature rising and falling with the shifts in elevation. The development was at the far edge of the city, which oozed out across the valley like slow-moving magma or an oil spill gone wrong. Someday it would probably reach the mountains in the distance, inexorably claiming acre after acre. And what of the spirits of the Apaches who'd lived here for thousands of years, never imagining what lay just over the horizon, danger approaching closer and closer? I thought of how a couple of the internment camps were set on reservations and what the Indians must have thought of these newcomer prisoners, looking almost like them, like distant cousins from a far-off shore. How the Navajo soldiers used their language to transmit messages in the Pacific that the Japanese couldn't decipher. How *nisei* soldiers helped decode and translate the messages from the enemy Nips. The ironies of history, a history of ironies.

At the far end of the course, I was about to turn back when I saw something moving out in the desert. A coyote trotting along, almost oblivious to my presence. Then it stopped and turned, staring at me. I mean you no harm, fellow, I said silently. I come in peace. But he knew better and he turned and scampered away at a brisker pace than before, trying to create distance between himself and this intruder.

For I *was* an intruder, in this city, in this desert. In my mother's life. In this country. I didn't belong here or anywhere. But I wasn't going to wander out into the desert like my brother. I didn't have the guts. I was only going to stand on the edge. I wasn't going to plunge in.

I thought of how those who guide people across the border are seen as predators, coyotes taking advantage of those who are desperate for a new life, another chance. I thought of the sheep who foolishly put their lives in the hands of those who only care about their own appetites and desires, whose only ulterior motives are themselves. Was my brother a coyote or a sheep? And what was my mother? Or me? Or was I neither, too timid to even consider any illegal crossing of borders, never venturing to see what was beyond the river, the next mountain range, the desert ahead? Never going off the reservation.

Too many questions, too few answers. Among the many questions I carried, among the many imbroglios I wanted to talk to my mother about, I knew I had to pick and choose. I wouldn't get to say everything, to ask everything. She'd never let me. She'd probably not let me get much of anything out. She'd clam up like a witness to an unspeakable crime, one whom the mob had called the night before and reminded that they knew where she worked, they knew where her family lived, they knew where she slept. She'd get amnesia all over again. There'd be nothing but blank slates on each page of her memory, all the books wiped clean.

As for me, maybe I was just as bad as my mother. I'd never talked to her about all the things Tommy had gotten into. How he might have turned out different if she or I had acted differently, chosen differently. How entangled we were in his fate. And yet how we stood outside it, mere witnesses—the way you might watch the car ahead on an icy road swerve and rip into a tailspin that sends it sliding off the road, through the railing and into the culvert below. But you're passing on before you know it, already far down the road and wondering if you should turn back or simply go on and call for help farther up, call for someone more prepared to handle such disasters.

I never did tell my mother about my suspicions. That perhaps there were other reasons for Tommy's disappearance. I didn't want to make it any easier for her, to say that Tommy made his own choices. I wanted her to live with her guilt. For Tommy. And my father.

I wanted to punish her. Just as I was punishing myself.

She was alone when I got back, sitting at the kitchen table. Marv had gone to bed. She was playing solitaire, the cards slotted up before her. She wet her finger and picked up a seven and dropped it in line, then slid that stack to the one next to it. It was a game for someone who can't sleep, who's used to staying up alone. I could tell from the way the cards had fallen she was probably going to win. I wondered if she ever cheated, like I did. No, probably not.

"You know, you really shouldn't go walking out there. It's a private course. Someone might see you."

"Who cares? I'm not hurting anything."

"Old people live here, Ben. They get nervous when they see someone walking out there."

"Ahh, yes, the cat burglar. I've always thought of myself like Cary Grant."

"Laugh if you want. I'm not going to go down there and bail you out if the security police pick you up."

"Yes, the wonders of the gated community. Keep all the riffraff out. All dos coloreds and Mexicans. It's a wonder they let me in, Ma. Maybe they thought you were Marv's maid and I was his gardener."

She looked up from her cards. "You think you're so funny." She threw down another three cards. "Besides, there are coyotes out there too."

"I just barked at them. And they barked back."

She was moving another stack now. The next throw came up an ace. She now had three aces up there above the stacks. She was close to nailing it down. I moved to the refrigerator and peered inside.

"There's some potato salad in there, if you want."

I came back to the table and sat down. She looked at my plate. "You're going to get fat you know. You've already put on a few pounds."

"Thanks, Ma. Good thing I'm not a girl. I'd be an anorexic by now."

Another ace. She snorted in recognition and put it up on top. "Look at Marv. He's in better shape than you."

"Hey, I'm a nose guard, not a wide receiver. But I suppose you're right about Marv. Old Marv will probably outlive us all . . . Over there, the second row."

"I know how to play."

I watched her finish up the game, moving the cards faster and faster as she cleaned up. When she'd won, she gathered up the cards and started shuffling them again, over and over, almost as if she were trying to calm herself down. At last she turned to me.

"You might as well get it over with," she said. "Whatever it is you came here to do."

My father once talked to me about hearing monks sing in a Buddhist temple, how the force of their singing penetrated to his bones. How it seemed so strange to him that these men with shaved heads and pale skulls and yellow teeth could make such a magnificent sound. How their robes were the color of dark wine and sunlight at the end of the day, and the smell of incense clouded his head and made it difficult for him to breathe. How scared he was of the stone lions in front of the temple. How afterwards he heard one of the monks playing a flute, and the notes seemed so delicate and forlorn, unlike the guttural sounds that poured from their throats, which seemed more like the deep iron tones of the bell they rang in commemoration for the dead. I don't remember how long it was into his description of that day before I realized that he was talking about his mother's funeral and that I hadn't known that his mother had died when he was very young and that the woman I thought of as his mother was really his stepmother. And this made me think of how my father had a stepbrother whom he never spoke of, one who died during the war, and I wondered what it would be like to have a stepbrother and not a brother-brother and whether that would have been worse or better.

I thought of all that the night I talked with my mother in Phoenix. Or rather, tried to talk to her.

She kept on saying it was late, she should be going to bed, and I kept on telling her, we have to talk, Ma, we have to talk.

"Who's going to come to the funeral anyway?" she asked. "You say he didn't really have any friends."

"I don't know. Aunt Satsu, Aunt Yo."

"They're back in Chicago."

"They can fly out here."

"That would be too much trouble."

I knew these weren't the real reasons for her reluctance. I could guess some of the reasons, but I really didn't know for sure. With my mother there were so many layers of secrecy and silence, it was hard to know where they ended, how deep they went. I could dig till morning and not get to the bottom of it.

"I don't care then, Ma. None of them have to come. It can just be you and me."

"But if it's just you and me, what's the use?"

"I don't know. It's what you're supposed to do, isn't it? Honor the dead."

"But suppose he isn't dead? You even said yourself you didn't know for sure."

She got up from the table and went to the sliding door to the patio and looked out at the desert dark. She sighed.

"What good would it do, Ben? It would put such a strain on Marv."

"Marv has nothing to do with this."

"He's my husband."

"You're Tommy's mother."

She turned and looked at me.

"You don't have to tell me that. You have no idea . . ."

I could see her body shake a bit and she stiffened herself and turned back to the window as if she were waiting for someone to arrive.

"I'm sorry, Mom. I know, I know."

"You don't know. Otherwise you wouldn't talk to me like this. You're just, you're just so selfish."

I knew I should have stopped then. She wouldn't change her mind. I knew that. No one ever changed Kimiko Richards's mind. Not even Marv. She was her own woman right until the end.

But no, she wasn't going to get off that easy. Why should she? She hadn't gone out and looked through Tommy's apartment. She hadn't questioned the cops who found his abandoned car. She hadn't been the one who listened to him late at night when he called about any one of the latest disasters that plagued his life, whether it be women or gambling or drugs or the downward spiral of his career. She hadn't gone in search of other reasons why he might have vanished, reasons that might have had nothing to do with our family. She hadn't tried to see if some honor might be brought to his demise or, if not honor, at least a sense of justice. And if not justice, at least some fuller explanation of why he had to go away so far from us he could never get back.

So no, I would not let her get off so easily. There were too many crimes to go over.

No, Mother, we've just begun.

I recall the barking outside. At first it was a dog, I was pretty sure. But then there was something else, whinier, more high-pitched, more strained. Not like any dog I'd ever heard. And when it broke into a howl, I knew what it was.

I was at the window then. My mother was back sitting at the table. I could tell she was going to start dealing again, and it made me so angry I walked right up to her and took the cards and flung them against the window. They splattered there like a flock of wings, as if a whole swoop of birds had mistook the glass for air. I thought of putting my fist through the glass too, as if that would do some good.

"Damnit, Ma. How can you sit there playing cards?"

"I beg your pardon?"

"What the fuck are you doing?"

"I'm going to bed . . ."

"No. You're. Not!"

She looked up at me sharply. "You can't talk to me like that. I'm your mother."

"Are you? Are you my mother? What about Tommy, Ma? Aren't you his mother too? Weren't you supposed to protect him? Weren't you supposed to protect me?"

"What are you talking about? I did protect you. Both of you."

"No, that's what you say, that's not what you talk about. You want to go around pretending as if your past didn't exist. But it exists, Ma. I'm here. And Tommy exists or existed, wherever he is. And he deserves a goddamned funeral. You didn't let him go to the first one, and that probably fucked him up for life, but hey, who cares, but you're going to give him a goddamned funeral if I have to drag you to it."

She turned away from me, frozen there, like a statue. As if she were alone in the room and there was not another soul there.

"Talk to me, Ma. Talk to me."

"Why should I talk to someone who uses a tone like that? Don't you have any respect?"

"Oh, I respect you. I respect you up the wazoo. After all, not just anyone could pull this second act off. Not just anyone could get off the canvas like you have and walk out of the ring and pretend the fight never even happened, pretend you never got into that damned ring at all. But I know you did, Ma, and I see the bruises, even if old blind-as-a-bat Marv can't see them."

"Leave him out. You have no right to bring him into this."

"O.K., yeah. Leave Marv out. But what about us? Where does that leave us?"

She was sobbing then, not loudly or hard. I felt something inside me that I'd never felt before toward her, almost as if I were seeing her for the first time, like a stranger, and it amazed me, how frightened she looked, how absolutely frightened.

"It's all right."

"You think . . . You have no idea how hard it was, with your father, not knowing what was going to happen with him, when he was going to be there, when he was going away, if he was ever going to come back . . . "

"Ma. I'm through. Let's forget it."

She looked at me, and what I saw there was pure steel.

"No, no, no, no, no. You wanted to hear this, you had to ask your questions, you had to keep pressing. Like some, some scavenger, you can't let it go. You don't see it, Ben, you just don't want to see it."

"See what? What the fuck don't I want to see?"

A fury crossed over her face, like a warrior launching into battle. "You're angry at me? At me? For what I've done? Who dragged you out of that store? Who told you to get away from that man?"

"But you didn't save Tommy, Ma."

"No, no, I didn't. And I'll have to live with that all the days of my life. Every single day. Every single day. Don't you know I think about that? Don't you think there are days when I wish that thought would go away? But it doesn't. It won't. It's like this animal howling in my brain and I can't let it go, it won't let me go. So I take it, and I go on. I take it and I go on. And that, that's what your father couldn't do."

"Oh sure, go after Dad . . ."

"Listen. Listen to me Ben. Your father left us. He quit. It got too hard, and he just quit. Just laid down and let it all roll over him. He took the easy way out. The easy way. But I couldn't take the easy way out, Ben. I couldn't take it out on you or Tommy, and yes, I know, I know, I could have done things better, I could have done things a hundred times, a thousand times, a million times better, but I didn't. So o.k. I'm sorry. I'm sorry. But I'm not your father, Ben. I didn't do that. I didn't take the easy way out and leave. And you have yet, once, in your ungrateful life to ever say thank you to me for that. Not once."

I couldn't answer her then. One more word and I knew something would have broken. Inside me. Between the two of us. It was better that way than thinking otherwise. That maybe it didn't matter. Maybe it already was broken.

A little while before she passed away, she wrote me a letter. It wasn't very long, and I didn't know what occasioned her to write it. She'd only written me a few letters in her life, mostly when I was in college and after that a couple notes on birthdays or anniversaries. Maybe she sensed what was already happening in her body. Maybe there are things about growing old that I don't yet know.

In the letter she told me that she was proud of me, that I was a good father—she could see that in the way I was with my boys. I was a good husband too. She was glad Grace and I seemed happy; she'd always liked Grace and felt she would be good for me from the time we first got together. At this point in the letter I felt appreciative but wary, as if the note had been written by someone I didn't know. I kept expecting the familiar subtle or not-so-subtle note of critique to slip in and take over.

When she said that she knew I was working on a book about suicides, I thought, oh yeah, here it comes. She didn't think it would do any good to write about such a subject—"why people always want to talk about the Japanese in this way is beyond me"—but she said it was my work, not hers. I was a grown man (thanks, Ma). Still she wanted me to know that "there are certain things that ought to be kept private." I knew then what she was warning me about, not that I wanted to go there either. "I want to make sure you understand this before I go on . . ."

She went into her old spiel then about not looking back and the need to keep moving forward, the familiar Kimiko Ohara litany. But then she surprised me. "I know you're a historian, so perhaps the past means something to you that it doesn't to me. And perhaps I know there's not much for me to look forward to anymore. At any rate, there are some things I think you ought to know. As you recall, my brother was killed in the war . . ."—But you never talked about him, Ma. I only found out about him years later from Auntie Satsu—"I was much younger than him and we were never really close. I barely knew him. But my parents were never the same after he died, especially my mother . . .

"Your father knew about all this. When he finally told me he'd been a No-No Boy I think he expected I would break up with him. Of course I was angry that he had hidden that from me. But there was no one right choice. I understood that. My brother joined the 442nd and went off to war. Your father joined the No-No Boys and went to prison. They each had their own fate."

Went to prison? Neither of them had ever told me that before. Why hadn't they said anything? No, I knew. It was all that *Shoganai*, and what can't be helped you don't talk about. *Kodomo no tame*. As if it were the kids they were protecting and not themselves. Or—trying to resist my own swift desire to indict them—perhaps was there some other reason for that silence, something right there before me and yet hidden, like Poe's purloined letter, something I was too dense or too far from them to see?

At any rate, it was all quite frustrating. I felt like I'd been stymied over a picture puzzle for years, and she'd just come up, reached into her purse and pulled out a missing piece, "Oh here, Ben," as if she'd just noticed what I'd been doing. Not that she was going to hand over much else, any further details. God forbid she should tell me everything I wanted to know and clear things up once and for all. No, she quickly moved on, as if she'd already said too much. Which, in her eyes, was probably the case.

"I suppose that's part of what's got me through all these years. I may be a Christian but I understand that each of us has his own karma. When I married your father I thought I knew how all those JACL-ers would look at us. I didn't like it, but there was nothing I could do about it. I didn't think it would make it harder for him hold a job but we dealt with that. Would I have married your father if I'd known what was going to happen to him? No. But if I hadn't married him I wouldn't have had you. Or Tommy.

"I'm sorry if you think we should have had a funeral for Tommy. But I couldn't have made it through. I just couldn't. It may have seemed selfish to you and perhaps it was. But I've sat through enough funerals for one lifetime. If Marv goes before me, well, I don't know what I'm going to do. But for some reason I don't think that's going to happen.

"You have one main job, Ben. Take care of Grace and your boys. Your father, Tommy, or even me, we're not your concern now. You have your own family. Take care of them and make sure nothing happens to them. That's all I ask."

After I finished the letter, I still felt so much was still missing, great stretches of the past left in silence. But this was it. And I had to admit she'd thrown down one last ace: my charge *was* to take care of the living and not the dead.

If only the line between the two was as clear as my mother would have it.

Over the years I've tended to avoid an obvious blank in my past: what drew my parents together, a query that quickly leads to the more specific question, what did she see in him? I know the two of them had problems early on in my childhood, and as my father sank into the living room couch, brooding in silence, his intervals of darkness and debilitation deepening, her exasperation with him only increased. And who could blame her, what with the burden of two young boys falling increasingly upon her shoulders—until the day, perhaps a day she came to see as inevitable, that she alone had to bear responsibility for our survival. (At least until she met her—the phrase "white knight" pops into my mind, but that seems a bit ludicrous given the mild and accommodating Marv, whose easygoing and deferential ways fit my mother's intensity and drive but who also possessed a solid, if rather dull, steadiness and a lightness my father lacked.)

But there had to be an earlier time when my parents' attraction overtook both of them and propelled them on an at-first mutual but eventually dividing paths. Of course it's easy to intuit how she dazzled him with her beauty. A beauty so insistent that years later, even widowed and with two young sons, she managed to attract a number of suitors. Add to that her incisive and practical intelligence, which later quickly helped her ascend at the post office and support herself and her two boys until help finally arrived. And I can only surmise that before my father's descent began to darken her worldview, she possessed a brightness and vivacity that I only caught glimpses of in my childhood, and picturing that which I have never quite seen, I can easily see how my father could fall for her, overlooking whatever whispered to him that perhaps they were not as suited to each other as he might have wished.

No, my father's vantage point here is simpler, and not just because it's male. And it's not that he didn't possess his own attractive qualities, something for her to grab onto. He was handsome, yes, handsome not in the way of a delicate court paramour like Genji, but in that rough, thickly bearded and gruff-voiced Mifune samurai way. And yet he possessed a gentleness and self-deprecating shyness. At the same time, he was capable of bursts of ebullience and even showmanship, as he demonstrated so often to Tommy and me in our bedroom, regaling us with tales, both Japanese and American, and his little bouts of amateur acting, reciting his favorite passages from

Shakespeare or the Gettysburg Address. Perhaps, during their courtship, courtship being what it is, he managed his own sort of charm, both the quiet and the loud, the retiring and performing striking a perfect balance. (And it was only later, as the former qualities began to overcome the latter, as he descended into his own personal dark, that things went off keel.) Then too he possessed an intelligence to match hers, if not one as practical; his acumen concerning character was as penetrating as hers, though he directed it, most likely to his detriment, inward, while she directed hers outward.

At any rate, given that they were both young Japanese Americans, surrounded by all that postwar America had to offer and settled in the Midwest where any anti-Jap prejudices had far fewer historical roots than on the West Coast, perhaps they could both feel they were starting fresh. A blank page. Out of the camps and unfettered by living in some ethnic enclave and with both sets of their parents no longer present, perhaps they sensed in themselves something unprecedented and promising; their own version of the American Adam and Eve, sole determiners of their fates and free to be with each other and make a new life, a sturdy, beautiful *nisei* girl and a strong, handsome *nisei* boy. And in this way, they were like so many of the other *nisei* couples around them, in Chicago and in other cities scattered throughout the country.

Only there was his past, his No-No past, his prisoner past. Which he had not told her about at first. Which he'd deliberately kept hidden from her, and perhaps even wondered whether or not he should ever mention. But he must have known that she'd find out eventually—their community was so small, and of course the way it had been scattered in the camps, that made it even smaller. Someone they'd run into was bound to have been in Heart Mountain, and if they'd been at Heart

Mountain . . . No, he had to tell her, it was certain to come out, and to be fair to him, perhaps he really felt a need to be honest with her, to let her make a decision with all the cards on the table, knowing everything, nothing hidden. Perhaps he could no longer carry his secret or continue his silence with her; perhaps he couldn't have gone through with the marriage otherwise.

Anyway, given all this, the inevitable question doesn't concern his motives or actions, but hers. Why go through with it? Why not take his not telling her immediately as the reason to call it off and thus not even face the implications of what he'd done during the war or making the decision about how she felt about it, his heavy historical load? Why not avoid all that?

I suppose that if I possessed a more detailed and intricate sense of her history and that of her family, I might be able to speculate more in-depth on the myriad reasons, psychological and otherwise, behind her decision. I might even wonder whether, given what had happened to her family during the war, particularly with her brother's death and her mother's reaction to it, she saw marrying my father as her own trial, her own loyalty oath. During the war, as a teenager in high school, she had been too young to make any significant decision—about the war and the camps, about her family, about what it meant to her to be a Japanese American. Faced with her fiancé's revelation, she suddenly knew that she was no longer her mother's child, no longer her father's child: she was on her own.

But was it simply a belief, as she seemed to imply in her letter, of *shoganai?* It can't be helped; this is his karma. But if it was *his* karma, why should it be *hers?* Or was it more her inherent *gambatte kudasai?* Work hard and you will make your luck? Or perhaps something more American, a belief that you need not drag the past along like a chain behind you, that you can always light out to the territories (though in her case the territories were east, in the Midwest, not on the West Coast)? Or was it—and given my mother's hard-eyed practical nature I know she'd never have put it this way, even to herself—that she was simply and deeply in love with my father? But why go on? There's no way for me to know the answer to these questions or to even investigate them any further than these brief surmises; most likely whatever I've come up with here is incomplete, if not entirely off the mark. How could it not be, given what little I have to work with, how little I've been told?

In the end, though, the fact remains: She didn't walk away from him. She didn't take the easy way out. No, that's not Kimiko Ohara. And I am her son.

5

WANDERING RONIN
(or WHY DON'T YOU GET DOWN
OFF YOUR HORSE, PILGRIM?)

From my notes for *Famous Suicides of the Japanese Empire*, written in the UCLA library, June 2, 1999, notebook No. 13:

Back when Grace and I were in college, they used to bring in all sorts of foreign films. 400 Blows, Black Orpheus, Closely Watched Trains. Chushingura, *the tale of the forty-seven* ronin.

Ronin were samurai without a master. In the case of these forty-seven, their master had been disgraced through a rival daimyo's *deceit. The master was forced to abandon his position and property and commit* seppuku. *Everyone expected the master's samurai to follow him into death. But instead, the* ronin *wandered the country, taking ordinary jobs. Their disgrace doubled, not only for their master's mistakes, but because they did not commit* seppuku *along with him.*

But slowly, undercover, they were gathering evidence of the rival daimyo's *treachery and their master's innocence. In the quiet of a midwinter snow, they attacked the* daimyo's *castle, wiping out both him and his men. Having avenged their master's death, having re-established his honor, the forty-seven then committed* seppuku—*no longer disgraced, no longer seen as cowards or traitors, no longer figures of scorn.*

I enjoyed the film, its bracing climax. A Japanese legend, like those my father used to regale me with. As I left the theater, I wondered why he'd never told me about it.

Now I know. My father knew how such stories really end. And though the end was seppuku, *it wasn't filled with honor. It was simply an end.*

Sometimes late at night I'll hear them, my dead. My mother, Tommy, my father. Perhaps their voices are part of some acid flashback, remnants of my brief psychotropic college days. Certainly, I don't believe in heaven or an afterlife. Tommy might say they were speaking from another dimension, some alternative universe where the history of our family unfolds in another direction, as a new, unexplored possibility.

At any rate, I know they're close by.

One more entry barely glancing at my official thesis.

Probably Grace would react to such jottings like Shelly Duval did in *The Shining,* stumbling upon the single sentence typed over and over by Jack Nicholson, when he was supposed to be completing his novel. (No, that's an exaggeration. I'm not that far gone. Yet . . .)

For years I've called myself a *ronin* scholar, as if that somehow excused or elevated my nontenure status. No permanent spot for me, thank you. I don't do well with institutions, with protocol and hierarchy, kowtowing to authority. And yet every year I've promised myself I'm going to finish the damned book. Yes, tear out that tome that's going to get me back in good graces with the *daimyo,* the dark lords of academia; make my return to the station my mother always envisioned for me and which she constantly reminded me I'd fallen short of. That's why I've set off once again to L.A., to the origins of my past. Perhaps I might find myself inspired amid the stacks of the West Coast libraries where all things Asian and Asian American are more common fodder, if not the coin of the realm. Or at least that's what I've told Grace. (Of course I didn't mention the boy at the

Adler Planetarium, waiting for his brother. Or my breakdown before him. Much less Tommy's lost postcard from Japan.)

But after a few days in the stacks at UCLA, whatever inspiration I'd been seeking still hadn't hit. My Japanese was rusty and translating the Japanese texts was tedious. I did find a couple interesting articles on Yukio Mishima and his paramilitary outfit, but that seemed off the course. I understood some of the impulses that drove him, including his middle-aged cult of the body, pumping iron and running up Mt. Fuji (for years I've been hitting the free weights in our basement, a holdover from my high-school football days, as if training for a big game that's never going to arrive). But Yukio's putsch for the revival of the sword and the Japanese Empire? That was a little *kichigai*, even for me.

So I put my research aside and, thinking it might clear my head, decided to head over to J-Town and the J.A. museum. I'd only been there once before, for a brief visit. Some part of me felt apprehensive, though I couldn't exactly say why. I suppose back in the Midwest anything concerning Japanese Americans always seemed not just obscure but nonexistent. Whatever brooding I've done about our history, I've done on my own, in solitude, in private. The idea of a large brick and mortar structure, funded to a great extent from the money the *nisei* received from reparations, felt alien to me. A bit too public, a bit too exposed.

I told myself I had no reason to feel that way. It was just a museum like any other. You've gone to the Getty and the MOCA, I thought. This is what tourists do.

The museum was elegant and tasteful, though as when I visited before, smaller than I'd expected. Lots of glass and natural light; open spaces; sandstone, granite, and steel; a Japanese rock and water garden. I had some miso soup and tempura at the restaurant, as if the food might serve as an easy transition. I took my time with the meal, lingering over some *genmaicha*, trying to empty my thoughts. Then I walked through an exhibit of some internment artists. Amateur work, visual documentation. Muted watercolors of camp scenes, like storyboards for a film that's never been made: A train at a station, a bus. People trudging toward their barracks, the barbed wire and rifle towers like after-thoughts in the distance. A woman sewing by the light of a window displaying a flag with a star. Ten *nisei* crowded in a barracks room. Two kids retrieving a kite tangled on a fence. A strike rally with indecipherable figures jousting about a flaming oil drum.

After that I could have left, could have headed back to my motel or to the UCLA library to bang my head again on my research. And I did think about it. Why go over it all again?

Instead, I walked upstairs to the replication of the barracks at the Heart Mountain Camp, and before I knew it, I was heading back down to the museum library. As if taken over by the dictates of my profession, I started to search for certain documents. In microfiche, on the museum computer, in books. In the permanent collection. Various official announcements for curfews and the internment. The Executive Order 9066 signed by Roosevelt. Responses of the JACL, sometimes seem-ing to placate or go along with the government, trying so hard to prove their patriotism. Even putting up the idea of some sort of loyalty oath. Letters from Mike Masaoka, the self-approving JACL president. And then the less famous documentation, records of the resisters. A copy of the loyalty oath. The mimeo-graphed broadside from the Heart Mountain Fair Play Committee, the group my father had been a member of: "We, the *nisei*, have been complacent and too inarticulate to the unconstitutional acts that we were subjected to. If ever there was a time or cause for decisive action, IT IS NOW!" Court min-utes. Interrogation transcriptions from the FBI, of when they tried to trap the No-No Boys into treasonous statements, ignoring their legal arguments, the rights they'd been guaranteed since birth.

The weight of those years, the lessons and laws and faith refuted.

I'd read about all these papers and documents before. But seeing the originals, I felt somehow deflated. I kept searching for the sense of outrage and anger I couldn't quite muster. I sympathized with my father and those No-No Boys, the impossible no-win situation they found themselves in, their refusal to back down. Their civil protest. And in a better world, their histories would have been honored, written down, part of what every American schoolchild learned. In a better world.

But as I always told Tommy, I live in this world. That's who I am. There is what, as children, like children, we wish for. And there is what is. And as I looked at those papers and searched inside myself for a response, I couldn't lie, I couldn't wish it away—how untethered I felt, how far away from it all, floating off into space. Just another postwar post-internment baby-boomer.

It didn't, I knew, say much about me, who I was.

But then, a little while later, I found myself looking at the less political records of the internment. Sepia photos, letters. The lists of family members. There was my mom's family, Aunt Satsu, Aunt Yo, Uncle Nobu. There was my dad's family, his father's second wife, his half-brother. The years they immigrated, the years they were born. All written down in the government's ledgers, keeping track of its prisoners. These were my people, people I knew—though perhaps, given their general and substantial silence about the past, I never really knew them at all.

I thought of all the deaths yet to be recorded, how they came after the war, including my father's. My lonely embattled father.

My sad noble father. My resister prisoner father. And my stoic silent mother. Survivor to the end.

And then there were the births, also missing from the museum's records. Mine, Tommy's. My cousins'. My sons'. The last of the Oharas . . . or were they?

How much I wanted to stop then, to stop looking. To just let it go.

No, the story was still unfinished. Stray pages unaccounted for. That was the real reason I'd come out here.

When I called, she pretended she didn't know who I was.

"I'm sorry," she said. "I don't know anyone named Tommy. You've got the wrong number."

"I looked you up on the internet."

"Well I'm sure there are a thousand Anna Delgados."

"You used to live in Oakland."

"I told you I don't know your brother."

"I didn't say he was my brother."

"Yes, you . . . I have to go now. Please don't call here again."

"Anna, Anna, don't hang up. Look, I know it's you. You were living with him. I came to visit when you were pregnant."

Silence. "O.K. But you have to come on Saturday. Otherwise I won't see you."

I wondered why she was so adamant about the day, but I let it go. It was enough that she'd agreed to let me see her. I got off the phone quickly, before she could change her mind.

I just needed to make sure. To clear my conscience. The visit wouldn't take more than a few minutes and I could apologize for bothering her and she'd never see me again.

I know that back in the days when my father would go to the hospital they didn't do much for mental patients. A sedative, perhaps. Nothing like the rainbow array of pills they have now, nothing like the treatment people go through with a therapist or a whole group of fellow patients, all that Oprah-like opening up of your history, rummaging about in childhood, looking for familial patterns, trying to seek out the origins of long-buried pain and misdirected compensating behaviors. I've never thought much about what he did there. He probably just sat around most of the day, watching TV with the other patients, just like he did at home. Certainly the origin of his own troubles was something he would never have talked about with anyone. Not that anyone there would have been able to make much sense of what he'd gone through, the ways his fate had been tied to his community's obscure history. He was probably the only J.A. in the place.

No, I don't think there was much back then that would have helped my father. Tommy was another story. I suppose there were various sorts of treatments available by the time he began to really drift away, but he wouldn't have even entertained such an idea. He was very much one of those who believed you keep your problems close to the vest, you solve them yourself or you don't solve them at all. He was very much like my mother in this, which is not surprising.

Sometimes Grace tells me I, or we, should go to therapy. Individual, couples, the mode depends on the issues that come up between us. Oh she's tolerant to a point about the way I can get into these low-pressure funks that hang around for days, always hovering around the potential for something stormier and more destructive. But if I go on too long or she's turned to me during the routines and occasional chaos of our family life and found I'm not really there, she'll start pressing, peppering me with questions that I can't or won't answer. I just tell her that that's the way we Oharas are, and that usually stops her for a while. I know she doesn't want herself to get into it with me too deeply, to start bringing up all the bitter brine and bodies of my past. All that's beyond her comprehension.

And yet I know she's right. There are times I am not here, present in this life of ours, the one we've built with Kengo and Takeshi, the present that presses in on both of us and demands and deserves an immediate response.

It's like she's saying, I'll let you take off occasionally. For a while. But don't ever, ever think of pulling anything like your . . . I will not stand for your vanishing, whatever version you might be thinking of.

Of course, she has no control over whether I do or not. And that drives her crazy.

As for my going off like this to L.A.? That puts her too close to the edge, that is, too close to a certain vision of who I am that she never wants to see. I could hear it in her voice as we talked on the phone.

"When do you think you'll be back?"

"I told you before. I'm not certain. Probably in a week."

"Kengo's school play is on Monday."

"I already told him I was going to miss it. Look, Grace, it's not like you don't go on your own business trips."

I knew what she was thinking: *her* trips possess a legitimacy that mine lacks; her trips don't require a whole other invisible set of luggage.

"Well, I just hope your research pans out. I'm all in favor of you finishing your book."

"Yeah, I know that."

Having reached at least some stance of temporary truce, I stopped. I didn't want to go into how I've always known she's been more than dubious about the subject of my book—if not quite as adamantly and openly negative as my mother, then with her own mostly silent Grace-like reservations. Bringing that up would only set things off.

Besides, I wanted the conversation to end as soon as possible; lies of omission are easier the less you talk. I knew how fragile our little truce was. I didn't want to take an axe to it by dropping in that I was headed to Vegas, let alone let on what I was headed here for.

I'm sitting across from her now. On the coffee table there's an overflowing ashtray and a tattered copy of *Glamour*. An empty can of Diet Pepsi. Out the window a battered vw bug in the driveway, its sides rusted and discolored as if with some disease.

It's taken me a while to get here. I got lost a couple times. The north side of Vegas, way past the line which used to officially segregate the town back in the old Jim Crow days and which still divides the town de facto. I keep thinking that I'm smelling weed, and I tell myself that's unfair. I don't even know her.

I remember Tommy said that her family came from way down south, somewhere in Chiapas. But that was long ago.

Already the day's beginning to heat up. We're way up in the hills, in a tiny rambler, just waiting for the developers to catch up and bulldoze all the riffraff away. The Strip, with its palatial hotels and monstrous multimillion-dollar shows, its whales and hoards of middle America taking a time out in our very own Gomorrah, sits simmering just a few miles back down the valley.

My body feels like it's still on the road, the asphalt vanishing behind me, miles and miles of desert. The ghost of my brother still wandering out there. I think I might have passed by him last night, still thinking I should have searched harder for him. But ten years ago I had told myself that it was too late for that. And yet here I am.

I can see the Indian in her cheekbones. Her face feels familiar, almost Asian, and yet there's something remote and untouchable in her beauty, as if you have to stare harder and longer to really encompass it. Not very tall, but there's a wiry tautness to her body, as if she's prepared for any sort of threat. She still looks young, I can't see the decade that's passed in her face. But then I've only met her once, and that for a couple of minutes in their apartment back in Oakland. She probably doesn't remember me at all.

Then again maybe she does. Admit it, Ben. That's what you're really afraid of.

Back in my twenties, just after I ditched grad school and first seemed close to finding my own way off the tracks, I worked at a nursing home as an orderly. I hated the work, hated the way the place smelled, the patients in various stages of dementia. The only appealing aspect was I didn't have to think, and after bashing my head about on my thesis and going nowhere for a couple years, it was a relief just to do what I was told to do. Simple physical tasks. Clean up the peach cobbler Mr. Jones spilled on the floor, empty Mrs. Warshowski's bedpan, change Mrs. McNulty's sheets.

There was old black man there, Mr. Clifton. He used to play the piano, quite beautifully, for the other patients. His hands were as large as Tatum's, though he didn't play like him. Mainly he did the old standards, Hoagy Carmichael, Cole Porter, that sort of stuff.

He could still play, but his mind was going. Very quickly. Some days he'd call me by someone else's name, as if he knew me. Others he'd ask if I could call a cab, so he could get to the Stardust—he was playing there that night. Someone told me the guy had actually once played in Vegas.

I thought of him as I drove here. I remember he looked a little like a black version of my father, only happier. I wondered if
my father had played an instrument, maybe things would have
been different for him.

That was before Mr. Clifton stabbed one of the other orderlies with a fork. It was something about a woman, but there was
some disagreement whether Mr. Clifton claimed the orderly
had taken his woman away or simply insulted her, called her
some name.

The next day I came upon him strapped to a wheelchair,
staring out the window. He looked more than a little drugged
up. He never played the piano again, whether out of punishment or because he had to be strapped down, I don't know.

I quit my job there soon after that. I remember wondering
if, after what happened with my thesis, I was establishing some
pattern.

In a family like ours, it's always hard to say when things
began to go off into space. There are too many moments, you
can't keep track of them all. I'm wondering if this visit with
Anna is another one of those.

She tells me that she and Tommy had broken up by the time he
went to Japan. She has some letters from him. Do I want them?
She goes into the bedroom. The other bedroom door's closed.

She hands me a small packet of letters held by a rubber
band. I think of Tommy's lost postcard from Japan, and I suddenly know it in my bones. He's not coming back. This is all of
him I'm going to find.

"I don't know why I kept them," she says. "Well, actually I do."

I want to ask her if she loved my brother, but I don't. I
remember Tommy talking about her on the phone. "I like this
girl, but I don't know if I love her. I know she's sweet on me."

Tommy told me she'd had a tough life, gotten married really young. "The bastard beat her. So did her father. So you see, I'm an improvement. Not that I'm giving myself any medals." She'd been a waitress. She probably still was. She still had her body, her looks, and Vegas sucked up girls like her as fast as it could use them and, after their looks ran out, spit them back out even quicker, like another sorry-ass boyfriend.

I put the pile of letters on the coffee table. I don't want to read them now. Or even later. Though I know I have to.

"He used to try talking to me about the work he was doing." She smiles. "Of course I didn't understand much of it. But I liked to hear him talk about it. And in a way, even though I didn't understand it, I sort of did. You know what I'm saying?"

"Yeah, actually I do. I never understood him either."

We sit there in silence, wondering. I'm thinking of the planetarium back in Chicago, that artificial plaster dome of a sky, the pinpricks of light shifting across the make-believe heavens, the constellations appearing and vanishing and appearing in their yearly path. I can't even begin to imagine what she's thinking.

She looks at me and nods to the closed door. "I suppose you want to ask me about Junior."

For a moment I can't quite process what she's saying, as if I'd already discounted that possibility.

My chest constricts. A wave of bad voices sweep over me, swirling out of my past, the loudest my brother, arguing with me the night he tried to punch out the moon, the shattered plate glass crashing through his yelps of "motherfucker, motherfucker . . ." The night I put away, along with what I saw half-hidden in a box on his bookshelf, an image that's stayed safely packed away for years. All I could make out was a brown tube of rubber, but I knew what the rest of the box held, I didn't have to look all the way in. It's coming back now, no matter how much I want to stop it.

"Yeah," I say, hoping my response has come quick enough. "I suppose that's why I'm here."

Back in Thebes and Athens, they denied funeral rites to those who killed themselves. In my worst moments, I've thought of my mother as one of that camp. But she was no Greek; she didn't possess that type of fury. In addition to denying a proper burial, they would also hack the hand from the arm that had accomplished the deed.

I sometimes think that I've done my own version of that.

Grace tells me that I've got survivor's guilt. She usually brings this up during our occasional discussions about therapy. I know she says this because it seems less accusatory, as if she wants to relieve me of something I don't have to carry around any longer. But of course that's not how I take it. There are so many things I've avoided carrying.

What was it like for my father those times he did go into the hospital? All I can muster is the image of him sitting and staring out the window, like Mr. Clifton, his face shorn of vibrancy, in a narcotic quiescence.

At the nursing home, I sometimes had to shave the patients. It always made me think of watching my father shave, and how he used to let me use the razor without a blade. How happy that made me.

I suppose that was another reason I quit.

She tells me that she doesn't know, for sure. She hasn't wanted to know. It's enough that the boy is hers and healthy. "And smart too. He's really smart." Then she stops as if she knows what I'm thinking, and I'm thinking too that I don't want to insult her—as if the kid's brains couldn't have come from her side or even from someone else.

"Does he . . ."

"Look like him? Well, you can see for yourself."

"I don't want you to wake him."

"Oh, he's not here—he's staying over at a friend's house. I was going to show you a picture."

"Oh yeah, sure." She goes into the bedroom again, and I'm thinking, what does a picture matter? There are scientific ways of going about these things; isn't that what Tommy, ever the believer in science, would have said? But then I think: Tommy gave up his rights in these matters a long time ago, even before he set out on his trek in the desert.

A dog starts barking somewhere over the fence out back. And then it starts howling like it's in some sort of pain, like it's being attacked, and I recall the coyotes that used to plague my mother's housing development in Arizona, occasionally picking off a stray cat or poodle. That night I howled back at them, walking alone through that alien landscape my mother had fled to.

Anna returns and hands me a photo.

I look down at it.

Instantly I know that I've seen this face before. He looks exactly like the kid I saw last March outside the Adler Planetarium back in Chicago, the day of my breakdown. I suddenly wonder if I'm losing it, the first inklings of psychosis or dementia seeping in.

Get a grip, Ohara, get a grip. I look down at the photo again.

Of course. The kid in Chicago was probably Filipino. Which equals Asian and Latino.

I look up at her, and she seems remarkably calm, as if she knows what I'm going to say.

"You knew it was his."

She gives a slight, almost imperceptible nod. A charge of pride on her face.

"So why did you tell me . . ."

"If you didn't see it—or if you didn't want to see it—I wasn't going to make you. I wasn't going to force you to recognize him. I don't need that. I've had enough of your family."

I can't think of what to say. Suddenly I start to cry.

The more I go over my past, scraping up memories and moments, the more often I feel like I can't remember much at all, that it's all—or the most crucial parts of it—slipped away. That I have no memories. It's like I'm someone other than who I'm supposed to be. Or that I've just woken up and found myself inside the life I'm living, and I've got to use what surrounds me to surmise what my past might be.

I do recall that back in college, after a night of partying, I'd have some mornings like that. But I never really got that much into partying. Like a lot of Asians, my body doesn't react that well to alcohol. No one ever drank much in my family. We had no problems like that. Nothing that clear. I'm told that in Japan that the *sarariiman* drink flagons of *shochu* and sake and walk through the streets late at night in Tokyo inebriated to their hearts' delight. And I know that in the early days of the *issei*, my grandparents' generation, the bachelor immigrants caroused at the end of their long hardworking weeks with Saturday nights at the bathhouses and bars and gambling dens, wasting away their hard-earned wages, sending their heads and stomachs tumbling into a sour and hungover Sunday morning.

Still, I never saw any such behavior growing up in Chicago among those in our family or other *nisei* families. No, if there was any drink we imbibed, it must have been a magic potion, the kind that lets you forget the past, that washes away not just its sins and sorrows but any particulars, any memories, places and people, stories and events, landscapes, weather, music, and smells. A long draught of forgetfulness drained to the dregs. So that there was no past, no childhoods, no family secrets, no looking back. Always the brightness and promise and plenty of the future, always the dreams of today for the imagined tomorrow.

I didn't know, of course, that we had drunk such a potion, that amnesia was our drug of choice (despite the heroin and others that Tommy took up). Perhaps if I could have kept imbibing that special *nisei* elixir of forgetting, I wouldn't have felt so lost all these years; I wouldn't have needed to ride into my own Western sunset like this. And whether it's been for fear or timidity, as Tommy often accused, or even from some inner strength I didn't know that I possessed, or just dumb luck, I couldn't take up my brother's way of forgetting. I've got my own karma to work out, whether I like it or not.

So, here I am, still trying to remember, to track down all that's eluded me. Or that I have eluded.

I ask a few questions. At first she's cautious, but soon she starts to open up. It's like she's been waiting for years to talk about him. For me to show up.

"Your brother used to say we're all made of stardust. You came to me out of a stellar wind, he'd tell me, blowing in from another galaxy. Oh, I knew that was bullshit, god knows I've heard my share of bullshit, but it didn't matter."

She pauses, as if she's remembering some moment between them.

"He had so many secrets I'm not surprised he didn't tell you about how it ended between us."

I can understand why my brother fell in love with her, though I would never have been attracted to anyone like her. Nor would I have approached anyone like her. Beyond my ken.

That night he smashed the window, after I left, she says he went on a tear. It didn't surprise her—she could see where they were going—but some part of her fought it anyway.

One night after he seemed to have gotten himself straight, they got into the car and started driving. He told her that they should go to Palm Springs for a few days. Or Vegas. They didn't have any money, but that didn't seem to bother him. He could lie so beautifully, she said. And sometimes you didn't even know it. He told her someone was going to wire some money. Maybe he was referring to me, she didn't know. She told my brother they'd agreed on what they were going to use the money for, but he didn't seem to want to listen to her. He just kept on saying they needed to get out of town, needed to make a fresh start.

After they drove a bit, they stopped at a gas station. He said that he had to make a phone call and went inside. After he came out, his mood seemed to have changed. She turned on the radio, and he told her to turn it off. Said he didn't want to listen to any of the crap she listened to. O.K., she said, you pick the station. I don't want to hear anything, he said. O.K., she said, why don't we talk. I don't want to talk. Then why are we driving? Where are we going? Just shut the fuck up, for once, will you? And so it went.

At one point he got off the highway. They were way up in the mountains. She wanted to ask where they were going, but she was afraid to make him angry. They were on a dirt road, and she wondered if he knew where they were. Then he stopped the car, and she thought he had to take a leak. After a while he called to her. She got out of the car and was suddenly scared. It was dark.

"He always had this edge about him. Like I didn't know what he'd do next."

I nod. Yeah, that sounded like Tommy.

And then, then he pointed up at the sky and started to outline the constellations for her. At first she couldn't make them out. They were just a bunch of stars, some brighter than others, some more clustered together. But there were so many, how could she pick out one from the other, how could she see where he was pointing? When she told him she couldn't see it, how could anyone see it, he got pissy with her and told her all these ancient people could see it, and she was just being lazy. But then he would calm down again, regaining his patience, and as she listened, he seemed to be talking in an almost childish voice, so eager with wonder, and she somehow got caught up in it, let it wash over her.

It was like, she says, I had to give up control to him, and then I could see it, what it was he was pointing out to me, and all these shapes and figures and creatures and beings started to appear, and she thought to herself that it was like being high, only they were both of them steadfastly sober, standing near the top of the mountain, looking up at the heavens, scrying like the ancients, who had all the time in the world.

But, she thought to herself, that's what we don't have. Time, time without end. We've got to make a decision, Tommy. Only she knew that she couldn't say that to him, that he knew that already.

At one point he said to her, "Why is there something rather than nothing? That's what's so amazing, Anna. Do you know if the forces of the universe, all those waves of energy out there and inside us, all the things that allow matter to come into being, were only slightly different, the whole universe would be inert? There'd be nothing, nothing happening."

"I had no idea what he was talking about. Somehow, though, I felt I understood. But I was such a stupid ass. I thought this was his way of telling me something. And it was. But he wasn't telling me what I thought he was telling me."

You and me both, Anna.

"You think you know someone, but you really don't."

She says when she was younger, her brothers used to get into fights, come home all messed up and bloody. It would drive her mother crazy. She'd rail at them, but it was no use. "I felt that way about Tommy. I could have spent a lifetime yelling at him but what good would it have done?"

It's like she is humming an old jazz tune, one I know. But no, the music is different and really isn't mine at all. Suddenly I feel I can see her face as it will be, years from now, wrinkled, ravaged, leather-tough. She is one of the survivors; she's not like her brothers. Or mine.

Sorry for your recent mishap. Thank you for your lovely story. The words spinning around in my head don't sound right, even to me. Tinny, off key. I feel sick from driving through the night, the veins in my forehead pumping some unbidden pain. And yet it's nothing compared to what she's been through. All the while she is telling me about my brother pointing up at the stars I can see that extinguished fire still burning in her face, the stellar dust. Winds out of space, out of nowhere, blowing through her, making her lighter and buoyant, despite all the time and shit that has flooded through her. Tommy. Tommy.

And beneath it all, trapped on this earthly plane, I see him with that strap of rubber around his bicep, pulling with his teeth, like a dog gnawing on one of its plastic playthings. Tapping the veins, a vivid blue delta on his forearm, letting them rise up and receive what momentary existence resided in the liquid sliding out the end of that needle. Nodding slowly then, as if in time to the beat, his own heart slowing. It is flashing before me now, everything I refused to see, though it was there before my eyes that night, bright as the full moon, swollen and heavy, and that plate glass he wanted to smash through, and all the while my thinking it was me he was smashing, as if I were that important, as if I mattered that much.

Of course. I was only his brother. I was trying to see some task through, some promise that I'd set out for myself back in childhood, when we were two boys whispering in that bedroom in Uptown, or listening to our parents argue, their voices coarse and angry and muffled down the hall. But we were boys back then, and I lost that point when he became a man—perhaps I never wanted to see it, what he'd become. Wanting always to have what he couldn't have. Going for broke. Hours of incense and smoke and junk years later, Anna knew him in this way and others I would never know. And if she didn't know him, neither did I. But we both loved him, and the contours of his missing form, and we were both here as he was not, and that I suppose says something about her (and perhaps even me).

Constellations above us, out of reach. Earth to Tommy. I miss you, bro. I really do.

It turns out that Tommy had lied to Anna, which wasn't surprising. They weren't going to Palm Springs or Vegas, but to the house of this guy he knew. Half-Chicano, half-Indian. His name was Martín. He had long hair, tied in a ponytail, not shaved like a cholo. He looked like a hoodlum, but when he and Tommy started talking, it was all about astrophysics, not anything she could follow, and after a while she fell asleep.

When she woke up, Tommy was gone. Martín told her to forget about him—he would drive her home. When she asked where Tommy had gone, Martín said it was better not to ask.

She realized then that she knew nothing about my brother. That Martín was right.

On the drive home, she wanted to ask again about Tommy but didn't. Martín said he worked at the observatory where Tommy had done his graduate work. Martín used to work for the military, and he and Tommy would talk about some of the things Martín had been working on, and Tommy would say that he already knew about all that, he'd been following those sorts of things for years.

"He's a bright kid," Martín said. "But we both know how messed up he is. He's trying to do the best by you. Really."

Don't bullshit me Martín, she told him. Yeah, he nodded. o.k. I'll just drive.

Later she got a postcard from Japan. From Tommy. Periodically he'd send her letters, and after the first couple letters, checks. Then after a while, nothing. But it didn't matter. Junior was a year old by then, and she had cleaned herself out, found Jesus. He was almost eleven now.

"Did Tommy ask about him?"

She shakes her head. I really don't want to say what I have to say next.

"Anna. I was the one who was supposed to send him the money."

I tell her that I was supposed to give it to him that night I visited. But after we had to go to the emergency room, I was too pissed at him. I wanted him to apologize, but of course he didn't. I wanted him to ask me again for the money, and when he didn't, I just forgot about it, like I wanted to forget about him. When he left the country, I said to myself that he must have figured out some other way, that things had been settled between him and Anna. Of course some part of me didn't want to find out different, and I excused myself by saying that when I called his old telephone number, it had been disconnected and she had obviously moved on.

"I suppose I could tell you I'm sorry. But that hardly makes up for it."

She doesn't say anything. For a long moment she looks down as if there is some book before her and she's engrossed in its pages. When she looks up at me, I can see something in her eyes I don't deserve, some tangled thread of knowledge that will never be untangled.

"Don't you see? That was meant to happen, Ben. That's the reason Junior's here. And he's the reason I had to save myself."

She pauses, then half as gentle afterthought, half as a spit in the dirt, "It would never have worked with Tommy around."

I keep wondering how I'm going to tell Grace about all this. When I first met her back in college, I didn't tell her much about my family. Only that my father had died several years before, and that my mom had remarried. I didn't know much about the No-No Boys back then, so we never talked about that. I can't remember when I actually told her that my father had committed suicide. But that's hardly surprising. I can't remember exactly when or how I proposed to her. I have a memory like a sieve.

But I do remember vividly when my boys were born. I'm not that lost. And in a way, this is another sort of birth, only a few years belated.

In the end I know what Grace's reaction will be. She couldn't have married into our scarred and enigmatic family without picking up a little *shoganai*. It can't be helped. Certainly that's the way I feel about all this, my trip out here, my meeting with Anna. I see now how I never understood the salt in that saying, the pride of the peasant, that endurance. How it resides in me, part of that inheritance that I was always trying not to claim.

There are those who go around proclaiming this country isn't what it once was. As if they really know what the past was. All I know is that there are histories that have never been told and some that will never be told (as a wise old Jew once wrote, history is the tale of the victors). So any speculation about what this country once was is just that. If not plain ignorance. And whatever we might say about history, the future will always be different.

I get in my rented Taurus, ready to light out on the road again. I fiddle with the radio, scanning for a channel that suits me. Nothing's there. I turn it off. I don't need any charging up; there's too much already running around in my head.

I drive down a street of Vegas dives, liquor stores, pawnbrokers, mom-and-pop slot clubs. Making my way to the freeway, I recall how Anna spoke of Tommy's friends. But they weren't really friends, just strangers he'd meet. In a pool hall. At the bar down the street. In places where he'd gotten his junk. She knew who and what they were the moment they walked into their apartment, knew the things they'd stolen and what they were going to steal. It was all too familiar. She'd had boyfriends like these friends, guys who'd take you to some rundown hotel or show up with a gash in their arm like someone had taken a meat cleaver and tried to see if it could make it all the way through.

I always told myself he wasn't like his friends, she said. She seemed to think a bit. He never beat me. And he was so funny sometimes. And so smart. And he didn't treat me like I was dumb just because I hadn't been to school like him. He was smarter than that. But so stupid, you know?

There were times, though, when he'd talk about things that made her wonder if he was going crazy. Like creating a suit that would make people invisible. Or drugs that would make you believe anything someone told you.

I told him there were already drugs like that, she said. He didn't think that was very funny.

Some nights, after she'd had a run of good tips, they'd go salsa dancing. That's when they were the happiest. It was then that he'd talk about leaving the country, seeing the world. Mexico City, Argentina. Benares. Macao. Japan.

"I thought it was all talk. Even about Japan. I mean, he always talked about moving out of Oakland, but we never even did that."

One night she walked in and found Tommy slumped over on the couch, drool running from his mouth. She tried shaking and slapping him. Nothing worked. She thought that he was never going to wake up. She wanted to call an ambulance, but he had warned her never to do that. Just let me sleep it off, he had said. I know what I'm doing.

"He didn't know what he was doing. I knew that. But I never thought it would come to that."

She sat there and watched him sleep. She thought of what he must have been like as a child, all that brilliance, all his charm waiting to be used. It made her furious, but there was nothing she could do.

That night at the restaurant, before she came home to find him like that, she'd met someone from the old neighborhood, someone who used to run with her brothers. He'd just gotten out of the pen. He said he was trying to set himself straight. She wanted to believe him. One of her brothers was in the same prison. She'd go to visit him a couple times a year. The others were scattered all over now, like they'd been caught up in some tornado like Dorothy and had landed in their various versions of Oz, still looking for a way home.

She served the man eggs with chorizo, breakfast food. He said that in prison his sense of time had gotten all messed up.

And yet every day it was the same schedule, the same routine, the same meals, nothing changed. Now at least he could eat breakfast whenever he wanted.

She was just beginning to show then, but the man didn't ask her. Perhaps he didn't notice. He was older than her and looked even older than that, and she knew even with the weight that she still looked good. He left her a good tip. She never saw him again. He was one of her own, but he was from another life, one that she'd cast off in order to survive. Perhaps it was time again to move on.

She took the bus home and nodded off. She almost missed her stop. There was a cat on the stoop of their apartment. It had been lounging there for days and she wondered whose it was. It came up to her and nuzzled her ankle, and she wanted to pick him up but knew what would happen if she did.

When Tommy finally woke, she wasn't relieved, only tired. Too tired to get angry or say a thing. He got up and went to the bathroom. Then he went to the bedroom. A minute later she could hear him snoring.

On the coffee table lay one of his books. She picked it up. The language was difficult, and she worked to make out what it was saying. It seemed to be something about the origins of the universe, the moment when matter, all the elements, began to burn off from that original uniform mass, a speck so tiny, so very tiny, that started it all. That's what surprised her, how small, how infinitetessimal it all once was. And out of that tiny, tiny dot all the universe exploded.

She looked at me then with eyes so clear and deep and dark that they seemed all pupil, as if trying to stare into the darkest of corners.

"I don't know exactly when I decided," she said. "I just did."

Before I left I asked her if I could see Junior. Maybe next time, she said.

"I have some things I have to tell him. I need to prepare him."

I must have made a face.

"Christ. You can't just come waltzing in here like this and expect things."

"I wasn't expecting anything, Anna."

She seemed to be holding herself back, as if she knew better. "Listen. I know what it's like to come from a fucked-up family. I don't want that to happen to Junior. I'm sorry. That's just the way I feel."

I couldn't argue with her there. I wasn't even going to try. Sure, I said. Next time.

From notebook No. 11, *Famous Suicides of the Japanese Empire:*

Say you're in early twentieth-century Nippon, and you plan to kill the emperor to free the Japanese people from feudal tyranny. You know you'll most likely be killed for doing so, but it must be done. Later you write in your journal random thoughts, stray lines of verse:

—The evening crow. It keeps solitary watch over the rain clouds floating slowly across the big sky.

—Autumn afternoon. In the hollow of the cherry tree, two tiny frogs are having fun.

—I remember when I said, "I'm going to end my life at twenty-two," and cut the strings of the violin and wept.

—You and I. We go to our graves feeling as if our hearts are separated east and west by the sea.

—The cherry petals fall on the stone-covered path of the Daihikaku Temple. And the temple bell peals.

Say you write these lines after your plot to kill the emperor has been discovered, after you have been sentenced to hang from the gallows. Certainly these lines can be read as a suicide poem.

The woman who did write these lines was Sugako Kanno, a socialist—or anarchist—of the Meiji era (1881–1911). At fifteen she was raped by a miner, a trauma that left her with a lasting sense of shame and guilt. Later she read an essay by the socialist Sakai Toshihiko, who advised rape victims not to let their feelings of guilt burden them. She sought more writings by Sakai and eventually joined his small circle of Japanese socialists.

Kanno went on to become an early champion of Japanese women's rights and lived, within the context of Japan, a rather bohemian existence, fleeing from a marriage, living with lovers, writing editorials and essays for a newspaper and political pamphlets—"Women in Japan are in a state of slavery. Japan has become an advanced, civilized nation, but we women are still denied our freedom by an invisible iron fence . . ." "There are these leeches: The emperor, the rich, the big landowners. They suck the people's blood . . . The big boss of the current government, the emperor, is not the son of the gods, as teachers have misled you to believe. The ancestor of the present emperor came out of the corner of Kyushu and killed and robbed people . . ." (Or, as the saying goes, behind all great wealth is an enormous crime; some criminals just hide that crime better than others.)

To most now, Sugako Kanno's words seem quite reasonable. But she was obviously too far ahead of her time. And she did not merely write against the emperor—she helped hatch a plan to assassinate him. Call her a terrorist then. But a suicide terrorist? It depends upon how you look at it.

At any rate, like the suicide bombers, she did die in peace, believing in heaven. Not a heaven of the afterlife with a hundred virgin lovers (what woman would want that?). Not even a heaven where her soul would dwell with her friends and fellow believers. No, this heaven was on earth, in the future:

I am convinced our sacrifice is not in vain. It will bear fruit in the future. I am confident that because I firmly believe my death will serve a valuable purpose. I will be able to maintain my self-respect until the last moment on the scaffold. I will be enveloped in the marvelously comforting thought that I am sacrificing myself for the cause. I believe I will be able to die a noble death without fear or anguish.

Say the temple bells, say the autumn afternoon. Say two tiny frogs behind the cherry tree are having fun. Two tiny frogs. Some forgotten image out of my past.

Often I've tried to convince myself that my father, like Sugako Kanno, was simply ahead of his time. The other day, in the museum library, looking over the documents on the Heart Mountain Fair Play Committee, I could almost believe that. In a new untitled notebook, as if already abandoning my original long-delayed thesis, I wrote this down:

"We, the members of the FPC, are not afraid to go to war—we are not afraid to risk our lives for our country. We would gladly sacrifice our lives to protect and uphold the principles and ideals of our country as set forth in the Constitution and the Bill of Rights, for on its inviolability depends the freedom, liberty, justice, and protection of all people including Japanese Americans and all other minority groups. But, have we been given such freedom, such liberty, such justice, such protection? No!! Without any hearings, without due process of law as guaranteed by the Constitution and Bill of Rights, without any charges filed against us, without any evidence of wrong doing on our part, one hundred and ten thousand innocent people were kicked out of their homes, literally uprooted from where they have lived for the greater part of their life, and herded like dangerous criminals into

concentration camps with barbed wire fence and military police guarding, AND THEN, WITHOUT RECTIFICATION OF THE INJUSTICES COMMITTED AGAINST US AND WITHOUT RESTORATION OF OUR RIGHTS AS GUARANTEED BY THE CONSTITUTION WE ARE ORDERED TO JOIN THE ARMY THRU <u>DISCRIMINATORY PROCEDURES</u> INTO <u>A SEGREGATED</u> COMBAT UNIT! Is that the American Way? <u>No!</u>"

All my life I wanted our father to be a hero. Perhaps he was.

And yet if history could be read as clearly as the capitals of the Fair Play Committee's declaration, there would be no need for historians or our constant looks backward, re-evaluating the past. Then too my father did not see himself as a hero (though perhaps some of his group did, for there were those who referred to themselves as the forty-seven *ronin,* as if taking up their own American *Chushingura).* In the end, even now, I know the world still isn't prepared for either the proclamations of Kanno Sugako or the No-No answer of my father; the emperor's still in his place and my father in his obscurity, and who believes the American public would not still celebrate the soldiers who upheld and uphold their marching orders over any resisters, no matter what those resisters might be making their stance against—whether it be the unjustness of some war or the treatment of their community back home.

Still, that's not the whole picture. After all, this wasn't just some made-up yellow-sheeted war of imperialism, some "Remember the Maine," or a second team effort of colonial expansion, driven by the fear of commies and dominoes run amok—no, this was the real thing, the closest to a just war in the whole century; this was the conflagration against genocidal Nazis and the rapers of Nanking, purveyors of fascist, racist ideologies with world domination as their goal; this was the war fought by the greatest generation, as Tom Brokaw would have it, against the greatest of evils. So, who were they, these *nisei* resisters, to put all the free world at risk, to question the efforts of Roosevelt and Churchill? Hell, even old Joe Stalin saw what sort of menace that mad mustachioed German presented (though it did take a certain double-cross to get the message into his thick Georgian skull).

No, you've got to look at the larger picture, what was at stake, the wartime hysteria and very real fears, to understand why any wrench thrown into the war machinery simply could not be permitted. In a time like that, so the reasoning runs, the fate of the nation goes before that of the individual, and some of these individuals, like some of the *kibei—nisei* who'd been sent to school in Japan—didn't even see themselves on the side of the nation, so why even trudge through the wasted motion of trying to separate the bad apples from the good patriots when they all looked from the outside like bad apples? Why take that risk? They'd been given their chance to take a side, and they'd done it, sealed their own fates by shouting back, No-No. No one forced them to answer this way; they did it of their own volition. During a time of war, they should have known what their fate would be and that it would most likely include prison. And given the various punishments and sufferings taking place throughout the globe at that time, including the likes of Belsen and Auschwitz, the absence of a fair trial or an eventually suspended sentence in a federal penitentiary could hardly be seen as anything more than a slight inconvenience. Or so one might argue. At least the No-No Boys survived the war, which you cannot say about hundreds of *nisei* from the 442nd.

But this overarching argument of necessity, however much I might rise up instinctively against it, doesn't really confound me. I've heard such reasoning before; I know the sophistry there on both sides, the politics of power and the politics of the sub-altern, each of course to be divided and complicated as any good historian must. No, it's not these larger questions and arguments that take me to task and unsettle me; it's the smaller and more personal ones, the ones that derive from considering not the fate of millions, but of one specific individual.

For Takeshi Ohara wasn't simply a No-No Boy. He wasn't an abstract argument on the merits of civil disobedience during a time of war. He was my father, so enigmatic in that role that to this day I cannot adequately explain why or how—or even if—his stance against the loyalty questionnaire affected my childhood, our family, or his solitude among us, who loved him and missed him long after he was gone. Did he carry with him a sense of shame, that emotion so tied to our conceptions of what is Japanese? (But he was not Japanese, he was Japanese American.) Perhaps, but from where did that shame derive? From the reaction of those of his community, the veterans and the JACL who saw him and others like him as traitors to America and to their fellow Japanese Americans, who wished to show themselves as patriotic or even more patriotic than the whitest of whites? Or did he even care how his fellow *Nikkeijin* felt and thought? Was his sense of shame something deeper and more personal, buried in his past before the war, in the complications of his family life and all that he rarely spoke of to me? Or did it have to do with the reactions of his wife or his sons?

More particularly, what of his older son who so loved America, who so wanted to invent for himself a glorious patriotic past, that he could not even imagine his father might be something else? A boy who could never even entertain the possibility that his father might have made some other decision than to fight, to stand with his uncles, in that most decorated unit in all of Europe, a group of heroes to march with the likes of Sergeant Saunders or John Wayne or Sergeant Rock, all the warrior icons of my childhood? Impelled by my own irrepressible urges to see myself as the All-American boy of boys, how often had I spouted off the deeds of real and fictitious G.I.s, playing war, pestering my uncle Elbert and recounting his stories to my father, turning the channel to *Combat* and *The Lieutenant* or the movies where some John Wayne or Robert Mitchum storms the sands of Iwo Jima or the beach at Normandy? And in that fervent worship of patriotic warriors, in my compulsion to recite the glories of battle and dying for the stars and stripes, how much had I myself contributed to my father's sense that he had somehow failed, that he had made the exact wrong decision at a time when his whole future and that of his unimagined family, his wife and sons, lay before him, asking him to become the hero they would want him to be? And if so, what of those fellow Japanese Americans, who may or may not have always directly shunned him but still left him knowing he had broken the pact they had made with America and so was no longer one of them and would never be again? Could it be that those who knew at least what the No-No stood for in his past and experienced the Kafkaesque contradictions of the camps, were not his most powerful and truest tormentors? For wouldn't it have hurt even more to confront in his own living room this unquestioning flag-saluting boy? This boy, who knew none of his past, who knew none of the factors behind that loyalty oath or his response to them, a boy of his own flesh and blood who, as most boys do to a father who is neither violent nor abusive but loving and gentle and understanding, looked up to him and saw him as a hero—to know that such a boy, his son, would have been ashamed of him, would have revolted from him, if he had known the truth about his father, if he had known what his father had done during the war, wouldn't *that* have been my father's greatest shame?

Wouldn't that have sealed in his mind whatever sentence he had been given by the government or whatever shunning he experienced from his own community? Wouldn't that have said to him that he should keep his status as an isolatto, he should not speak about his past, he should remain encased in the silence that was his proper and just prison, for all he had done? And why have I never seen this all before? How have I been so blind?

Please forgive me, Father. Decades too late.

After I return from Anna's, I brood about my brother, about my father and my mother, all the unresolved ghosts of my past. I write in my notebook, exploring the myriad indirect and crooked paths through which I've arrived here, alone in a Vegas motel, letting the knowledge of Anna's revelation and my visions and versions of my father settle into my bones. A deep exhaustion tumbles upon me, and I lay back on the bed, staring at the plaster ceiling before sleep overwhelms me, like a powerful wave.

Waking I feel relieved and unnerved, resolved and jazzed, as if my journey still isn't finished. What should I do next? Head back to LA and continue my research? Return home? Stay in Sin City, diving within its whirling waters, gambling and giving in like Odysseus to the call of the sirens?

At a certain point I pick up again the documents and articles I've had copied from the Japanese American National Museum archives. I bought a couple books from the museum store, and I browse through them too. I don't exactly know what I'm looking for. Something's nagging at me, some sense that I haven't put another part of the puzzle back together quite right.

And then glancing at one of the articles, I see it. Almost all the No-No Boys were sent to the Tule Lake internment camp by 1943; some were repatriated to Japan, some simply kept there or shipped to "punishment" camps. But the No-No Boys weren't sent to prison like my father (as my mother belatedly informed me in her letter just before her death). And though the No-No Boys had refused to serve in the armed forces on the loyalty oah, Japanese Americans weren't being drafted at that time. Then in 1944 the draft for Japanese Americans was reinstated. Uncle Sam needed the troops and it didn't matter if they came from those the government had put behind barbed wires. It was the draft resistors like those of the Fair Play Committee at Heart Mountain who were sent to federal prison, and Heart Mountain was where my dad had been interned.

So was my father technically a No-No Boy? Perhaps my mother's reference to prison in her letter was to Tule Lake or some other special detention camp. Then again my father turned eighteen in 1944; he wouldn't have had to sign the loyalty oath until that time, so that was the reason he wasn't sent to Tule Lake. Or maybe he was a draft resister. Maybe, after the war, others in the community regarded his draft resistance and imprisonment as akin to the stance of the No-No Boys. Certainly that's what many JACL-ers believed. But what did my father and my mother think? Particularly for my mother—No-No Boys, draft resisters, it might have all seemed the same to her. What exactly did my father tell her about his past? How much did she want to know? Were there lies or omissions or conflations between them? Or with those around them? Or both?

All the questions I still don't have answers to. And may never answer. But that's no reason to stop asking them.

Double down. Go for broke.

Tonight, on the road out of Vegas, it's his voice I hear, louder than I've heard him in a long time. As if he knows where I'm headed. Or maybe it's up to me to fill in the stories, all he never told me, all he could not say. The words bring with them images or rather the ghosts of images, as if on an old Zenith, catching stations from another time zone.

There's this scene I keep going back to, boichan. *Of forty-seven young men, standing in a room in winter. Forty-seven who've decided to say "No." Some sport a* hachimaki *roped round their foreheads. Some have shaved their heads. Wind whistles through the cracks of the barracks. Their breaths, little exhalations of steam, puffing in the cold.*

What were we doing there? Were we there to say no, to say that things had gone far enough? To lodge a legal protest? Or were we merely there to take revenge against the JACL, the inu, *the traitors, the dogs? Those who called us traitors, who accused us of thinking of nothing but ourselves.*

"Kill the sons of bitches," said Jimmy Fujita. "Let's get rid of them. Goddamnit, when I saw those MPs haul away Omori-san, I wanted to jump on them and rip their guts out. And I would have done it too, if all those families weren't there."

A couple weeks before, some of the guys had caught a JACL-er in this little alley between the last two barracks. He had to be hospitalized. The camp authorities came down on us hard. They began shipping guys out of the camps, and they arrested one of the cooks, who'd been mouthing off to the authorities for some time.

Jimmy said worrying about getting hurt had gotten us nowhere. That was JACL garbage. "So what should we do? Nothing? We're just sitting here. Like lambs to the slaughter," muttered Jimmy. "Like lambs to the slaughter."

"Jimmy's right," said Hiyama. He wrote our camp newsletter. Or did until the authorities closed it down. "They've made it so we can't even speak to our own people."

"They kept Omori-san locked up for a week," said Jimmy. "Wouldn't let his wife or any of his family see him. And then they simply shipped him out. No explanation, no reason, nothing."

"*You know the reason,*" *I said, jumping in.* "*It was his speeches. People were listening.*"

"*And what about Nishimura?*" *said Jimmy.* "*They dragged him in for questioning.*"

They kept asking Nish to name the members of our group, kept hinting that there were consequences that he'd want to avoid. They kept reminding him what had happened to Omori-san. You don't want to leave your family all alone, do you? they told him.

Hiyama swiped a match against the wall, lit a cigarette. "*Yeah, then there's Izu. Izu won't talk to any of us now. He's scared shitless.*"

Boichan. *It was so much easier to turn on those around us, on the ones who looked like us, who shared our fate. It was like our own civil war, right there in the camps. Some to one side, some to the other. Some sided with the government, no matter what the government had done to us. Some, like me, said no, we won't, we can't join in the fight against our country's enemies. As much as we'd like to. Someone has to stick up for our rights . . .*

They sent the ones who weren't married to the penitentiary at McNeil Island. Up in Puget Sound. Not much happened there. The Big House was large and cavernous and depressing. Rows of cells, stacked cages. Somebody from Seattle observed that two years before they'd shipped him out of the area because he was so dangerous, and now they'd shipped him right back. There was a guy there who tried to fight the camps in the courts. He told me how he'd walked into a police station in Portland and demanded that they arrest him for violating the curfew for nihonjin *. . .*

We weren't paroled until more than a year after the camps closed and the war ended. I guess the government finally figured that there was no use in keeping us.

No, the government no longer saw the need to fear or hate us. Not like some of the veterans or the JACL-ers . . . It changed me, prison, though I don't exactly know how. Mostly I tried not to think about it. It wasn't something anyone wanted to talk about, including myself. I suppose that's why I never mentioned it to you. I don't think it would have made much difference if I had, do you?

No, you've been judged enough, Father. If nothing else is clear, that is.

The scene has shifted now. We're in Chicago, the lake endless as an ocean, stretching its blue out to the horizon, waves smacking against the giant blocks of concrete that form the shore. Only I'm not there. Or rather I seem to be incredibly tiny, almost the size of an insect, looking up at the looming giants whom I know are my father and mother. Two silhouettes against a backdrop of water and sky and clouds. A voice faintly singing, growing louder and louder. And the tiredness in my body deeper now, unsettling.

There is so much there, too much to tell. And what comes to my mind is something that might seem odd to you: she had such a beautiful voice. A truly beautiful voice. I recall the first time I heard it. We were walking along Lake Michigan, the waves lapping in on a windy spring evening. She wore this white polka-dot dress that brushed her legs, and she skipped along the stone walk and twirled and broke into a Broadway show tune, "Oh What a Beautiful Morning." I couldn't believe such a powerful voice could soar out of such a slight body. I could have listened to her the whole night.

But it wasn't just show tunes. She had studied lieder by Schubert and Schumann and Brahms, a whole classical repertoire. When she first sang one of those to me, it felt even stranger and more wondrous. The notes sailed through the air as if buoyed by the breeze, a clear contralto colored by the waves and the white clouds heaped on the horizon and the sun setting behind us and the sky blue and pure like the timbre of her voice. I heard beauty there, and sorrow, and I saw she was showing something of herself to me, and

I knew I should treasure not just that moment but what she was showing me.

So how could I sully it, how could I tell her what I had been thinking of telling her, coming clear at last with what I had done, who I had been, where I had fled from? No, that would come later, too late.

Soon after that, her mother died. Of throat cancer. A gruesome horrible death, the tissues in her esophagus growing blacker and blacker, choking off her wind, racking her with coughing fits, making it difficult for her swallow. She visited her mother daily until she died. Sometimes her mother broke into hacking coughs, seizures struggling to clear her throat, gasping for breath.

Of all her daughters, her mother turned to her most. At the end her mother grew more and more irrational and started speaking more and more in Japanese. Weeping for her son killed in the war, cursing in ways neither her husband nor father or anyone in the family could stomach or even believe they were hearing, and still her mother called for her, and she had to go, and stand there and listen. It was like listening to the wailing of a demon in one of those Noh plays. And then her mother began to speak of her fears during the war, fears for those she had left behind in Japan, fears of the guards and the rifle towers, fears for her boy who had entered the service, fears of being imprisoned forever in the desert. And her daughter would try vainly to calm her, to ease that voice, to bring it back to the present and to life, all the while knowing she would fail.

You can see all this in her expression in the funeral photo. It's not just the somber grief in her gaze but the icy placid cast to her face, not peaceful but not bearing any emotion at all. It's no longer a girl's face. That girl singing that night on the pier jutting out into the wild of Lake Michigan, she's gone, vanished.

She never sang much after that. She quit her music classes. She took classes in bookkeeping and shorthand, practical things. When I asked her about it, she said she needed to prepare herself for a job, not some pie-in-the-sky dream. What about her talent? I asked. She said she had no illusions about her talent. She had a pretty voice but what did it matter when pretty hakujin *voices were a dime a dozen.*

When I finally told her about who I was, how I had refused to serve, she accepted it. Accepted it the way she accepted her mother's death. Shoganai—*it can't be helped.*

But I don't think, no, I know she never saw it through my eyes, what I had done, what I believed about our country or the words we had been taught in school. How could she? She was so young in camp, all the arguing among the grown-ups passed her over. And of course I didn't want to go into it much. The war, the camps, the loyalty oath, my imprisonment, they were all in the past. We were starting a new life.

I know now, boichan, *I should not have left you. Or Tommy. Or your mother. That my real shame was not in answering No. But instead in not also answering Yes, Yes, Yes. To all of you.*

But you know that.

The voice is fainter now and I'm falling back asleep. I'm in our old apartment in Uptown, listening to him at my bedside. My eyes closed, hearing him as he sits on my bed, that nightly ritual, a voice in the dark, almost without a body. A ghostly presence, lulling me, but never quite taking away the pain.

So tell the story. Tell it to your sons. Let it be passed down from generation to generation, like Momotaro, like Issunboshi, like Popeye or the Incredible Shrinking Man. Like Chushingura.

Yes, Father, I will.

It's not an easy place to get to, tucked up in the northwest quadrant of the state. Cody was the last town whose name I recognized. In the early morning sun, the macadam looks black as oil, threading out in the distance. Flat, flat land. Wisps of clouds brushed on a vaulting blue sky, some failed attempt to break the monotony, to scale down the immense emptiness. Now and then a few clumps of cattle, black hunks of fur and flesh. The day's heating up. Nothing but static on the radio. I get the feeling that if I keep driving in this direction, I could slip right off the end of the world, swallowed by the continent, as if I never existed. I pass by what might be elk. Or antelope. So here I am, home on the range, like I once dreamed of as a boy. I'm sure Grace would think that I've finally lost it.

I ease off the two-lane and down a greasy drive of gravel and into the parking lot of a Conoco. There's a trailer home at the edge of the lot. Beyond it a pair of grain elevators, like thick twin smokestacks of some sunken ocean liner. Giant sentinels. A surreal feeling. I've been driving all night, and I've got that slanty dizziness I get when I haven't slept enough. I grab a couple doughnuts, a cup of coffee, and a Mountain Dew, sugar and caffeine jolts for the last turn of the trek. Dentyne for the sour taste in my mouth, not that I'm going to be kissing anyone anytime soon.

The woman at the counter is wider than me, with hair bleached into some awful artificial aubergine. A face lined with smoker's wrinkles. She could be anywhere within twenty years of my age. Eyelashes as thick with mascara as you get without being false. She looks at me as if she knows me. It's not quite a smile, just a sly recognition. Before I can say a thing, she names my destination.

"We don't get as many of you around here as we used to."

For a second I wonder if she's referring back to the war years, but of course she's not.

"Where you from?"

"Chicago."

"You're a long way from home."

She doesn't pursue the usual follow up question: No, where are you really from?

"Actually I drove up here from Vegas." I tell her I've always wanted to see this part of the country. Where the real cowboys come from.

She laughs. "Real cowboys? There hasn't been a real cowboy around here for a hundred years. You're as likely to find a real cowboy out here as you are to find a real Indian. I mean, look at me. What do you think I am?"

She looks to me generically white. Not pure Aryan but even Eva Braun was a little dark.

"I've got some Native blood in me. Crow mostly. Maybe a little Cherokee. You never know what went on back then."

I wait for her to take my goods and total them up. She just stands there, like she's the one waiting for me to do the tab.

"You don't know where you are, do you?"

"Isn't this Rowel?"

"Sure it is, but that's not what I'm talking about."

I'm beginning to wonder if she's all there in the head. I really just want to get my doughnuts and coffee and go out into my car and enjoy my half-assed breakfast.

"Look, I'm kind of in a hurry."

"No, you're not. You ain't got but a forty-five minute drive left, and it's only what, nine o'clock? You got all day."

"Really, I'm on a tight schedule," I tell her. "I've got to be in Chicago by tomorrow." Yeah, tomorrow. Just in time for Kengo's school play.

She just stares at me, like she's appraising some piece of lawn furniture. "You know you don't look like the usual visitors of your kind."

"Well, we don't all look alike."

"That's what I'm telling you. You look different. A little slicker."

She smiles. I've sometimes been told I look a little like Beat Takeshi, but she's probably not familiar with Yakuza films and Beat's sleepy-eyed gaze or lumbering bear-like gait.

"Course you look the same, too," she adds.

"And how's that?"

"Like you're still trying to figure out if you really want to see it."

I think about this. "I can't imagine there's much there to see anymore."

She gives a small laugh and points her finger at me. "Now that's just what I'm talking about, enit."

She rings up my meager provisions. I feel like she's laughing at me. Look, ma'am, I want to say, I don't mean to be impolite, but you don't know a thing about me. I just came in here to buy a few doughnuts and some coffee. And I want to get out as soon as possible because, well, this really isn't a place someone like me should be, even now, much less fifty-five years ago. I just want to get there without running into some skinheads or good old boys who might flail my ass and leave it hanging somewhere out on a fence in the middle of the prairie, like some rabbit on a gibbet. Scared? You bet I am. And you'd know that too, if that Indian blood you claim runs in your veins actually showed up somewhere in your face as something other than a paleness that matches the neon bulb back in your men's room. You don't know a thing about my fears.

She sacks my purchases and fists them over.

"Sure, honey," she says as if there's been no break in the conversation. "I may look white on the outside, but that don't matter. Sometimes you got to take on the skin of your enemy. Like the way the old ones used to put on buffalo skins to hunt."

I stare at her. Suddenly I'm feeling the long drive and the night miles, and my skull's a bit woozy. Like a running back who's just been helped to the sidelines. I shake my head, then my shoulders, trying to knock the grogginess out.

I glance at my cup. As I lift it to my lips, I look at her face and see it now, what she's talking about. A wonder I didn't see it before. The coffee burns my tongue, better than I'd have a right to expect in a place like this.

"Thank you, ma'am. Hope you have a good one."

"You too," she says.

Back in the car, I take a bite of a bear claw, wash it down. That old Indian warrior saying pops into my head. Yes, it's a good day to die.

A pickup truck squeals across the gravel and comes to a halt. Four guys pour out, each bigger than the other. Two with base-ball caps, all in jeans, two in T-shirts and one with a plaid work shirt with the sleeves ripped off at the shoulder. Various tattoos. The bulkiest is built a little like Ray Nitschke, the same bald dome as the old Packer's middle linebacker. He notices me munching away in my car and gives a stone stare like there's a prison yard between us. Fresh meat. He nudges one of his friends and says something, and the friend laughs. But the other two are already in the Conoco, and they move to join them, though Ray keeps on staring at me, all the way to the door.

I eat the second doughnut more slowly, savoring the glaze. Sip the coffee with smaller sips, making it last. I catch the smell of grain in the air, filtered through the reek of gas and oil. Dandelion puffs float by, like bobbing bubbles. A car whizzes past. Another. I'm thinking of that game where Gayle Sayers scatted for six touchdowns, and I'm trying to recall if that was against the Packers or not. Probably not. Old Ray wouldn't let that happen.

New Ray comes out of the Conoco bearing a six-pack in both fists, his buddies armed in the same way. New Ray sees that I'm still there, and he stops. He's still staring, and I stare back and nod my head. He starts walking toward me. His friends look at him like, what the hell?

He's a few paces from the car now.

I'm telling myself this is stupid. I look him straight in the eyes. No, Ray, I'm not turning back.

"What you lookin' at, chink?"

I don't answer.

"I said, what the fuck you lookin' at?"

He stands there like he's waiting for me to get out of the car. His friends start to amble over. To help or to hinder I don't know. "Come on, Bill," one of them says, but Bill doesn't seem to hear him.

"You scared to get out of the car?"

Damn right, I think. I count to three, each breath, like a quick individual meditation. I find myself opening the car door. I step toward him and stop. He drops his six packs. One of the cans fizzles open, hissing like it's suddenly come alive.

When he swings I duck and he lurches forward, his breath radiating a beery stench. I start bobbing from side to side, and the fact that he's already drunk is about all I've got going for me.

Another roundhouse and I jump back. "Come on, you chink," he mutters, "stand and fight." I hear his friends shouting—at him or me, I can't tell. His next punch smacks my arm, a glancing blow, but it hurts. Drunk or not, his right's got some power. The longer this goes, the more chance he'll catch me with a bomb. I can only rope-a-dope so long. And what happens if his friends jump in . . .

He swings again, and as my forearm blocks his blow, I see his shin almost before my foot cracks it like a toothpick. He howls and bends to attend to the pain, and my uppercut plunges his solar plexus, soft and cheesy, and I hear the breath pop out of him. One rabbit punch to his neck spills him to the ground. I'm about to kick in his sotted face when something stops me. I look up at his friends, huddled about us now, and I wonder if one or all of them are going to step forward to take his place. The adrenalin's roaring through me like a race car, around and around and around.

"Jesus Christ, Bill. What the hell you doing?" He says it in a way that I know that this has happened before.

"Just let him lie there," another buddy says. "Serves him right."

"We can't do that. It's his car."

"Christ. Jesus fuckin' Christ."

They're standing over him as he moans a little and lies there in the dust. I keep waiting for them to turn to me, but it's as if I'm wearing an invisible cloak. They don't even see me. Or maybe they're taking me for some kung-fu kick-ass monk, as if, for once, the old stereotypes are looking out for me.

I don't wait around for them to think up some other response. I slip into my car and drive off. In the rearview they're helping him up, like a player who's been injured, but the din in my head isn't some hometown good sportsmanship, giving the opponent his due. I know I'm the lucky one. I should be the one lying there in the dirt.

It takes me a while to recall where I last used that maneuver. Some things, I guess, you never forget.

It looks just like I've imagined it, and yet it doesn't. The mountain jutting up in the distance is actually purple, like in the song, an odd outcropping of limestone amid miles and miles of flat prairie. Acres of dry wild grasses, halfway to straw. A patch of black-eyed Susans along the dirt road. Forget-me-nots and goldenrod. A tree here and there, barely scraping the horizon line. I'm not surprised there are only a couple buildings left, both tarpapered and boarded up, one with a huge brick chimney. Have they been remodeled? Mostly there are scattered blocks of stone and remnants of foundations. Our own *Nikkeijin* Stonehenge. Railroad tracks where they got off in the middle of nowhere, wondering where they were and what was going to happen to them. The barbed wire fences and rifle towers are gone. Were they torn down, or did they simply dissolve on their own?

I feel like I'm all alone (I am). Like I've survived some great vanishing, a figure like Ishii, the last of his tribe. There's no one in sight. Who'd come to a place like this? And yet there are these various signs, outlining what was here, telling visitors to recall this "tragedy" and warning of the need to practice "tolerance."

Tolerance, hell. They'd do it again if they wanted—it's still constitutional, still on the books, the good godly Supremes never completely ruled against it, refusing to knot up the legal loopholes. The powers that be have their laws, and we get these cheap placards. Some bomb or something else really scary goes down, they'll be ramping up for the next roundup, Jap *keiretsu*, Arab terrorists, Chinese spies, all those dark hordes streaming up from south of the Rio Grande.

At the center there's a flag and a large sign, with the heading "Honor Roll." It lists the names of all the soldiers from the camp who "gave their life for their country." Despite being imprisoned, despite being denied their rights as citizens. The heroes of my childhood, back when I wanted to be a soldier, when I dreamed of killing Gerries and Japs, just like Sergeant Saunders or my uncle Elbert.

Of course there's nothing here about the No-No Boys, black sheep to the end. As if their double negative rendered them invisible, forgotten, an errant stain that needed to be erased. Nor is there mention of the Fair Play Committee, the draft resisters and their dual incarceration.

But who did the erasing? And why? Perhaps that's a question I can answer. After all, I am a historian.

Then again, I know who did the erasing. It was me.

I glance back at the sign at the entrance. Heart Mountain. Once there were almost fourteen thousand here, among them my father. And I don't know what it all means or what part of me belongs here. I don't exactly know why I've come here. And yet it seems strange that I haven't been here before.

I've fought against them for so long and have never seen how much stronger that's made me. I've never seen how I've managed to go on, despite it all.

I'm like a dog or a coyote, trying to sniff out some prey or danger, hidden in the brush. A rabbit scurries out from my feet and darts away, rattling my nerves. But who is the intruder here? Who's the one trespassing, so far from home?

This is it, the heart of a ghost town. Or the Twilight Zone, as Tommy might have put it, laughing his ass off at me.

Yeah, bro. The one who survives, he's the one who tells the tale.

Suddenly I rear back and let out a howl. It flows from my chest, up through my throat and out my mouth like a great exhalation of all that's inside me, all that needs to come out and yet will always be there. I think of those Buddhist monks my father once told me about, chanting sutras for the dead, and how I really need to say good-bye to my brother. (Oh, I could say it was my mom who never wanted a funeral for him, but I didn't have to give in to her. I didn't have to let it go.) I suppose I'm no different than back when Brother McConnell first confronted me about my faith, certainly not a Christian but not really a Buddhist either, just some confused soul who can't claim any one place to stand. But somehow—why do I see this so clearly now?—I managed to fend off his missionary urgings, both in terms of the spirit and the flesh. Once upon a time there was some fight in me. I said my No-No, and now I am standing here, aren't I? And isn't this where my father once stood? It's as good a place as any for a ceremony, as good a place as any to release my dead. And yes, it is a good day to die.

So I howl again and then once more. I kneel and take up a fist of the dusty dirt before me. I let it fall through my hands, once for my father, once for Tommy, once for my mother. Then a fourth time, commingling mine with theirs, knowing that my time will come in its course—I don't have to hasten it, though it's always there for the taking, as is my legacy. I can put the tip of my finger to my tongue and taste it, dry with a touch of salt. I wish I knew a hymn or a sutra to sing, but I don't. I'll just listen to the silence, feel the breeze flowing about my face, its hymn and sutra all I need.

I walk around some more, aimlessly drifting. These stones here are all that's left of a huge fruit and vegetable house. They made things grow here, even in this wilderness. And someone spoke out, against the government, against why they were here. And someone went off to war and fought for their country. And someone wept. And someone prayed. And each of them left something here that no one wanted to remember. And yet they all did. Remember.

And then they moved on.

I'm going to sit here till night comes. I'm going to let the heat of the high plains sun sink deep into my skin, and I'm going to walk around and around this prison, until I feel lost again, and then, then I'll know that I'm home, then I'll know that I can go home. I'm going to watch those far mountains in the west as the sun slips down, that burning globe of gases and nuclear explosions that Tommy explained to me when we were kids. I'm going to lie back and watch the dome of the stars come out, so much clearer and brighter and more myriad than in the skies of my childhood, back in Chicago. I'm going to see them against the palimpsest of the constellations, all etched by a trick of light on the dome of the Adler Planetarium, and I'm going to remember the brilliant boy who was my brother and the boy who was waiting outside the planetarium for his brother to bring him home, and I'm going to do the best I can to bring those in my charge safely through this world, marking this promise like a bedtime tale as I fall asleep so I can wake in the morning, after a day of walking in circles in my own version of a ghost dance and doing nothing but remembering. And then I'm going to get in my rented car and drive back east, past the deer and the antelope and the purple mountains majesty and the amber waves of grain, and I'm going to take it all in, bearing the boy that I was, and the man that I am, back to my boys and Grace, and I will tell them in their turn, as the time comes, all these stories, every one, including that of their newfound cousin, the one they never knew they had.

Last there's a book I've got to write, only it's not the famous suicides of the Japanese empire, and it's not Japanese at all. It's Japanese American, a book for my father and my mother, for the camps and the No-No boys and the draft resisters, and perhaps even for the two boys who grew up amid that history and knew so very little about it.

ACKNOWLEDGMENTS

I want to thank my parents for their support and love.

I could not have written this novel without my aunts—Ruth, Miwako, Sachiko, Ruby, Yoshiko, Yukimi, Baye—and my uncles—Lou, Elbert, Dick, Byron, Tad, Ken. Thank you for your stories and your legacy; you and my parents lived through what I am still struggling to understand.

My brother, John, and my sisters, Linda and Susan—though the story this novel tells is not ours, it arose out of our childhood, our lives together. You and our cousins—Marianne, Sharon, Debbie, Diane, Mark, Kent, Brian, Paul, Ernie, and Steve—shared the legacy of the camps and those years in Chicago.

Along with my wife, four people read this novel in manuscript:

For giving me the title and for his indispensable reading of this novel and for our late-night conversations, my deepest gratitude to the genius of Junot Díaz.

For being my collaborator, supporter, insightful reader, long time dinner companion, and great friend, my everlasting thanks to Alexs Pate.

Juliana Pegues provided me with both support and critical readings from her perspective as a fellow writer and a scholar.

Sandra Zane, for believing in me and this novel—thank you.

My thanks to my friends and fellow artists in the Twin Cities community for their companionship and encouragement; you've helped remind me that I'm not alone and have given me hope: Ed Bok Lee, Bao Phi, e. g. bailey, sha cage, Ka Vang, Bryan Thao Warra, Sun Yung Shin, Katie Leo, Heather Wang, Soo Jin Pate, Mai Neng Moua, Sandy Augustin, Sherry Quan Lee, Marlina Gonzalez.

Diem Jones, Elmaz Abinader—thanks so much for your friendship and for bringing me into the VONA family. Chris Abani, Suheir Hamad,

Ruth Foreman, Willie Perdomo, Tim Seibles, comrades and presences of light and delight.

Garrett Hongo has been a longtime friend and fellow *sansei* writer, someone who's thrown me a lifeline when I needed it.

Thanks to the Asian American artists, scholars, and writers who've helped me over the years: Philip Kan Gotanda, Kelvin Han Yee, John Jang, Traise Yamamoto, Stan Yogi, Xiaojing Zhou, Gayle Issa, Li-Young Lee, Sarah Gambito, Marilyn Chin.

Cindy Gehrig of the Jerome Foundation has been a warm and welcome presence in my artistic life for a number of years. Jerod Santek of the Loft—you're a gift to our community. Allan Soldofsky—a generous soul and one of the angels of literature.

The Montalvo Arts Center gave me time and space to work on this novel. A grant from the Loft and the McKnight Foundation provided me with needed support.

I'm grateful to Roger Shimomura for allowing Coffee House Press to use his wonderful artwork for the cover.

I especially want to thank the staff at Coffee House Press and their wonderful organization: Allan Kornblum for so readily taking in my book and for his extremely helpful reading of the novel, as well as for all the great support he's given to literature over the years; Christopher Fischbach for his close reading and edit; and the supportive and professional staff who were so helpful and easy to work with: Molly Mikolowski, Esther Porter, Linda Koutsky, and Diana Heim.

Frank Chin's writings and talks on the history of Japanese America have been instrumental to my understanding of the internment, the role of the JACL, and the stance of the No-No Boys. So has Michi Weglyn's *Years of Infamy: The Untold Story of America's Concentration Camps*. I adapted William M. Tsutsui's anecdote about his childhood costume from his *Godzilla on My Mind: Fifty Years of the King of Monsters*. Other sources of material were *Reflections on the Gallows: Rebel Women in Prewar Japan* by Mikiso Hane; *Six Lives, Six Deaths: Portraits from Modern Japan* by Robert Jay Lifton, Shuichi Kato, and Michael R. Reich; *The Big Aiiieeeee! An Anthology of Chinese American and Japanese American Literature* (1991), edited by Jeffery Paul Chan, Frank Chin, Lawson Fusao Inada, and Shawn Wong; William Weatherall's account of the trial of Fumiko Kimura; Bill Gordon's translation of the letter of Lieutenant Sanehisa

Uemura; Lawrence Fouraker's article "'Voluntary Death' in Japanese History and Culture"; Kay Redfield Jamison's *Night Falls Fast: Understanding Suicide*.

Finally, I want to thank my children, Samantha, Nikko, and Tomo, for their love and support. My deepest gratitude goes to my wife, Dr. Susan Sencer, for reading countless versions of this manuscript and for loving me all these years.

◼

This is a work of fiction. Names, characters, places, and incidents in this novel are the product of the author's imagination or are used fictitiously. Certain historical events and facts have been altered or are viewed through the lens of individual characters.

With that caveat, I wish to note that the No-No Boys who answered negative to questions 27 and 28 on the loyalty oath were one distinct group. They were not the same as those of the Heart Mountain Fair Play Committee who resisted the draft. However, certain members of the Japanese American community, including Japanese American Citizens League officials, viewed both the No-No Boys and the draft resisters negatively. In the novel, Ben grows up believing his father is a No-No Boy. It is only near the end that he realizes this may not have been the case, and he envisions his father as a member of the Heart Mountain Fair Play Committee. But which group his father was a member of remains uncertain, as does his father's motives.

COLOPHON

Famous Suicides of the Japanese Empire was designed at Coffee House Press, in the historic warehouse district of downtown Minneapolis. The text is set in Caslon.

FUNDER ACKNOWLEDGMENTS

Coffee House Press is an independent nonprofit literary publisher. Our books are made possible through the generous support of grants and gifts from many foundations, corporate giving programs, state and federal support, and through donations from individuals who believe in the transformational power of literature. Coffee House Press receives general operating support from the Minnesota State Arts Board, through an appropriation by the Minnesota State Legislature and from the National Endowment for the Arts, and major general operating support from the McKnight Foundation, and from Target. Coffee House also receives support from: two anonymous donors; the Elmer L. and Eleanor J. Andersen Foundation; Bill Berkson; the Buuck Family Foundation; the Patrick and Aimee Butler Family Foundation; Jennifer Haugh; Joanne Hilton; Stephen and Isabel Keating; the Kenneth Koch Literary Estate; Allan and Cinda Kornblum; Seymour Kornblum and Gerry Lauter; Kathryn and Dean Koutsky; Ethan J. Litman; Mary McDermid; Stu Wilson and Melissa Barker; the Lenfestey Family Foundation; Rebecca Rand; the law firm of Schwegman, Lundberg, Woessner, PA.; Charles Steffey and Suzannah Martin; the James R. Thorpe Foundation; the Woessner Freeman Family Foundation; the Wood-Rill Foundation; and many other generous individual donors.

This activity is made possible in part by a grant from the Minnesota State Arts Board, through an appropriation by the Minnesota State Legislature and a grant from the National Endowment for the Arts.

To you and our many readers across the country, we send our thanks for your continuing support.

Good books are brewing at coffeehousepress.org